The Journey Prize Anthology

Winners of the $10,000 Journey Prize

1989
Holley Rubinsky (of Toronto, Ont., and Kaslo, B.C.)
for "Rapid Transits"

1990
Cynthia Flood (of Vancouver, B.C.)
for "My Father Took a Cake to France"

1991
Yann Martel (of Montreal, Que.)
for "The Facts Behind the Helsinki Roccamatios"

1992
Rozena Maart (of Ottawa, Ont.)
for "No Rosa, No District Six"

1993
Gayla Reid (of Vancouver, B.C.)
for "Sister Doyle's Men"

1994
Melissa Hardy (of London, Ont.)
for "Long Man the River"

1995
Kathryn Woodward (of Vancouver, B.C.)
for "Of Marranos and Gilded Angels"

1996
Elyse Gasco (of Montreal, Que.)
for "Can You Wave Bye Bye, Baby?"

1997 (shared)
Gabriella Goliger (of Ottawa, Ont.)
for "Maladies of the Inner Ear"

Anne Simpson (of Antigonish, N.S.)
for "Dreaming Snow"

1998
John Brooke (of Montreal, Que.)
for "The Finer Points of Apples"

1999
Alissa York (of Winnipeg, Man.)
for "The Back of the Bear's Mouth"

The Journey Prize Anthology

Short Fiction from the Best of
Canada's New Writers

Selected by Catherine Bush, Marc Glassman,
and Hal Niedzviecki

M&S

Canadian Cataloguing in Publication Data

The National Library of Canada has catalogued this publication as follows:

Main entry under title:

The Journey Prize anthology :
the best short fiction from Canada's literary journals

Annual.
1–
Subtitle varies.
ISSN 1197-9693
ISBN 0-7710-4423-2 (v. 12)

1. Short stories, Canadian (English).*
2. Canadian fiction (English) – 20th century.*

PS8329.J68   C813'.0108054   C93-039053-9
PR9197.32.J68

We acknowledge the financial support of the Government of Canada through
the Book Publishing Industry Development Program for our publishing
activities. We further acknowledge the support of the Canada Council for the
Arts and the Ontario Arts Council for our publishing program.

"Doves of Townsend" © Timothy Taylor; "Hearsay" © J.A. McCormack;
"The Heart of the Land" © Andrew Gray; "Onion Calendar" © Karen Solie;
"Pope's Own" © Timothy Taylor; "The Premier's New Pyjamas" © John
Lavery; "Sheep Dub" © Lee Henderson; "Sightseeing" © Andrew Smith;
"Silent Cruise" © Timothy Taylor; "Swan Street" © R.M. Vaughan; "We Move
Slowly" © Jessica Johnson; "Your Mouth Is Lovely" © Nancy Richler
These stories are reprinted with permission of the authors.

Typeset in Trump Mediaeval by M&S, Toronto

Printed and bound in Canada

McClelland & Stewart Ltd.
The Canadian Publishers
481 University Avenue
Toronto, Ontario
M5G 2E9
www.mcclelland.com

1 2 3 4 5   04 03 02 01 00

About the Journey Prize Anthology

The $10,000 Journey Prize is awarded annually to a new and developing writer of distinction. This award, now in its twelfth year, is made possible by James A. Michener's generous donation of his Canadian royalty earnings from his novel *Journey*, published by McClelland & Stewart in 1988. The winner of this year's Journey Prize, to be selected from among the twelve stories in this book, will be announced in October 2000.

The Journey Prize Anthology comprises a selection from submissions made by literary journals across Canada, and, in recognition of the vital role journals play in discovering new writers, McClelland & Stewart makes its own award of $2,000 to the journal that has submitted the winning entry. This year the selection jury was Catherine Bush, the author of two novels, *Minus Time* and, most recently, *The Rules of Engagement*; Marc Glassman, the owner of Pages Books and Magazines, who is also a journalist, film programmer, and associate producer on several documentaries; and Hal Niedzviecki, the author of *Smell It*, *Lurvy*, and *We Want Some Too: Underground Desire and the Reinvention of Mass Culture*. Niedzviecki is also the founder of Canzine, the annual festival of alternative culture in Canada, and the editor of *Broken Pencil* magazine and *Concrete Forest: The New Fiction of Urban Canada*.

The Journey Prize Anthology has established itself as one of the most prestigious anthologies in the country. It has become a who's who of up-and-coming writers, and many of the authors whose early work has appeared in the anthology's pages have gone on to single themselves out with collections of short stories and literary awards. The Journey Prize itself is the most significant monetary award given in Canada to a writer at the beginning of his or her career for a short story or excerpt from a fiction work in progress.

McClelland & Stewart would like to acknowledge the continuing enthusiastic support of writers, literary journal editors, and the public in the common celebration of the emergence of new voices in Canadian fiction.

Contents

INTRODUCTION

Surprise us.

That's the first thing we ask of any story. And we don't mean a jump-out-of-the-closet-and-shout-BOO! kind of surprise. Give us surprise mixed with wonder. Take us in hand and show us something we haven't seen before.

Surprise as discovery. Arouse an intense sense of curiosity. Seduce with words so precisely and energetically chosen that the skin tightens down the back.

Reading the stories for this year's *Journey Prize Anthology*, we were consistently engaged. Certain things also became clear to us. We realized how much we like stories in which we learn something — not in any didactic sense, but by being plunged into a world of intriguing information through which the writer's own fascination pulses. In this way, the known world grows larger and stranger and more convoluted than we could ever have imagined on our own.

None of us could have said that we were fascinated by the processes of cheese-making, until we read the story "Pope's Own." Read it and you'll never look at ash in a cheese again.

We collectively agreed that stories simply about families, particularly dysfunctional families, are becoming ever less interesting. Because we've all seen so many. Then again, surprise us — there'll be an exception to every claim. Of course, we each have our biases.

Catherine found "Your Mouth Is Lovely" to be a thoughtful inversion of one kind of family story, the archetypal nasty-stepmother tale, this time set in a nineteenth-century Russian shtetl. Searching for fictional worlds where the drama extends beyond the merely domestic, she was drawn to stories in which people's lives and work become passionately entwined, as in "Hearsay" or "Silent Cruise" or "Doves of Townsend," also one of Marc's standouts, which operates on that level while confounding our ideas of what a gift can mean. Marc enjoyed "Doves of Townsend" and "Pope's Own," two tales about people in the process of reinventing their lives. He is interested in stories of characters in flux and was enchanted by the idea that these protagonists' inner lives would be profoundly affected by new choices of profession. Other stories succeeded by stretching and playing with our notions of the real: for example, the delicate dream imagery of "In the Heart of the Land," or the peculiar but precisely rendered antics of the suburban yak in "We Move Slowly," one of Hal's favourites, which steps a little further into the surreal.

What all the stories gathered here share is their unpredictability, which we believe to be at the heart of good fiction. A deep and resonant sort of surprise. They offer us the experience of complexity. The writers of these stories render complicated emotional lives and at the same time are brave and confident enough to leave space around their characters through which this sense of complication – and mystery – pulses. Each story is alive with conviction, its voice and language the agency of this conviction, word by word by word.

The three of us came to the task of choosing the stories for this year's anthology from divergent aesthetics. Marc is a bookstore owner, cultural community organizer, and film critic. Hal is a small-press agitator, critic, and author of always lugubrious, often experimental works of fiction. Catherine is a novelist whose most recent book explores the points of connection between the world's war zones and the sheltered surreal of a comfortable everyday life. Though we all respect each other's work enormously, we also expected that our judgments would diverge considerably. (Each of us secretly harboured the suspicion that the judging process would descend into a shouting match.) And yet in the end we were surprised by how easily we reached our decisions. The standout stories stood out. When we argued (and we did argue) for different stories, we fought for them on similar grounds.

The stories in *The Journey Prize Anthology* are chosen from ones submitted to McClelland & Stewart by literary magazines across the country. While impressed with the selection, we would at the same time have welcomed a greater diversity of stories to choose from (not more, just more variety). Different voices. More formally adventurous stories. Sharp little short-shorts. After all, it's a big (and unpredictable) country. Too often, an imaginative premise was diminished by a dull, predictable writing style. Great beginnings would peter into dim endings. Or, even worse, sparkling, exciting prose was held back by the effort of trying to conform to an idea of what the Canadian short story should or could be about.

We end, then, by thanking both McClelland & Stewart for their support of new writers, and the editors and publishers whose journals and magazines allow us to have a Journey Prize each year. These are the unnoticed workers-in-words whose unrecognized efforts allow the young Canadian writer to grow and learn and, most importantly, find an audience. Their presence is crucial in nurturing talent and extending the grand tradition of the Canadian short story. In some small crazy way, we can't help but envy the job of these editors who, every day, return from their mailboxes, arms full. We too, however briefly, now know the feeling that is sitting down to read a stack of stories all the while hoping, demanding, to be surprised.

Catherine Bush
Marc Glassman
Hal Niedzviecki
Toronto, August 2000

ANDREW GRAY

The Heart of the Land

Before I travelled into the North I lived in a small apartment in the suburbs. I was not working any longer, and I walked down to Lake Ontario every morning and fed the Canada geese. I moved slowly through the forest of their undulating necks, sowed bread among them and listened to their plaintive honking. During the day I ate soup from cans and made phone calls and wrote letters to people who were embarrassed to hear from me. They would not even let me through the hospital doors.

Before I lived in the apartment, I had a condominium at the Harbourfront, facing away from the Gardiner and out to the lake and the small tufts of island anchored in front of the city. I cycled the paths beside the water on mornings I wasn't working or on call and drank coffee and ate breakfast looking across the water. In winter I walked. I loved the way the lake changed with the seasons: the glitter it had in summer when sails skimmed across it; the grey cast it took in autumn when the wind ruffled it; the cleanness of snow on ice, broken only by the winter trails of the island ferries.

Water has always calmed me. Paradoxically so, for I have never learned how to swim. When I was a child it was all I would drink, and this calmed me too. Glass after glass of it, cold, straight from the tap. I never developed a taste for soft drinks or even milk, though my mother worried and tried for years to change this. Now that I am up north, canoeing, I drink water with iodine tablets in it, mixed sometimes with Gatorade crystals to

I

keep my electrolytes up. I must be swallowing two or three litres a day.

When I lived in the city, my job was to open people's heads and look inside. Sometimes I removed cancers the size of golf balls; sometimes portions of the brain itself – knots of tissue that had rebelled and were issuing conflicting orders. Once I put an electrode directly on the surface of a man's brain, right at the speech centre, and he said "fuck your mother," in a clear, precise voice. I moved it a millimetre and he said "problematic." Then he said "pop, pop, pop," until I removed it. Part of me wanted to keep it there and see what else he might say, as if there was something profound waiting inside him, words the right person could bring out with a spark.

I did not know then that my life was perfect. It was perfect the way the lake is perfect in winter when it has frozen in the harbour and the snow has just finished falling. Of course there is still water moving darkly underneath, toxins in the sediments, and the ferries soon carve their tracks across it, but for that brief time it has no flaws.

The first time I saw Susan she had a Medusa-tangle of wires writhing out from her head. There were no cards or flowers beside her bed; she seemed to have no family or friends. No one took her hand; no one sat and talked to her as people often did to the comatose.

Wayne, a colleague of mine – almost a friend – called me in to have a look at her. She lay there pale and motionless. Wires like coloured, flowing hair led to a cluster of computers beside her. Bright lines moved rapidly across a set of display screens.

"I'm in a hurry," I said.

"Stay a minute," he said. "I think this will interest you." He pointed to one of the screens. "Remind you of anything?"

The lines moving across it had the bumpy look of REM sleep. "Looks like an EEG of someone dreaming."

"Right," he said. "But she's comatose. She's got a brain tumour. There's not supposed to be that much activity in a comatose brain, not in her state."

"So that's why she's wired up?"

He nodded. "Partly. We're also trying something new. We're trying to read her mind."

I looked at him, waiting for the smile that would show he was joking, but he simply nodded. "Seriously. We're not actually reading her thoughts, but we've got an electrode grid over her Broca's Area. If she is dreaming, she might vocalize something. I'm hoping that with the computers we'll be able to translate the electrical patterns there into speech."

I looked at her again. Under the wires and the blanket she seemed frail and threatened. "How did you get authorization?" I said.

"She's got no family we could find, no guardian." He shrugged. "She's going to die soon anyway. The Ethics Board finally said it was okay, as long as we weren't invasive."

The confidence we had. It startled me sometimes, thinking of it. The heart was a pump, the liver a sieve, the brain a fleshy computer. With the right keys, all their secrets would come tumbling out.

The next day I had an eight-hour cancer operation. Afterwards, as we were all changing, Maria the scrub nurse pulled out a photograph. It was the graduation picture of a woman who looked to be in her early twenties. Her hair rose in a blonde cloud over her head. "She's my cousin," Maria said. "A teacher. What do you think?"

Maria was always mothering me, bringing food, winter scarves and pictures of her various female relatives. "Maria." I smiled at her. "You know I'm married to my job."

"You've never even met her."

I peeled off my gown and dumped it in the bin. "Maybe when I finish my residency. I'll have more time then."

She shook her head. "All the good ones will be gone, you know."

I went up to Neurology and looked in on Wayne's patient. One of his medical students was there typing something into the computer. The woman lay unmoving, the sheets like snow over the land of her body. Watching, I finally saw the gentle movement of her chest that showed she was still breathing.

"Hello?" It was the student. I'd been standing at the doorway for long moments, unaware of him.

"Sorry," I said. "Just curious. Tell Wayne I stopped by."

At home that night in my condominium I sat at my dinner table eating some microwaved pasta, trying to concentrate on a new journal that had come in. After a few minutes I found myself looking out across the water, thinking of the comatose woman again, her frailty, the machines that were trying to eavesdrop on her thoughts. It seemed indecent to be intruding on the end of her life. Such a private thing.

I was dozing, coming off the end of a long shift. I had sore eyes from looking through the operating microscope, an aching back from standing all day. I dropped into a chair in Susan's room to watch over a new program the computers were chewing through; a favour for Wayne since his students were busy. The computers woke me. One of the machines was beeping, and when I tapped gently on its keys I heard a voice whispering from the speakers. "Don't worry," it said. "I'm changing. Go down to the beach." The voice of a dream; I scarcely believed I was awake.

She lay there unmoving, still as water. The voice of her thoughts wound through the air like smoke, and I watched her. "Leaves," she said. "Leaves everywhere." She must have sensed autumn in the air. "The sky is dark today. And that's smoke on the wind; can't you smell it? I think the fires are coming closer."

I examined the computers, reviewing the programs they had been developing. Wayne had been using a type of software evolution, running through hundreds of slightly different programs a week. The thought came to me that if I marked this one down as a failure, they would move in a different direction and perhaps never succeed. I knew it would be a strange, reckless thing to do, but it seemed so wrong just to let them listen to her, to let her expose herself to them. I looked over at her wan face.

I carefully copied the program that was running, the one that worked, then told the computer it had failed, and that it should try another.

As I prepared to shut down the system, she spoke again. "When you took me away," she said. "Why did you leave me there? Where's everyone else?" It was so hard not to talk back to her, just to leave her there in silence, locked in her skull.

I saw her there in her room, alone. It was night, the halls were quiet and I was tired and a little depressed from a long operation that hadn't gone well. Wayne's project was still running, the computer humming uselessly beside her bed, no longer a conduit for the words she couldn't say. Then suddenly I understood – I could be a witness; I could be there for her. And so it was that I was lost.

Nights when I had finished working and should have been sleeping in my bedroom by the cold face of the lake I sat in Susan's room, listening to her dreams. I told Wayne I was interested in his project. I told him I'd monitor his equipment when he or the student assisting him was not there. But all I would do was load in my program and hear her voice, watch her still face and imagine her lips moving in speech.

Almost without thinking I began to talk back to her. Just murmurs at first, but the more I spoke the more it felt as if we were actually communicating. One night she said. "Will you swim with me?"

"Of course," I said.

She hummed a tune for a few seconds. "The water is so beautiful." Then, "Where are you?"

"Beside you."

"Isn't the water beautiful?"

I sat on the edge of the bed and held her hand. Somehow I expected coldness, but it was warm, full of life. She didn't move, but she said, "It's beautiful." She said, "Nice." She said, "Where are you?"

The next night when I finished changing the computer program, she said, "Tell me something true."

I told her about my childhood, about how I had been shy and clumsy and spent all my time indoors reading and playing with computers. I talked about my condominium and the expensive kitchen equipment in it that I'd never used; the way the lake looked under bruised autumn skies. I told her things I'm not sure I had ever thought about before. Sometimes she said, "Tell me something true." And sometimes she said, "Peter, come back to bed," or "Why are you like that? You look sad."

I held her hand each time I saw her, each time surprised by her warmth, her vitality. I could see the rivers of blood under her translucent skin; the blue in her wrists startlingly bright. I read her charts, examined her CAT scans, the MRI images that glowed from the hospital computer. Inoperable, they said, no matter how often I stared at them. Inoperable.

Susan's tumour grew larger, and more and more her EEG showed the deep, slow waves of true coma. Wayne started winding the project down, and he told me I didn't need to help any longer. I found, however, that I couldn't stop visiting her room. I tried once, not going for three days, but I became anxious and worried. I imagined she'd died, and no one had been with her. Or that she'd had some message for me, and it had gone unheard.

To evade Wayne, I began coming in after midnight and staying for hours. She talked less frequently, but she still talked, if I waited long enough. I stopped reading my journals, and takeout containers began piling up in my garbage.

One day during an operation I fell asleep. I had been operating with another surgeon, and as he worked I closed my eyes and let my head rest against the microscope. I woke with a jerk when he said my name, realizing I'd heard it several times already. "Sorry," I said quickly. "Thinking about something else."

He looked at me for a few moments. "You're not an intern any more," he said. "Get a full night's sleep before an operation or you won't be operating."

Maria came up to me afterwards. "Are you okay?" she said.

"Sure," I said. "I'm fine."

"I'm meeting my cousin for a bite; why don't you come along? Maybe it'll perk you up."

I looked at my shoes, noticing a small spot of blood on one of them. I wiped it carefully against my pants. "Okay," I said.

At the restaurant across the street her cousin was already sitting in one of the booths. I realized she was the woman from the picture; I remembered her hair. Her name was Mary, and she taught third grade.

"So," she said. "You're the brain surgeon."

"No, I'm a Neurology resident."

"Oh." She looked sheepish.

I felt sorry for her for a second. "It's almost the same thing," I said. "I'll be a brain surgeon when I finish."

We ate, and slowly the conversation slipped away from me until I realized that only they were talking. Something about Mary's students. I finished my overcooked burger and watched them for a while. They seemed so flat and unreal compared to Susan.

On the way back in to the hospital, Maria said, "She likes you, you know."

For a moment I was confused, unsure who she was talking about.

"Mary asked if you wanted her phone number."

"Her number?"

Maria shook her head. "So you can call her. So you can ask her out sometime."

I couldn't quite imagine it. "Maybe later," I said. "I better do my rounds now." I hurried off before she could propose anything else.

I came in again that night, after two. To my surprise, I bumped into Wayne near Susan's room. "Awful late," he said, looking at his watch.

"Checking a patient," I said. "He's been trying to die on me for the last couple of days."

He looked steadily at me. "You're all right?" he said.

"Sure."

"You just seem very distracted lately. You look run down."

I looked nervously at Susan's door. "A family problem," I said. I'd told him once how little I talked with my parents, how far apart we were.

"Oh," he said, embarrassed. There was an awkward silence for a moment, then he looked towards Susan's room. "Did I tell you we're stopping the monitoring?"

"What?"

He turned back to me. "She's fading fast. We won't get anything else out of her. My med student Michael's going to take the computer out tomorrow morning."

I made some meaningless response, my mind numb. When he had left, I went in and took Susan's hand and sat beside her on the bed, muttered into her ear. The program ran for an hour until she spoke. She said, "Turn around, let me see you." And she said, "This room, you know, it's so small. I can barely see you."

Then she said more. She said, "You know that time I was alone, when I was young? I was lost, I was surrounded by people who towered over me like trees. Maybe I was in a forest, I'm not sure. And I kept tugging on sleeves, pulling on arms that felt like bark. You went away. I was looking for you and you weren't there."

"I'm here," I said. I touched her forehead gently, brushed her thin hair from her eyes.

"The ground was so soft. I wanted to sleep, but I knew if I lay down the forest would swallow me – I'd grow into it like moss and I'd sprout roots and I'd never come back."

I thought I saw her eyelids flicker a little then, but I can't be sure.

"All I wanted was to touch someone, to feel real skin. To see a face."

I pulled the blanket down a little and opened her gown. Her breasts were veined ivory and I touched them gently. She needed human contact so badly.

When I had imagined romance before, the woman had always been a blurry, passive figure, not quite real. Susan, though, was so real I almost couldn't contain myself. I kissed her warm lips and moved clumsily over her, trying to be careful, stunned by her beauty.

Early the next morning, Wayne and his student found me asleep in the bed beside her.

She said, "You'll look for me in the forest, but you won't see me. I'll be a sapling in a grove of trees. I'll drink water from the ground." She said it as I sat there and looked at Wayne, at the strange, stiff expression on his face.

He said, "Why?" He said, "Do you know what you've done?" But I didn't try to explain. I knew it would do no good. I knew he wouldn't understand.

After I was asked to resign, then told to leave the hospital, I wrote letters and made phone calls, and couldn't imagine I would never see her again. When I finally heard of her death, months later, I watched the island trees bowing under the invisible hand of the wind and wished it would descend on me until I too was part of the earth.

Out in the middle of the water the wind picks up and pushes the canoe around like a leaf: each stroke is a battle. Every day my shoulders burn and my neck stiffens so much during sleep that I must stretch and stretch in the morning before I set out again. I follow a chain of lakes, bumping against inlets and bays until I find the rivers that link them. When I track across the rocking centre of a lake I think of the cold depths, the bass and muskellunge nosing through them, their bodies a single flexing muscle with one intent. At my best moments I join them, imagine myself a fish sliding through life, food and motion a thought I repeat with every breath.

At night I sit in front of my small tent and hear her voice whispering through the trees. I stare at the stars splashed carelessly across the sky. Their ancient light pins me down.

The water is deep everywhere. I rarely see bottom. Finally, I take my wristwatch off and drop it over the side of the canoe. It falls like a fishing lure, twisting and glinting, diminishing. It winks out and I am freed from time.

The same day, I reach the end of a lake and find the river again. I paddle downstream for hours, then after I follow a bend in the river I realize the water is flowing downhill. It is as if I am descending a flight of stairs. Behind me the land rises; ahead the water gets rougher and rougher. The river pulls me through itself, a needle on silver thread. Around me its banks rise up like buildings. As I am swept along, I see trees climb the rocky walls on twisted feet, half-remembered faces surfacing from the stone. The sun appears and disappears over the edge of the gorge, and I feel the water surge around me like a living thing.

And I come out again. The river widens and is flooded with light. The water slows and the roar of the rapids fades behind me. Trees crowd in close along the banks of the river and I know I am in the secret heart of the land. I know I have found her at last.

The water below me is black and deep. I bend over towards it and see my face staring back at me. I cup my hands and drink and drink.

TIMOTHY TAYLOR

Silent Cruise

Sheedy was a meticulous handicapper. He had a CD-ROM library of past performances and an index of tracks with pictures and lay-out diagrams. He downloaded race results off the Internet directly to the Psion palm-top computer he favoured track-side.

Dett was prostrate before the altar of a more compulsive method entirely, the mechanics of which he didn't understand or question and about which Sheedy respectfully did not ask. And yet, they needed one another.

In the Fat Choy Lounge at 13:01 Saturday September 6, 1997, Dett was engaged in the habitual translation of analogue detail into digits. It would be impossible for Dett to be in the Fat Choy on a Saturday, or anywhere else on any other day of the week, without yielding to the delicious impulse: the sixth day of the week in a place named with the sixth and third letters of the alphabet, waiting for the third race.

Sixes and threes, two sets.

"What are you getting in the third, Dett?" Sheedy was asking, pecking at the tiny black palm-top. The overhead TV was providing Cantonese analysis of a race that ran at 12:43 in Santa Anita. Around the subterranean Fat Choy, Chinese men (23 of them) in patched grey cardigans and battered hats were fanning their forms up and down, beating them silently into their palms, conducting as the timbre of their luck resounded faithfully in the replay.

Dett looked down at his program. The third race at Hastings Park had a post time of 14:23 with 12 horses running. The 14, the 23 and the 12 linked themselves to the sequence of sixes and threes – Dett visualized this in three dimensions, the multi-coloured numbers re-clustering like evolving DNA – each addition reconstructing the predictive significance of the strand.

These were Dett's numbers. Spools of digits, a numeric cascade inspired by every ambient detail. A "bit-snow," as he came to think of it, that had alarmed him only once. He had played the ponies since high school, betting a combination of handicapped picks and selections made through the sifting of these compulsive numbers. But in second year university – Dett was studying mathematics – he found himself losing, all at once, plunging below the payout of random picks. There were ancillary problems, he was failing his exams.

He couldn't fault the handicapping. His own spill of numbers had increased in manic intensity to the point that they emitted a noise. He was driven to numeric fixations unlike anything he'd seen: the day of the week on any date in Julian or Gregorian history? Despite a compulsion to solve this problem, a compulsion that lasted in full flower for many months, eliminating friendships, disturbing professors whose lectures might be interrupted, it wasn't particularly relevant to any of his courses. The question wasn't on any of his finals.

His Non-Parametric Methods professor took him aside at the end of second year. A tobacco-stained Irish mathematician whose advice had been compacted down in Dett's memory to a single string of words: ". . . the most unusually gifted student does not necessarily succeed . . ."

Indeed, he flunked third year. And although the noise eventually abated, the obsession to precisely calendarize everything calmed, he still invested some time researching Repetitive Word Disorders which he learned were clustered under Obsessive Compulsive Disorders, themselves a strain of Thought Disorder. Was he sick?

It was true the numbers tumbled ceaselessly, and his various personal and academic embarrassments satisfied the requirements of the Diagnostic and Statistical Manual of Mental

Disorders, which stated that obsessions must be "intrusive or inappropriate." But Dett didn't think the American Psychiatric Association's catalogue of disorders captured his mental action in total. On occasion his numbers persisted in sprinkling a pattern of meaning across the situation at hand (mostly at the track where they had thankfully resumed their function). If "bit-snow" were a sickness, then he had grown to like the numeric frost on his mental peaks, it was a key feature of his personal topography and screw the APA anyway.

Sheedy never asked about it directly. It was enough that at a crucial moment he sensed a facility soft-wired into Dett's cranial gore, and on that uncharacteristic, un-handicapped hunch had picked Dett to fill a vacant Financial Analyst position for which the advertisement had expressly stated "MBA required."

"You have second sight," Sheedy said during the second interview. Dett remembered that he was wearing a hand-me-down suit of his father's from Eaton's Pine Room.

Second sight, second interview, second-hand suit. Dett asked Sheedy to repeat himself.

"Second sight," Sheedy said for the second time. "You see shadows behind the numbers, which is rare."

He could never have predicted this. 13 months of unemployment living in a friend's basement next to a thicket of home-grown. 64 applications. 19 first interviews. 18 polite rejection letters. One lonely second interview and this strutting Vancouver Stock Exchange peacock in a bottle green suit actually understood his numbers.

"You like the ponies?" Sheedy asked him.

It had been good to get out of that basement on his own terms.

Sheedy sent him on the Securities Course, basic training for financial analysts, brokers and investment dealers. It had been 47 years since anybody scored 100%, you just didn't get everything right in this world.

Dett got everything right.

Sheedy took his new protégé to Hy's Steak House to celebrate. Sent Dett staggering home early with a pound of beef and a half bottle of Chilean cabernet sloshing around his gut. Dett was thinking: 100% every 47 years. 100, 47, 100, 47. 1997–47 makes 1950. Today was January 13th, so back-calculating the day of the week he established that January 13, 1950 was a Friday.

Friday the 13th. He liked that. The last idiot-savant had nailed it on Friday the 13th.

Fat Choy is Chinese for good luck.

"Who do you have in the third?" Dett asked back to Sheedy now, sitting across the lino-top table in the smoky track-side lounge.

Sheedy straightened his gold tie against his French blue shirt, shot cuffs out the sleeves of his Prince of Wales double breasted. He had a distinct Boss aura despite being a Little Man. (He inspired in Dett the auto-thoughts *proportional* and *lifelike*.) Black brush cut. Black eyebrows. Olive skin and a straight nose to match his straight teeth which were also very white. He walked everywhere like he was pissed off, shoulders hunched, legs and arms straight. The MBAs who worked at Sheedy-Mayhew called him Bucky Badger after the mascot of his Wisconsin alma mater.

"Got spanked by Bucky this morning," someone would say.

"Yeah he looked pissed," would come the response.

"A badger is always pissed, you know that, I know that . . ." So it ran.

"A Little Risk," Sheedy said now, the palm top having endorsed one of the favourites.

"Ooooh. Ballsy," Dett mocked gently.

They were the only suits in the Fat Choy, ever. This was where Sheedy brought his hot prospects for a couple of laughs before signing up a new account. Dett rode data-shotgun from time to time. The two of them would drive out to the track in Sheedy's leased metallic green Porsche Carrera 4. Dett would run the conventional numbers for the client, establishing base confidence in the firm. But Sheedy also knew Dett could run his stranger numbers and pick a winner on occasion, and if he picked one of Sheedy's hot prospects onto a winner – a placer, a shower, anything that demonstrated Sheedy-Mayhew was also a *lucky* firm – well then Sheedy could pitch any woo known to man. Sheedy could wax the sale.

"Who is it?" Dett asked.

"Andrew Xiang for the third race. I need second sight."

"And you like A Little Risk?" Dett asked, scanning the program.

"I do," Sheedy answered, squinting at his six-inch screen.

"Does Andrew know the ponies?" Dett asked, changing tack.

"A little gaming itch, like you or me, nothing big time. You want another?" Sheedy produced a money clip from which he delicately extracted a twenty.

Dett got Sheedy his drink. Southern Comfort and Coke, no ice. "But Andrew isn't a new account," he said as he sat down again.

"Have a drink for Chrissake." Sheedy said, staring at the empty table in front of Dett.

Dett shrugged. "It's only one o'clock."

"Fuck one. We gotta have some fun sometimes. You're not having fun?" This was classic badger, displaying a small wound for emotional leverage. Dett thought all the blood that had cumulatively seeped from Sheedy's wounds over the nine months he'd been at Sheedy-Mayhew wouldn't moisten the pecker on a Brazilian needle-tip mosquito. But Sheedy was also recently divorced (again) so now he was going to riff on How Important It Was To Just Have Fun Once In A While until Dett broke down and had the drink.

"What're you having?" Sheedy said when Dett returned with his glass.

"Southern Comfort and Coke," Dett said. "No ice, boss."

Sheedy laughed, and reaching a manicured hand across the table he gripped Dett tightly by the back of the neck.

"We're having a good year," Sheedy said, and here Dett found himself staring into his mentor's cold brown eyes with a pound of Rolex clicking audibly in his right ear.

"Bre-X," Dett said. He wasn't above reminding Sheedy once in a while that he had counselled selling the infamous gold stock a full month before the geologist went airborne, falling only slightly faster then the share price eventually did.

"You're the best. How much do I pay you?" Sheedy said, releasing him.

"Not nearly enough, but let's not talk about it here," Dett said.

"I'm just asking because you look so raggedy-assed all the time."

"This is Armani," Dett said, touching his lapel and recalling the sticker shock.

"You take your own action I hope, take care of yourself with the things you learn," Sheedy said, between sips.

"I take care of myself," Dett said. It was true. Information trickled through and you didn't need much to beat the house.

"And I facilitate this," Sheedy said.

"You do," Dett said, wishing to move on. "I was asking why we're trotting Andrew Xiang out here when he's already a client. Are we selling something hard?"

Sheedy grimaced slightly and leaned forward again.

"OK," he said, pressing his palms together in front of him. "We have to . . . evacuate somebody."

"Liquidation sale," Dett said.

"Not a liquidation sale," Sheedy said, lowering his voice. "Christ don't even think that, our seller is still very liquid."

"So who fucked up?" Dett asked, thinking: one of the MBAs.

"The seller is *my* client," Sheedy answered.

Dett regarded his boss who just briefly pushed a hand through his black hair, straightened his shoulders and gathered himself. Sheedy only had a few clients and they were all guys who lived on very quiet properties in the hills around Whistler and paid commissions in cash.

"Remember Jimmy?" Sheedy asked. "He has to leave the country. It's legal."

Jimmy was one of those clients. When money or signatures were required he flew down from Whistler in a chartered heli-jet. He had an impenetrable sleepy expression and a discordant predilection for angry expletives like "cock-sucker" and "whore." On the one occasion they met, in connection with a deal Dett was working on, Jimmy had shaken his hand limply and said only: "Sheedy mentioned you. So let's put this whore to bed then, all right?" He pronounced it Hoo-Er.

"So sell the stuff," Dett said to Sheedy now. "What's the deal?"

"The shares in concern won't trade openly until the fall by which time he has to be out of the country. The fall is too late, by then he'll be banned in Vancouver and probably everywhere else."

"A private sale then," Dett said.

"A mandatory sale," Sheedy answered, staring intently at Dett. "He has over four hundred thousand tied up here and he wants his cash."

"Best-efforts," Dett said, shrugging.

"You're not hearing me," Sheedy said. "We sold him these shares and he was more than a little reluctant at the time. But he trusts me, understand? Now he has to do a runner on 48 hours notice and I have to produce his cash."

"Is he threatening you?" Dett said.

"He doesn't have to," Sheedy said, shaking his head. "We are fucking hooped here Dett."

"I see it," Dett said, imagining the quiet phone call that Sheedy had received at home last night. It wouldn't have been Jimmy calling either, some associate nobody had ever heard of before. "It's critical we move on this . . ." Words of elaborate politeness.

"There's an upside, naturally." Sheedy tried to lighten the tonc. "Double commission. Undying loyalty of the client's friends. All that shit."

"Fantastic."

"Hey," Sheedy said. "You and I have done this before. Your brains, my good looks."

"So what do we have here?" Dett asked.

"A couple of months ago we took Jimmy deep into two positions. If we unload even one of them he'll be happy," Sheedy said. "You feel like selling some healthcare or some technology today?"

Dett pretended to look out the window, as if the answer to this question lay somehow in the weather. High light blowing cloud, cool and pleasant. It meant nothing.

Sheedy swung his case onto the table, tore open the Velcro side pouch and produced the fax-smeared stock exchange fact sheets.

"This is all I get?" Dett asked, incredulously. A prospectus was normally six pounds of paper. If Dett was going to do numbers, conventional or otherwise, he preferred more of them. It inspired him, he waded into them and paddled around.

"What do you want?" Sheedy said. "Xiang knows these companies up the yin-yang. We need second sight today, so pick me the winner. Health care or technology. And a horse in the third. I gotta take a leak." And here he snapped shut the palm top, slid it into a side pocket of his suit, de-perched from his chair and stalked off to the johns.

Dett glanced down at what Sheedy had left for him on the table.

Commerce-Net provided Internet marketing solutions. Yawn. Who didn't? Expected to open at $3.80 in late November. Zero revenue. Zero track record. About the only thing Commerce-Net had were some "channel partners" as they were known, heavy hitters like Microsoft who backed the technology without a direct investment. When Dett had skimmed to the bottom of the sheet he got to the phone numbers. CEO Bertie Perkins could be reached at 1-888-555-0000. Who picked a number like that? Dett closed his eyes. 3.80, 0, 0, 18885550000. It all flattened out and left him in a single void place.

Halox Inc. was developing a bowel cancer marker which, if it were picked up by one North American hospital in one hundred would make everyone connected with the company a millionaire – legitimate investors, Sheedy's drug dealer clients, nieces and nephews of the CFO. Of course, at the moment Halox was hacking and bunting its way through the bush-leagues of level-two clinical trials. This would be considered still a long away from the show. Another zero going public with zero. Pure speculation.

Dett looked around the room, his eyes red from the smoke of the endless collective Fat Choy cigarette, some foul brand these old guys favoured.

Three minutes to the first post here at Hastings Park. Sheedy would be at the window putting down a hundred dollars on whatever horse the palm top picked to win. Sheedy bet all nine races every time, an indiscriminate strategy that lost him about 20% a year. Dett knew that random bets and the barest trace of luck would get him into the same tax bracket.

Sheedy once said to Dett: "When my old man went to the ponies, the stands were full of honest people and the game was totally crooked. You could actually play a game like that."

Exactly. Dett folded up the Halox and the Commerce-Net papers and went outside and watched the changing odds on the board across the stretch. Rumsey favoured in the first at lean odds of 8:5, which Dett took as emblematic of how the game had diminished. All these hard-core track guys scanning the same numbers, picking the same winners, same losers with the same information. It was hard to win any money in this environment without second sight, something that could cast a shadow behind the numbers the handicappers had factored down to value zero.

So now Dett looked around himself and the nearly empty asphalt yard, not yet littered with torn betting slips as it would be over the next hours, and he started spontaneously counting heads. 26 people on the benches. 18 people at the fence. He averaged the people in the grandstand with a sweeping glance. One person per ten seats.

Rumsey was at the pole, position number one. The heavy favourite according to the form, which said "Rumsey is the one-to-beat." Dett thought: horse number one, the one to beat, over $1\frac{1}{16}$ miles.

He won by one-and-a-half lengths.

"Did you have that action?" Sheedy asked him after Dett had descended again into the Fat Choy Lounge.

"Did you?" Dett asked back.

"You had it you fucker, why didn't you tell me?"

"You didn't ask."

"I'm slumping," Sheedy said, staring at his little screen, entering the results.

"He was the favourite," Dett said.

"Who picks a favourite? You can't make any money doing that."

"Most people pick the favourite," Dett said. "That's what makes them favourites. You just have to bet a whole lot."

Sheedy made a mental calculation. "I'm thinking at 8:5 I would have had to bet about three hundred grand to get us out of our little situation here."

Which brought to mind Jimmy packing crates for the midnight float-plane south of the border. Glued to his cellphone, waiting for news on the matter of his available cash. "Hey Eddie, did we get a call from that broker down there?" "Nothing yet." "Well you phone that cock-sucker and rattle his fucking chain."

"Do you want another drink?" Dett asked Sheedy now.

"Naaa," Sheedy said and looked at his watch which Dett already knew read 1:43 PM. Ten minutes to the second post. "So what is it, health care or technology? I like technology myself. I met Bertie Perkins at a trade show once. Sharp guy, respected. Xiang will know that."

"Commerce-Net and Halox," Dett said. "They might as well be identical."

"I'm not talking fundamentals, I'm talking gut."

"Either way they're zeroes, Sheedy. Total specs. I would advise a client to buy based on how much long-shot money they had to piss away."

"If I wanted MBA answers at a time like this, I would have brought an MBA to the track with me," Sheedy said.

"Sorry," Dett said. "This is not a fuzzy logic problem."

"Which one can be sold more easily, then?"

"Same answer," Dett said.

Sheedy flopped back in his chair. "Maybe you need the drink," he said. "You need to loosen up."

"You're not listening."

"Talk."

"We sell him both. He knows the companies so he knows they're both spec zeroes. We tell him it's a hedge, like betting a box, two horses to finish, any order. The Internet breaks up, people will still get colon cancer. The marker tests come up blank, you always have the Net. Technology-healthcare. Optimism-pessimism. Shoot him some of that stuff."

Sheedy went up and got the drinks.

"Will this work?" he asked, sitting down.

"Christ Sheedy, I can't promise. We've done it before, I can say that much."

"Un-hoop me, I can say that much. Do you have my horse in the third?" he asked. "We're going to need that horse."

"I'm waiting for it," Dett said. "But I'll get one."

"What about the second race?" Sheedy asked him.

Dett just shook his head. He was going to sip this drink and think about nothing and then go over to the parade ring and have a look at the runners in the third.

"Come on, give me a pick on two," Sheedy said. "I need a win here."

Dett sighed. Outside, he looked across the track up high to the blue mountains opposite and breathed in deeply. 11 horse field. Horses six and five were the favourites. 6 plus 5. 5 plus 6.

Sometimes he didn't need a big pool of numbers.

He went inside.

"Springhill Billy," he said to Sheedy.

"Horse number one?"

Sheedy bet a hundred dollars and Dett went track-side in time to see the horses pass the grandstand. Croy Lightening by a head on Springhill Billy.

"Interesting," Dett said out loud.

Springhill Billy was holding third at the halfway point.

"Fade baby," Dett yelled.

Springhill Billy was sixth in the stretch, and seventh at the wire by seven lengths.

"What the fuck was that?" Sheedy said when he sat down. "The thing sprang a leak."

"Sometimes you just bet a hunch."

"Everything you bet is a hunch," Sheedy said, face back over the palm-top. "Number six won."

"And five?" Dett asked.

"Showed," Sheedy said, looking up suddenly, "How are you feeling partner?"

"Don't sweat it," Dett said. "We saved the win for the third race."

"I sincerely hope so," Sheedy said.

Andrew Xiang was standing at the top of the steps for several minutes before Dett spotted him.

"Do you guys like this place?" he asked when he sat down and had a look around himself.

Sheedy shot a look over at Dett.

"I like it," Dett said, taking the tag.

"Why not sit in the clubhouse? You can get a sandwich up there," Andrew Xiang said.

Sheedy was on his feet, "That's a good idea. Let's go."

"These guys are the only real bettors left," Dett said, looking around himself as he got up, as if he were seeing the room for the last time.

"Quirky," Andrew said, still seated. "I wonder who'll be betting down here after they all die of lung cancer."

"Hey, it's the Fat Choy room, maybe they won't die," Sheedy said.

Andrew Xiang laughed.

"It has to be the room," Dett said. "You never see the old guys anywhere else."

It turned out they could get sandwiches at the Fat Choy bar.

"Do you wager Mr. Xiang?" Dett asked. The use of Mr. might have been spreading it a bit thick. Andrew was only a few years older than Dett and although he had a lot of money he didn't have what Sheedy called "a roasted fuck of a lot of money."

"Andrew. Sure I like to bet."

"I'm losing today," Dett said, avoiding Sheedy's curious gaze.

"Too bad, who did you like in the second?" Andrew asked.

"Number one, Springhill Billy," Dett said.

"He faded," Andrew said, wincing sympathetically. "I listened in the car. Long shot though, I can relate. It's hard to make money against your old guys here."

"You're exactly right," Dett said. "The game has changed. More professional and yet harder to play. Bigger house take, narrower odds. It's tough."

"That's business right there though, isn't it," Sheedy was leaning forward on the table now, picking up Dett's leave. "Bigger house. Competition. You know what I'm saying?"

"It's true," Andrew said.

"I find myself betting the box more," Sheedy said, warming up. "Cover myself off a little."

"How is it going today?" Andrew said, smiling broadly. He knew the answer already.

"Well, I'd like to be up on the day, if you understand what I'm saying."

Now Andrew was laughing. "I thought you might want that," he said.

Dett excused himself. Sheedy was at stride, talking about three-horse wheels now. Dett figured he might as well go over to the parade circle. 15 minutes to the third post, time to listen to those numbers, time to take a slow walk in a flurry of bit-snow.

Crossing in front of the grandstand it occurred to Dett that the scary part was the thought that it might stop snowing all at once. Even while researching Repetitive Word Disorders he hadn't actively wished the bits to stop. He always had a sense of how the silence might ring on and he imagined what mental fixations might fill such a void.

With two scratches there were ten horses running, which suggested immediately three significant numbers: The One, the Ten, and the difference of nine.

Dett watched the grooms leading the horses out of the paddocks and around the small dirt parade ring. It wasn't his habit to note the beauty of a horse but Dett couldn't deny that they were all exquisite. A chestnut. A grey. A muscled one, a lithe dancer. Long of body, high of haunch. Was it femininity people saw, Dett wondered, or masculine power? The meekness in the slow step or the wildness in the eye?

Ten horses walking slowly in a circle. Ten glistening coats. Ten horses and One would win. Nine losers. With the scratches, the ninth horse was now Silent Cruise.

He found him in the parade. Silent Cruise was a deep mahogany, muscled and powerful. His head tossed. He appeared impatient. Silent Cruise wore deep purple silks, Dett noticed, a kingly colour.

He glanced at the racing form. Silent Cruise was picked to win and to place by the two race columnists.

He walked back slowly towards the Fat Choy. Pausing briefly in front of the grandstands, he wondered how long the track would survive with nine out of ten seats empty. One seat in ten.

The One in Ten. The empty nine. Those numbers again.

Sheedy surprised him.

"Sheedy," Dett said. "Where's Andrew?"

"Still downstairs," Sheedy said. "Pick please."

One in ten was all he was getting. One in ten and the nine left over. That integer string plus an image of a favoured horse with a rich royal purple silk. Horse number nine.

"Silent Cruise will at least show," Dett said. "Get him to take Silent Cruise."

"Show?" Sheedy asked.

"It's a safe bet and I'm getting it hard," Dett said. "It rings for me. Drop Silent Cruise on the table with absolute confidence like you never thought of another horse. And make a deal about putting down some of your own money."

"I need a winner," Sheedy said.

"No we don't Sheedy," Dett said. "We need to show luck which means we have to Be In The Money. There's more luck picking a show and showing than there is picking a win and getting beat by a neck."

Sheedy became a very serious badger.

"It's not going well down there," Dett said, interpreting the look.

"He thinks they're both dogs," Sheedy said. "I mean real dogs. He hasn't made his final decision yet but I don't feel good about this. If we don't show him something amazing in the third, I think he may walk away from both of these stocks."

Sheedy's cellphone bleated.

"Damn," Dett said, looking away.

Sheedy stood adrift on the sloping asphalt.

"You have to take it," Dett said.

"Hello." Sheedy said, and Dett retreated a few yards. Now Sheedy was nodding, cellphone to one ear, left hand up and over his other ear to block out the track noise, to make sure he caught the quiet words, the quiet non-specific words spoken across the insecure cell frequencies. Words which Dett imagined stringing themselves along the issues of "our agreement" and the "paper concerned" and "the cashflow aspects of the situation."

1 in 10 in 1 in 10.

Sheedy clicked the phone shut, pocketed it and stood for a second with his hand on his lips.

"Our guy?" Dett asked, consciously drowning out his numbers.

"We have to pull something out here," Sheedy said.

"Lower the price."

Tough-looking women on quarter horses were escorting the thoroughbreds down to the gate, the jockeys standing in the stirrups, the wind rippling the silks. The squat working horse and the thoroughbred side-by-side highlighted the rare beauty of the racer, high-strung creatures prancing and skittering next to their serene companions. As Silent Cruise passed – the deep shining brown, the vivid purple – the thoroughbred laid his head piteously against the neck of the smaller horse as though seeking a reprieve. It brought to mind how young they were, all of them, the equine equivalent of the 14-year-old super-model backstage with her teddy bears.

Sheedy was talking: ". . . totally wrong signal to lower the price at this point."

Dett flashed on something Sheedy had said earlier. The undying loyalty of the client's network of friends which suggested the obvious downside corollary.

"These really are dogs aren't they?" he said, as it dawned on him.

Sheedy paused and stroked his small, symmetrical chin.

"Commerce-Net lost both its channel partners in some legal dispute this morning. Microsoft is going to sue. Halox is a fucking placebo. The word is that the trials are completely flat."

"Christ Sheedy," Dett said.

"These puppies are going to sewer on Monday when it hits the street. Jimmy has to be out." Sheedy's speech slowed. "He simply will not take a four hundred grand hit the same week he's doing a runner and leaving a dozen houses behind."

"When were you going to tell me this?" Dett asked.

"I wasn't," Sheedy said. "Did you want to be privy?"

He had a point, and he also looked more than a little scared now. "Wax this sale for me Dett and your efforts will not be forgotten."

"And him?" Dett asked, nodding his head towards the Fat Choy.

"Fuck Xiang," Sheedy said, the badger was back in an instant. "Don't even ask that question. If it wasn't him it would be some other loser, like on every bet you and I ever made together. You were born knowing this shit. That's why we're a team."

Sheedy stalked off a few yards, hands stiffly at his side. Wounded. Then he stalked back.

"Now give me my winner," he said.

Dett wasn't sure that he had ever used numbers to consciously screw somebody before. On the other hand, he'd never been forced to.

One in ten then, he thought, at the moment of truth this is all I get? A string of 1s and 10s which might be mathematically expressed as (1, 10, 1, 10, 1, 10 . . .)

1, 10, 1.

January 10, 1901 let's say. Well January 10, 1901, as it happened, was a Thursday.

10, 1, 10.

October 1, 1910 was a Saturday.

Thursday to today, Saturday. A 3-day spread.

Today and the holy number 3.

3rd letter = C.

Saturday and a C.

S. C.

SC.

Silent Cruise.

"This is insane," Dett said, and it seemed to his ears like he was speaking from inside a steel drum.

Sheedy was waiting impatiently.

"There is no rigour in this," Dett said.

"Has there ever been?" Sheedy asked.

"Silent Cruise," Dett said, by way of an answer.

Sheedy was appraising him. "You said Show before."

"Silent Cruise is the One in Ten, Sheedy. It's what I'm getting."

Sheedy faced him squarely. "Don't you start guessing on me."

"He's the One," Dett said simply. "The One in Ten."

"Who's the jockey?" Sheedy asked, digging in his pocket for a racing form. Mysticism was one thing, but corroboration never hurt.

Dett gave him the name, having checked.

"Same guy who rode Rumsey to win in the first," Sheedy said, handicapping aloud and liking the result. And with that, the decision made, he turned and marched back towards the Fat Choy room. Ten yards off he stopped and turned. Yelled back: "Are you watching out here?"

"Where else?" Dett said.

Sheedy was back in 145 seconds with Xiang. Dett had counted the seconds. 143, 144, 145 . . .

"This is much better," Andrew Xiang said. "I can actually breathe out here."

Sheedy squinted in the milky sunshine, a little out of breath from trotting in to the windows and making the last minute bet.

"Did you make your bet?" Dett asked Xiang.

"I got a tip," he said. "You have to bet on a tip."

"Silent Cruise," Sheedy said, leaning in as if to deliver this information to Dett.

There was the gunshot sound of the gates slamming open and in an instant Dett could feel the vibration in his soles.

"Here's to Sheedy's luck," Andrew Xiang said. "Here's to mine."

Dett turned back to the track in time to feel the breeze as the horses hurtled past towards the first turn. Canadian Diamond and Haida Bells, stirrup to stirrup. New Blazer was third by half a length on Silent Cruise.

"Come on now. Come on now," Sheedy was chanting quiet encouragement to the jockey from just over Dett's right shoulder.

Into the back Canadian Diamond and Haida Bells pulled away to one-and-a-half lengths, and the pack squeezed up on New Blazer and Silent Cruise.

"He's flattening out. Don't let him flatten out now. Take him in. Come on, take him in."

Entering the straight the four had again pulled free by a length, and Silent Cruise was moving confidently to the outside on New Blazer.

Thunder to the soles of my feet, thought Dett, his mouth unable to open. Thunder in my empty insides. Thunder you beautiful beautiful thing. Thunder home baby. The One in Ten.

"Ride him home," Sheedy was screaming now. "Ride him home. Come on. Take him in. Take him home." And there was an instant after Sheedy said this that Silent Cruise moved on Canadian Diamond and Haida Bells, in third just half a length off the leaders. But it was only an instant, and then Dett could see that the horse was going down.

"Ride him. Ride him," Sheedy was pouring out his final supplication.

Ten yards off the wire Silent Cruise abruptly fell, half a ton of horse crashing chin first into the dirt. His jockey spilled over his head and into the track, curled already in a defensive ball. Haida Bells ran into the tangle of legs and hooves and also fell, his rider sprawling through the rails and onto the infield turf.

The field surged past. Tulista from fifth to win, followed by Canadian Diamond and A Little Risk.

Haida Bells surged to her feet, swayed, staggered and cantered away. Eyes spread wide and white froth streaming from her nostrils. Silent Cruise struggled on his side, then rose.

From down the grandstand fence, Dett registered a woman's shout. Disembodied. The words released into a hovering silence: "Don't look Maggie," she cried. "Don't look."

And Dett did turn away, pushing his back sharply to the track. And from this swivelled position he noted how Sheedy stood defeated. The crumpled basketball leather of his cheeks, the false pearl of his tiny teeth hanging dryly beneath a thin bloodless lip. Andrew Xiang stood blank-faced, wooden next to him.

Dett turned back to the track. Silent Cruise was standing on three legs, staring slightly upwards without comprehension. His front right leg was shorn off almost cleanly twelve inches above the hoof and from his bloody leg protruded a stump of bone. The hoof and fetlock were still connected by a visible sinew, and the piece flopped brokenly onto the dirt as Silent Cruise looked for footing, weakly finding none, only the emptiness under his right foreleg and what must have been the eclipsing pain of contact between open bone and earth. As the crowd surged to the rail around them, Dett felt a complete silence descend into his insides.

While the horses galloped in, the track crew circled the damaged thoroughbred, their calm ponies sidling in obediently around the staggering racer, penning Silent Cruise against the inside rail. A rider dismounted and took Silent Cruise by the bridle, holding his head as he reared tentatively, losing strength, and then he was helped down to his side. Around him rose the wall of ponies and crew, backs to the crowd, shoulders and flanks together. A wall of respect, thought Dett, although through the legs of the horses he could still make out the needle, and the operation that was quickly performed. A tractor pulled a covered trailer onto the track, and the crew held up a blue tarp in front of the dying thoroughbred as he was loaded. A very slight heave of the flank was the final thing Dett saw.

Dett looked around himself numbly. The two thrown jockeys were on their feet. Fragile as the very elderly, supported by crew. One had made it to the grandstand fence and now stood, muddy circles around the eyes, leaning and shaking. Sheedy and Xiang were gone.

Dett walked back to the Fat Choy in silence.

"No, I like that pick Sheedy," Xiang was saying. "Thanks very much."

"How much did you bet again?" Sheedy was asking, laughing falsely.

"Two hundred and fifty dollars."

"I went down a hundred myself."

Dett watched this jocular exchange, staring at Sheedy and seeing the re-animated fear under his waxy pretence of humour. Even now, Dett knew, Sheedy was trying desperately to find his angles, to return the conversation to Halox. To Commerce-Net. Counting on Dett to assist in re-aligning the conversation on the axis of the sale.

Dett thought only that Sheedy had walked away from track-side, Silent Cruise down and the results in. And he imagined walking away from Sheedy in the moment of his breakdown, imagined vividly the enraged badger hurling abuse at his retreating back.

"I liked that horse," Dett said.

There was a polite silence as the two men regarded him.

"He was coming on," Xiang said finally. "What can you say? It's racing."

"Running fourth," Sheedy said shaking his head. Disappointed with the dead horse's performance.

"Third," Dett said.

"A Little Risk would have caught him. You could see that, which I mean as no disrespect to your pick," Sheedy said.

Xiang chuckled. "I figured it was Dett's pick," he said. "People are always taking credit for their employee's work."

Sheedy made an insincere face like *Guilty, what can I say?*

"You picked the one to die," Xiang said, looking over at Dett.

"An interesting skill," Sheedy said, preparing to riff.

"I thought Silent Cruise would win," Dett said, cutting off Sheedy and returning Andrew's stare.

"You don't handicap at all," Xiang said.

"Nine times out of a ten," Dett returned, "handicapping is a crock of shit. The punter is gone and there's no one left to take advantage of."

"In your view."

"In my respectful view Mr. Xiang, yes."

"And your method instead?"

"I prefer," Dett said, "interpreting the insane pattern of my own numbers."

Sheedy was wincing behind an open palm.

"I am sincerely impressed with that," Andrew Xiang said, nodding slowly as if he had just figured something out. "It's brave and rare."

Sheedy couldn't watch this anymore, and leaned forward, palms pressed tightly together. "Could we return to the matter at hand?"

"I can't help you guys," Xiang said quietly.

"Help me?" Sheedy said, flushing and going rigid.

"I'm just not interested in either," Xiang continued calmly.

"Fine," Dett said.

"Fine," Sheedy said, nodding vigorously up and down, his face heating visibly.

Xiang raised his shoulders and smiled. "I suppose there is one way I *could* help you."

Sheedy was beginning to vibrate with escalating badger rage but he stayed in his chair.

Andrew Xiang leaned across the table and whispered. "Get out of Halox. Get out of Commerce-Net."

It was Dett's turn to freeze. He knew.

"Bad news on both," Andrew said. "Obviously I can't say what precisely, but if you have clients long on either, I would back away. Since I won't buy yours, you should know I'm not shitting you. End of help."

And here Andrew Xiang left.

Dett didn't say a word all the way out to the car. The sale had been dead before it started and Sheedy hadn't seen that at all.

Sheedy riffed on a simple hostile theme, time and the sexual preferences of Andrew Xiang: "Waste of my fucking time. Faggot wasted my fucking time." All the while walking rigidly, hands in his pockets, jaw thrust out, head jerking from side to side as he scanned his memorized client list for the Plan B sucker.

Dett was flooded with images. Silent Cruise in the stretch, gaining on the leaders, the envelope of his spirit like a sonic boom through the air and soil and echoing off the far hills. Approaching the wire, veins all over the thoroughbred's body had bristled under the mahogany surface, marbling his hide.

"Gilbert Bligh maybe," Sheedy said when they got to the car.

I turned back, Dett thought, standing silently at the passenger door. I turned back to the sight of his breakdown, to the sight of his pain. Was there a trace of disrespect in watching Silent Cruise die? In not leaving him with the track crew and work ponies, in the company of his own?

"What do you think of Gil Bligh?" Sheedy repeated, louder.

Or had the fall pushed the duration of the race out beyond its strict borders? Would it then have been disrespectful to turn away, to treat wire results as the entirety of the event itself?

"Answer me!" Sheedy shouted and he thumped his hand on the Porsche's roof, which brought Dett's eyes sharply up from the green surface.

"What's the question?" he asked.

"We are emphatically not out of this yet, you hear me?" Sheedy was yelling at him from what might have been a great distance. His voice came through a kind of static. A static bristling with a thousand digits, rising to the surface of Dett's subconscience. 1s and 10s. 9s and other shadowy figures.

"We were punished," Dett said, hardly hearing his own words.

"Give me a freakin' break," Sheedy said, angrily popping the locks.

"I actually got that horse. I *got* it."

"Oh yes," Sheedy said, stepping away from the car, circling with his head lowered, arms rigid and balled in fists. And then after two or three circles, when his fury hit some glass-breaking pitch, he looked up and screamed across the car: "I've been meaning to *thank you for that*."

"Those *were* the numbers though. Those were the real numbers."

"Evi-fucking-dently." Sheedy said, spit flying from his lips and speckling the metallic green surface between them.

"The One in Ten," Dett said. "One in Ten."

"Shut . . ." Sheedy had to back away from the car again and circle. He couldn't complete the sentence.

"One is the full number," Dett went on. "The number that eliminates the other. The One that casts the shadow across the remainder."

Dett felt a delicious impulse rise within him as he continued. "The numbers 1, 9 and 10 can give us various dates in the 20th century," he said. "Like, say, September 10, 1901; October 9, 1901; January 10, 1909; October 1, 1909; January 9, 1910; and September 1, 1910. That's Tuesday, Wednesday, Sunday, Friday, Sunday, Thursday."

Sheedy continued to circle, now making a noise from his throat that sounded like a leaf blower. His arms were still stretched down at his sides but his fingers were spread as widely as he could. He might have been psyching up to break bricks with his head.

"But all along it was only the 9 I needed," Dett went on, oblivious. "9, 9, 9 . . . September 9, 1909 was a Thursday! A Thursday Sheedy. The 3-day spread. It corroborates."

This all burst from him in a hail of internal applause. He thought it must have been like this to crack the Weirmach encryptions. A room full of jumping, hugging bodies and flying bits of paper.

"The remainder was 9 and I didn't understand it. 9 was the empty set, the left out number. 9 was the shadow. I was shown the shadow and we used it wrong, we tried to fuck someone over and the numbers fucked us back. It is so beautiful."

Sheedy continued to circle, his Samurai cry rising, cresting, then fading off into a plaintiff ululation of grief which itself wound down after a minute or two.

"Get in the car," Sheedy said finally, his face drained. "We have work to do."

"So beautiful . . ." Dett was saying to an audience of billions of digits which swarmed in appreciation.

". . . phone calls to make, markers to pull in, numbers to run . . ."

"You're wrong about numbers," Dett said, and a brief silence descended in him. "You think numbers are bits and pieces."

Sheedy put his elbows on the roof of the car. Leaned his face into his hands.

"Numbers," he said, his voice muffled. "You see, Dett, you swim in a sea of friggin' numbers. You float in a data cloud, my young friend."

And here Sheedy lifted his head from his hands, fixed red eyes on his protégé and held up a single quivering finger to emphasize his point.

"And that Dett is a *good thing*. That makes all the molecules in your universe the same thing, little snips of data, numbers, digits, bytes. You have the building blocks and you can put them together one way and you have an interest rate swap. Another way and you have a derivative based on the price of Argentinean Black Angus testicles. A third way and you have the Argentinean Black Angus testicle itself. It's data. *Your* data *your* world. There isn't an MBA in a fucking thousand who is as stripped clean as you. I hired you because I envy you."

"You're still wrong," Dett said. It was amazing to him how insight, when it arrived, threw a brilliant light across every particle in the universe. "Numbers are perfectly analogue," he announced. "Not bits. Not pieces. Perfectly analogue."

"We're both going to be bits and pieces if you don't get in the car," Sheedy said. Then he climbed into the Porsche and slammed the door, which in a car of this price and parcelled engineering, produced a sound like: Snick.

But Dett couldn't hear most of this anyway. The gentle cascade of his numbers had started again and grown to a thunderous noise, the numerals spilling out of him like some kind of anchor chain, screaming and clanking as the linked steel integers fell into the depths. 1 in 10 in 1 in 10 in 1 in 10 in 1 in 10 in 1 in 10.

It still had a new car smell, this Porsche 911 Carrera 4, which could do 0–60 miles per hour in about 4 and ½ seconds flat. But these were meaningless numbers to Dett at the moment, who was busy pondering, musing, smiling, thanking the great host of numerals that arrayed themselves around him on a never-ending, seamless plane.

9, 9, 9 . . . I would just like to *thank* the number 9.

LEE HENDERSON

Sheep Dub

Whose baby hands were soft and instinctive, clenching indiscriminately around fingers laid in her palm, whose legs shot into the air like sensitive feelers, probing and tasting the air of her crib; whose stomach was as soft as kneaded dough and bare for a mouth to press against and make loud raspberries; whose baby cry she never lost even when she was six, crying when I forced her out of my room and pinched her toe when slamming the door, crying when I told her she was stupid, crying when I strangled her, and crying when I told her I didn't like her; whose memory was idiot savantish, or photographic at least, remembering things from when she was less than a year old: the colour of the shirt I wore the first time she had a fever and was taken to the doctor, the name of the dead barber that used to cut my hair, before he died – who she had met once when she was two; whose hair, as a baby, began to grow in leafy tufts from behind her ears and turned long and flowing and the colour of bittersweet chocolate, whose name for fear was "the Sheep"; whose nightmares accosted us both because she insisted on sleeping in my bedroom; whose first word at five months(!) was "Ben," my own name; whose favourite food was bananas; whose smell was always slightly of bananas; whose constant reminder was that I didn't like her, that I was as close to hating her as a brother could be, that she was not wanted around me; whose own name was Christine, is now long dead.

I wasn't far enough away from the maternity ward, not far enough away that I didn't have to hear my mother's shrieks, the high, anxious noises like the kind she made when she'd almost cried enough and was about to fall back asleep. I was in the hall, on a folding chair a nurse had opened for me, so that I could see into the room where my mother was birthing my sister. Inside, my father wasn't making any sound and I didn't know what his role was in the delivery – if he was necessary the way he was for the conception. Now and then a nurse jogged by me, one slipped on a streak of coffee I had seen a man loose from the geriatric ward spill earlier. The old man had passed me, shaking, and as I watched him and heard at the same time my mother's screams, it seemed as if it was all coming from him. He was screaming, he was shaking, he spilled some coffee, kept walking. I was supposed to be reading an X-Men comic. A family of mutants. The blue beast.

Next day I came back with my father to visit for the second time.

"You'd like to see her," my mother said.

Made my way across the room towards her stirrupped bed and saw at once that my mother had huddled against her the baby swathed in hospital towels. I hooked my hands around the cold railing above the mattress and stood on my toes to see my new sister's face.

"Meet your brother, Christine," she said, tilted the baby towards me. She had eyes that were puffed and shut, and twists of blue and red veins like hair all over her skull. Her mouth was tiny and caked with stuff, as was her nose.

"I saw her yesterday," I said.

"Did you. I can't remember."

My father folded onto his knees and petted his new daughter's face, casually wiping some of the stuff from her nostrils and lip corners.

"The most beautiful baby," he said carelessly.

Blocking my own view of her, I saw for the first time the bare patch of skin on my father's scalp and the thinning striations of hair surrounding. He was ambling towards baby himself, the way Christine was bursting away from it.

My mother said to him, "Hope your hands are clean."

Whose memory was idiot savantish, or photographic at least, whose favourite flavour of ice cream was banana-mint, whose designated bowl for eating banana-mint ice cream was an old ceramic onion soup bowl with a chipped handle. At three years old, her nose met the edge of the kitchen table so that it looked as though she were peeking up over the top to pilfer the food before her. She swung a spoon up and dipped it into the bowl and brought a dollop of the dessert down to where her mouth was, out of view.

She said, "This is our medicine." She picked out a nugget of mint and held it. Then with two fingers she placed it at the back of her throat the way she'd seen it done. The way she'd seen it done with medicine.

The wicker garbage basket in the bathroom was always filled with empty amber bottles, all labelled in dot matrix print with my mother's name, the doctor's name, the name of what the bottle used to contain.

It was a game she played. Standing at the window in the living room while I puzzled over math problems or the loops and hairpin turns of p's and z's, she would press her finger against the glass and point to something outside.

"What's behind that house?" she would ask.

"Shut up," I said. "I'm working," I said.

"What's behind it? Nothing?"

"Shut up."

"If there was two of me, I could find out with no one knowing."

She turned to the window again and looked out past the glass.

"What's over there, behind that?"

I stood up from my math book and kicked it aside, went to her, took her arms in my hands and shook her. She saw me coming and flinched, wound her shoulders up to her ears and opened her mouth to cry; I shook her, saw her eyes stutter and toggle. I could feel that she was small; her bones clacked together like the joints of a marionette. I shook her like that, there.

Told her, "Shut up."

Letting her go she throbbed, dizzy on her feet. Christine welled up in the eyes with tears, and before I could make it back to my homework, she had me at the waist. Wrapped around me and crying or about to cry, her open mouth allowing drool to dampen my shirt, she stopped me from moving.

"Please, Ben." She hugged me tightly.

I gave her a knock on the head with the heel of my hand. "Let go."

Her crying worsened and she said again, "What's behind that?"

I said I didn't know, I didn't know what was behind the hedge-wall that she pointed to because I'd never been allowed across the street.

I could see the coin-sized grease marks her fingers had left on the window.

The glass and wood that separated us from outside was thin and delicate.

"Never," my mother said, "ever – cross the street. Alright. Follow the sidewalk."

In bed – when all light aside from what my nightlight cast had been carved away and we could see one another only by the rare shapes relieved of shadow – she would attempt to mimic the inflections of our mother's voice.

"Never ever," Christine would say, pausing to sigh, letting her eyes shut and open like someone veering too close to sleep, "cross the street. Alright. Follow – the sidewalk."

She also said, "What's that?" whenever there was a noise. And I could hear her frantically twisting in her sleeping bag, unleashing her arms and sitting up.

"What was that, Ben?"

Whose name for fear was "the Sheep"; whose nightmares accosted us both because she insisted on sleeping in my bedroom; whose first word at five months(!) was "Ben," my own name, whose sleeping bag was kept unrolled below my bed, with a pillow and a plush E.T. doll.

"What was that, Ben?"

The doorbolt sliding back, a knife lifted from a kitchen drawer, the creak of a knee-joint. The Sheep: she could hear it raise a heavy front leg and drop a hoof to the carpet, and then another leg, and another, another. Each hoofstep, a muffled thud coming closer, up the stairs two at a time, the hard blow of nostrils becoming audible as it made its way to the door of my bedroom.

"Can I sleep with you?" she'd whisper. "Ben."

"Stay in your sleeping bag," I said, "on the floor."

But now even I could hear the Sheep's nose sniffing at the door, smelling us through the cracks; it sucked the doorknob between its big lips and spun its tongue along the brass to taste where the palms of our hands had lain; it bit down and tried to wind the handle open.

She was in my bed, beside me under the covers, without my noticing how she got there, and I could feel her shaking, could feel her fingers clench and tug at my pyjamas.

"Oh my," she said like our mother said it. "Oh my," and then my sister started to cry. Her crying was severe; I'd wipe away the hairs that webbed her eyes, which remained wide open, dilated, black and raw.

She once described every pattern on every one of our father's ties. She drew them with Crayolas on loose-leaf and we hung them on the fridge with real estate magnets.

Whose hair began to grow from behind her ears in leafy tufts and turned long and flowing and the colour of bitter-sweet chocolate; whose job it was – in return for candy – to regularly inspect the wicker garbage basket in the bathroom for our mother's empty bottles. She fished them out from the pool of Kleenex, mint dental floss – and I kept them in an old sewing box under my bed. At five I learned to crack their childproof caps.

I kept mostly candy inside our mother's discarded vials. Like a pharmacist, I used a letter-opener to divide a selection of the candy between us and we surreptitiously ate as we sat and watched the television.

Jellybeans, Mike & Ikes, Nerds, Tart 'n' Tinys, Sweet Hearts, Runts, Pez, licorice Goodies, Rain-blo.

"Let your mother sleep," Christine would say and lie back on the carpet, fold her hands behind her head – slaked, coloured sugar-powder crusting at the sides of her mouth.

At six I was allowed to visit the confectionery at the foot of our block without being accompanied by my mother. Christine was also invited so long as we held hands through the entire trip.

We followed the neat lawns and fork-tined fences to the confectionery, dustbowls raising themselves in cones off at the horizon where houses had yet to have been built, where the construction workers left their trucks when they came in to pave the new roads or wire new lamp-posts. I choked up Christine's hand inside my own as punishment for walking too slow. I made my grip so tight her fingertips flushed purple, squirmed.

She didn't complain.

"Hurry up," I said and yanked her forward.

At the store, the boy behind the counter – whose thin moustache disappeared completely at the centre, and whose breath smelled of digestive biscuits – tipped towards us, smiled and said, "Looking for the rush?" and we nodded shyly, made for home with our candy where I would fill the amber bottles with the confections and catalogue them accordingly. Certs, Tic Tacs and other mints were separated, as well as the more serious collection of sneaked Tylenols, Anacins and Rolaids – which our father left around in half-eaten rolls.

There was also, in an amber bottle all to its own, pressed against the bottom by six lumps of cotton, a single white pill that I had found below the sink. This was one of our mom's real pills. Christine and I often thought of that pill, and we regarded it as a treasure, studying it every day; I constantly scrutinized it to ensure that it hadn't been pilfered. It was very small.

I had a friend over from school, a boy named Andy. And we sat in my room and I doled out my drugs to him and he pretended to be affected by their properties. I carved out three Sweet Hearts, four Certs and a Rain-blo, and told him to take them all immediately or he would die. He did so, and then, with a burp, went into a clonic fit, a brief and comedic seizure that portrayed the drugs' side effects.

"Thanks, Doc," he told me and shook my hand.

I served myself a prescription of Runts, swallowed them fast. The more prescriptions I filled for myself and Andy, the wilder the side effects got, until Andy was flailing about, slamming against the walls and pulling his cheeks out as far as they would stretch, as I butted my face against the mattress of my bed.

"What are you doing?" Christine came in without knocking.

"Help," I screamed to Andy, "I'm having a streak of violence. Get me some drugs before I kill her." I leapt from the bed and came at my sister with both arms raised, hands splayed and ready to strangle.

"Help," I cried. Andy worked fast at designing a prescription for me; not fast enough. I had her against the wall, my fingers locked into a tight cage around her neck. Her face puffed and the capillaries in her cheeks came to the skin; her eyes watered and became ringed with blood. She made little gasps and her teeth drew shut. She kicked weakly at my shins, her fingers hooked to my shirt. I could feel I was holding her from falling, that her body was giving way.

I swallowed what Andy put to my lips, and once sated, released her.

She found her breath again while holding me, still, holding me. Her head against my chest. Not making a sound aside from the sound of air climbing in and out of her lungs.

"Leave," I told her. "I have a friend over," I said.

Whose first word was "Ben," my own name, and then more words, "banana" (a command), "David" (our father's name), "six" (the news at six), until she began to repeat the monologues on afternoon soap operas, the lyrics to songs on the radio, or the number of times the phone had rung in the last three days. By the time she was five she would give me a synopsis at the end of the week of all that had happened in the last seven days. Her degree of accuracy astounding, she seemed to clone our lives, doubling every event. She would perform, verbatim, dialogues between our father and mother, fights and capitulations; she would describe scenes in microscopic detail; she would, in effect, dictate her diary to me.

Christine came to me, knelt down to where I was working and said, "I feel bad-weathery." It was something our mother said if we asked her why she had just swallowed some medicine. Watching her raise the heel of her hand to her mouth and swallow with her head cocked upwards, then massaging her throat with her knuckles. A glass of water afterwards.

I invited Christine to my room, showed her a bottle with dot matrix type on it reading: Take two daily. A.m. then p.m.

"Take two of these every day." Uncapped the bottle, handed it to her. "One in the morning. One before bed."

She nodded. "It's nothing serious." She twisted the bottle in her hands and considered the contents.

"Thanks, Ben," she said.

I waved her out of the room.

She was to take Junior Mints for the next month or so, and I made sure that she did not take more than she was allowed. I counted them.

Watched her drop them in her mouth as our mother did, with the heel of her hand. A glass of water afterwards. Twice a day as prescribed.

The Sheep made the wind howl, made the tree outside my window scrape its stiff elbowed branches against the pane of my window, made the high heels click on the sidewalk. The Sheep made these sounds.

Two minutes later, two minutes past any sound, a cough cloaked by doors and walls, a car passing with a swim of light across our ceilings, any sound, and two minutes later – the time it would take her to gather the courage to get out of bed and go to the hallway – she would knock on my door. A series of tiny, one-knuckle taps like code. Tap tap tap. Tap tap.

I said nothing, did not reply to the knocks, knowing it was her. I imagined her head screwing around in the darkness of the hallway, alert to the Sheep, waiting for a serrated tooth to carve into her back.

She knocked again.

"Ben."

The door opened, hissed as it brushed against the carpet of my room.

"Ben. The Sheep. I heard it."

But she imagined something more feral. A sheep with dense, oily wool, stained with ash and mud, smelling of the bitter held-in upchuck of nausea, with jagged coiled horns like nautilus shells, and joints as stiff and rotten as old wood. It would trample her, kick its front legs into the air and hammer them on her neck and ribs, snapping her, then bite at the split skin to tear chunks off to eat. Its breath was cold, loud, its eyes like black beans.

"Ben."

"Shut up," I said, did not move.

"Can I sleep with you?"

"No."

She took the sleeping bag and pillow from beneath my bed, slid into it on the floor. I heard her fishing for her doll and then putting it beside her head as she always did.

"Stay there," I said. "I don't want you near me."

Found her the next morning up against my back, making noises in her sleep.

She said that our mother's hair was "auburn" and then asked me what the word "auburn" meant.

I remember at night, when our father came home, he was in clothes I never recognized, their pleats, their tailored seams. They were as unfamiliar as he was. The front door would open and at first I wouldn't recognize him. He would go to our mother on the sofa to kiss her and wake her, and then soon after, to the shower.

"Don't kiss my lips," she said and rubbed her mouth with the back of her hand, "you've been out all day."

He put his hand on her forehead, she pushed it away.

"I feel bad-weathery."

"I'll have a shower," he said and left to start one running.

Beside the toilet there was a rack of race car magazines, some with women on the covers dressed in bathing suits, some without.

"Come to me," she said and barely moved her hand. Her palm cupped, scooping. I came towards my mother, stood beside the couch where she lay.

"Be good to your sister," she said.

"I am," I said. "I'm good," I said.

"A hug." She raised her arms for me to climb between them, hold her.

"No," I said.

"Leave then." She let her arms fall, elbow then wrist. Her chest rose, her mouth opened as if to release a sigh but no sound came. I felt I had hurt her feelings.

Stayed beside her a moment more and considered giving her the hug she had asked for, thought about it, walked away. Went to my room and shut the door, attempted to think about nothing.

For Hallowe'en Christine wanted us both to go as Ghostbusters, and my mother offered to make us the costumes. She built us special backpacks made of cardboard and Tupperware – all painted black – with vacuum cleaner hoses fastened to them that fit into loops on our belts at the other end. We had matching grey outfits and rubber boots. Christine had never walked our neighbourhood aside from the route back and forth to the confectionery, and she sat beside the window in the living room on the day of Hallowe'en and followed the sidewalks with her finger against the glass, planning the areas she would cover.

"What's behind that house?" she asked me. "Can we go there?"

"I don't know." The television was on.

"Are there houses behind?"

"Don't know."

"Mom coming, or just Dad?"

"Dad."

When the sun fell and the street became dark it was harder for her to see across the road to where she imagined we would start our route – the place she first put her finger. Squinting, she saw the lamps outside flicker and glow, spreading cones of orange light down on the sidewalks.

A child came to our door and rang the bell.

"You're a ghost," my mother said.

"Tick or teat," the ghost said, one eye-hole around her nose. Christine stared at the child, watched the girl follow the

candy bar our mother gave her down into her pillowcase.
Watched her run back down our driveway.

She didn't eat dinner; wasn't hungry.

Mother put us in our costumes, attached the hoses to their
proper places and fussed with the collars of our suits.

"Take a picture," she said.

"No film," our father answered.

"Great." She stood up and went to the kitchen, filled the
dishwasher.

"Let's go," Father said and went to the door and put on his
shoes. He looked to his watch. "Let's go," he said once more.

Christine pulled me down to whisper something in my ear.

I came home an hour later and showed her all I had gotten. She
looked back at the window.

"All this came from our block?" she asked.

"Didn't even finish the block," I said, started sorting the
candy.

"Going to bed now," our mother said once she'd seen my loot.
Heard the door shut to her bedroom.

"Thirty-two kids came," Christine told me. "Want to know
what they were?" She was still dressed in her costume, though
she had not left the house.

"No." I put my candy into the medicine bottles.

"Can I have one?"

"No."

Before going to bed I studied the single white pill that was our
mother's. Its edges were soft; it could easily dissolve.

That night there was no moon. It was cold. I had blankets up to
my chin, and I rubbed my feet together to keep them warm.
There was no sound.

I looked to where my closet was, expected to see nothing. My
closet where I kept my clothes and a basket of old toys. Light
came from within the closet, breaking through the slats of the
door. The light was whitish-blue and dim. When I attempted to
look away I found that I was not able to move, paralysed.
Something was inside my closet.

From outside my room a sound came and I forgot about the light as quickly as it dimmed. There was no light.

I heard the noise again, and then soon after, Christine tapped on my door, opened it, hissing as it brushed against the carpet of my room.

"Ben."

I felt like crying for some reason, but didn't let on.

"Go away," I whispered.

"No, Ben. I hear the Sheep."

"Don't worry about it. Go back."

She came inside and shut herself in the sleeping bag. We listened to the noise again.

"What is it?" she asked. It was coming from our parents' bedroom.

"Shh." I looked to the closet again but it was normal.

"Ben." I could hear her sniffing back tears. "Can I tell you what came to our door tonight?"

"I don't care," I said, having difficulties breathing.

The sound came louder now.

Christine whispered, "A cat. Three pirates. A television set ..."

"Oh," the sound said; the silence afterwards ate everything.

"I'm scared Ben," Christine said, "can I –"

I was scared too. I hadn't moved and I was frightened to try. She opened the blankets and fell in beside me, breathing hard through her mouth. She took my hand. I could see the Sheep.

"Christine," I said, "it's in Mom and Dad's room."

"It is?"

"It's killing them."

"Oh," the sound said.

Christine squeezed my hand. We continued to listen.

"We have to save them," I said.

"I'm too scared."

"Come after us next."

"Oh," the sound said.

We opened the door, peered into the corridor. I put my hand out, watched it being swallowed into the black. The hall stank of soap and something foul. The Sheep. Christine clamped my hand as we stepped out of my room. The whitish-blue light now came from the slit between the door and carpet of our parents' room. The tufted hair of the carpet was flickering in light from the source.

"Oh," the sound said.

Christine pulled me down to whisper something in my ear.

She said she couldn't remember anything any more, felt guilty, was frightened. I put my finger to my lips to tell her to be quiet. I saw that tears were streaming down her face.

Our feet made no sound as we made it from my bedroom to our parents'. The door knob, cold and brass, made no sound as I wound it open.

"Oh."

Neither of us were breathing. I opened the door.

"OH." The sound was louder now. We saw that our parents' television set was on, with the sound turned down to nothing. On the screen a woman's face was burrowed in the belly of a man.

I could feel Christine's knees knock against me as they shuddered.

"Oh," our mother said, sitting on top our father.

She would tell me all that had happened in the last seven days, the Hallowe'en. She would describe everything that she could remember, every microscopic detail, every word. But she wouldn't remember much other than a cat, three pirates, a television set.

While our mother was in the hospital, near Christmas, I found Christine on the floor of my room, lying flat with a hammer beside her. She had broken open every bottle, had eaten all the candy. A dusty purple film coated her lips. She looked sick.

"Those were mine," I said. Saw wrappers from the candy I had received at Hallowe'en, saw the remnants of what I had bought from the confectionery, and all else gone as well. She had eaten everything, not a thing left.

"I'm overdosing," she said.

"Get up," I yanked her arm and lifted her to her feet. She repressed a belch and ran to the bathroom. I shut the bathroom door, and then my own door so I wouldn't have to listen.

Christine had been given a few tranquilizers, was asleep in her room.

"We all need some rest," my father said and squeezed his temples. "Go to bed." He smiled a small smile and folded down to his knees to look me in the eyes. Put his hands on my shoulders, opened his mouth to speak, didn't. Casually, he wiped my face, though I don't know why. He stared at the floor, and when I looked down too, saw that there was nothing of consequence there. He took his eyes from the carpet, and looked at all that was in the hallway besides me – didn't look at me. Finally he laughed. He made a single, numb laugh come out.

"Ha." Stood up again and shut the door to his bedroom behind him.

I lay in my own bed, the covers up against my chin. I wasn't asleep.

Soon I heard the door to my bedroom slide open, saw my sister, her head drooped.

She said, "Can I sleep with you." Her voice was slurred and slow. She said, "don't feel so good."

"Yes," I said.

She stumbled over, almost tripping once, and fell down beside me, and as I covered her over with the blankets, having to move her arms and legs into more suitable positions, I saw that she was already fast asleep. The medicine my father had given her to relax her combined with my entire stock of pills had made her drowsy. She had barely made it to my room. I knew that she had also eaten that single white pill of our mother's, because it too was gone.

I tried to sleep, but couldn't.

When I opened my eyes it was as dark as when they were closed. The air was crisp. I looked to where my closet was, and since it was dark, expected to see nothing. My closet where I kept my clothes and a basket of my old toys. There was light coming from within the closet, breaking through the cracks in the door. The light was whitish-blue and dim. It did not frighten me. When I attempted to move towards it I found I could not, was paralysed. Saw from between the slats of the closet door a slight movement, like an animal shifting its weight from one heel to the other. I could see the Sheep in the whitish-blue light.

I rolled Christine against my back, her head towed along behind, draped her arm over me, tested the skin at her wrists, the thin tendon cords there, and the pulse of blood. I held her hands inside mine the way I did when we went to the confectionery, I held her that tightly, and I felt the slow, shallow exhalation from her mouth against my neck. Each breath coming later than the one before.

J.A. McCORMACK

Hearsay

By April I was sick and tired of waiting for Garnet to get out of jail. He had been in so many times that I was used to it, but there was a difference between being used to it and liking it. He was never in for very long because he never did anything very bad, so it was more of an inconvenience than some kind of sour sad thing the way you might think, but it was still a pain in the butt.

It wasn't so much the money, because I had a job and that was what we mainly lived on anyway, although we were a lot better off when he was working as well, but the fact of it is that even when he was out of jail he often didn't have a job because Garnet was a pretty touchy guy with a temper, maybe because his life to date hadn't exactly matched up to his view of himself. This made him nervous that maybe he had the wrong view, but he didn't like the one his life seemed interested in giving him, so he would get into a stupid fight with some sonofabitch supervisor just to prove his view was right, with the result that if we'd had to rely on his paycheque we would have been up shit's creek without a paddle a long time ago.

The one good thing about him being in jail was that he always came back in a kind of glad mood. He was so tickled to be out, it was like everything was new and gorgeous to him and he was sort of in love with his own clothes and eating non-jail food any time he wanted to. I guess this last part wasn't surprising since according to him, the jail had contracted out the food services a few years ago so that it was all pre-frozen and then microwaved or else reconstituted from powder or flakes or concentrate, with the result that the scrambled eggs were like lumps of yellow rubber and the mashed potatoes had potato juice leaking out of them, and the Jell-O was like slime, which he felt was kind of an insult to it because he liked Jell-O, although who the hell knows why because it's not exactly my idea of something great. Of course all this gladness would only last for a few days, then he would go back to his usual crabby self.

Now there was something he was really good at. He almost had a gift in that direction, he could complain from morning until night and never repeat himself. Everything was goddamn shitty, everybody was assholes, according to him, starting from the coffee in the morning, moving on to the weather, the seams on his jeans, the super, it was as if he had made himself judge of everything, and everything was guilty. If he was in a fairly good mood, it was just habit, but if he was in a bad mood, he could tear a strip off someone like his tongue was a buzzsaw.

So maybe somebody else wouldn't have missed him, but I did.

Every once in a while he would look at me in this leaky kind warm way that made me feel like you do when there's something you wanted all your life and didn't think you would ever get and hardly recognize because it's been in such short supply. Whenever I started thinking that maybe I didn't need to be with someone who had a personality like a scrub-brush, I would see this look and end up thinking differently.

I used to visit him in jail but it was a long bus ride and at the end of it you just got to speak on this telephone and look at the person through this plastic barrier, and then I could never think of anything to say, so we'd make small talk, and to tell you the truth the whole thing drove me goddamn bonkers, I would keep thinking about breaking the plastic just so I could just get a little feel of some of his important parts and maybe a little sniff of the way he smelled. The fact was that it was worse than not seeing him at all to see him in this chopped up little boring way with all the juice sucked out of it, and so after a while I stopped going.

While I was sitting at my kitchen table thinking of how tired I was of waiting for Garnet, Denzie banged on the door and I let her in. She was carrying all our stuff for doing our hair, rubber cap with little holes, crochet hook, Sunkissed *Colour by Numbers*. I put the kettle on and made her instant coffee with sugar. She needed sugar almost continuously, it was some kind of medicine for her, like her body was deficient, sort of like diabetes, but not yet discovered by medical science. This meant that she was pretty big though, lots of wobbly flesh, and the biggest boobs I've ever seen, a ledge coming out at her chest, even bigger than her stomach, and the whole thing moved together most of the time and swayed up and down or from side to side when she walked. I don't know how she stood it, although I was no slenderella myself, big thighs, a few rolls here and there but I was minor league compared to her. It was hard not to look sometimes, her fat just seemed kind of hypnotizing, most of the time she didn't mind if she caught me staring, although sometimes if she was feeling bad anyway she snapped at me. Then other times she would tell me what it was like, people looking at her in a disgusted way all the time and she had to powder all the creases with talcum powder because otherwise she would get rashes there, so she always smelled like Lilac Spring or Wood Rose or whatever she could get on sale at Shoppers Drug Mart. The thing is that she would sweat a lot too, so usually it was Lilac Spring mixed in with the skunky smell of sweat.

I went first, so I pulled the cap over my head and she started pulling strands of hair out of the holes with the crochet hook. I could do the ones in the front myself, but I needed help with the back, and she just found it easier to do it all over once she was up there hanging over my head. It made her feel like a real hair stylist, which she had always been interested in but figured she couldn't be because she was so fat. The truth is that she could have been a lot of things because she was smart as hell, and she let you know it, because she was tired of being treated badly. But it was probably true about the hair stylist because let's face it, you need to be able to stand between the styling chairs, and they don't make the space for someone her size. Not to mention that they liked people who were so thin and fashionable they looked like they could slip under the door to get to work.

In fact, she once applied to be a manicurist at Pearl's Unisex down the street, and they said no without giving any reason and they never asked her to demonstrate her manicure skills, even though the manicurist works while the person is under the dryer and there was plenty of room there, I know because I went and checked it out for her before she applied, so we figured it was prejudice, not a doubt in our minds. I felt really bad for her because I knew she was hoping this would be the thing that would get her ahead, but she wouldn't admit it, just pretended it was no big deal, I guess because she had a lot of hopes burnt up like that, and couldn't afford to admit that it got to her.

Anyway, Denzie painted the Sunkissed on to the hair sticking out the holes and set the timer and we sat by the kitchen table, which in my case had a grey and white plastic top and drank some more coffee and each wondered to ourselves whether it was too early to have a drink, and decided it was and besides we didn't have any, so we smoked like chimneys instead. The window was open and the air that was coming in was warm and a little spongy since it was spring. The sun was out but it was kind of wet-looking too and we sat and yakked and watched the smoke from our cigarettes curl and twist around and hang in the usual smoky way.

When the timer went, I washed out the Sunkissed and rinsed the cap and dried it as well as I could, and then it was her turn. So I pulled the cap down and pulled her hair through the holes, and she sneezed, the way she always does when I do the part on the right front side of her head, and so we got that out of the way, and then I spread the paste on and we set the timer again. By this time, we had covered recent events, like who was moving in on the fifth floor and whether Carlene's son really was dealing, which I thought was pretty goddamn obvious because he had too much money, and he spent too much time hanging around outside at night meeting strange people, but Denzie was a friend of Carlene's, so she just said he was a smart kid, and was good with a buck, so it didn't actually prove anything, which I had to admit, but it was sure suspicious, which she had to agree with. Anyway, the conversation was running down a little while we waited for Denzie's hair to bleach although by this time mine was drying, and looking blonder, and it made me feel like I was growing a bunch of daffodils on the top of my head the way it always does, like maybe if my hair was newer and yellower everything would be different, although you would think by now that I would know better since I had been doing it every two months for the last four years and nothing had changed.

"So when's he getting out?" Denzie asked.

"Two months, four days, but who's counting," I said.

"Seems like he just went in," she said. She had the usual friend-of-the-girlfriend relationship with Garnet, where they basically like the man because he's the kind of person that the girlfriend likes and so normally the kind of person they would like too, but on the other hand, they've had to listen to the girlfriend bitch and complain about the man and be loyal to her, and also they know all about the man's bad points.

"Seems like it's been a hundred years to me," I said. The room stank of the chemical smell from the Sunkissed.

"So do you think he'll stay out this time?" she said. This showed that the conversation was really running down because she knew Garnet and I had gone over and over this trying to figure out where the goddamn problem was, was it bad luck or judges who were against the little guy or being in the wrong place at the wrong time, or whether there was something he could do to avoid all his problems. Basically we were stumped, and not because we were stupid either, because we weren't, it was because each time there were so many different things involved that all seemed to come from different directions, but all landed up together to screw things up royally.

"Beats the hell out of me," I said. It always seemed like he would start out in the best way but then things would fall apart like a pear going rotten, brown spots appearing all of a sudden out of nowhere but some parts still good and then the brown spots getting bigger and joining up together until you had to throw the whole pear out.

He had made so many brand new starts and they had all gone so bad that he was starting to lose faith in the whole thing and feel jinxed, although I tried to keep him from thinking this way because I was afraid that if he did, it would come true just from him thinking it. But even I had to admit that the optimistic viewpoint had less and less support.

Sean came in then. He'd been running around outside and he was hungry but all I had was bread and peanut butter which isn't so bad and is better than nothing but he was tired of that, although he ate it anyway but it meant that he was grouchy, and Denzie ignored him because she looked after him after school while I worked as a secretary for Meyer Kaplansky, barrister and solicitor, and she told me she had to save all her patience with Sean for those days and not use it up when he had me around, because there was only so much Sean patience in the world, or at least between the two of us, and we had to be careful not to use it up at the same time.

This is because Sean is a very energetic kid, even hyperactive some of his teachers said, and also has very strong feelings so that when he's feeling bad he howls at the top of his lungs and when he's feeling good he's the king of the castle and bounces around like a goddamn Mexican jumping bean which can be just as tiring. When he was younger and couldn't go out and play by himself in the courtyard, I used to have to take him out every day and kind of run him around to work off his jumpiness or else he would wind himself up and whirl around in the apartment like a dog chasing his tail to the point where the thought came into my head that one day he might go so fast he might disappear in a puff of smoke.

Once the school wanted to put him on drugs to slow him down, and I was against it because I thought that it was just that he was kind of exhausting to deal with as opposed to anything being really wrong with him, and they were just being lazy, and besides he was quite good at the school work itself because he loved to count things over and over and repeat words and put things that were the same together, which pretty much took care of kindergarten and the first couple of grades. I might have done it though, because they were pushing so hard and I wasn't sure I was right and I figured that they knew quite a bit about it, but actually Garnet was the one who was dead against it, which was helpful in terms of propping me up, and good considering Sean wasn't even his but had come along before him. So Sean never went on the drugs, and he's gotten a little better, but all you have to do is spend an hour around him to see

Denzie's point. Although every once in a while he says something that makes you feel achy and kind towards him, and this helps to make up for the times you feel like smacking him because you're at your wits' end. I try not to smack him because I figure I don't like to be hit and fair is fair, and besides I'm bigger than he is but that kid could try the patience of a goddamn saint, and I'm not a saint so a couple of times I've lost it, but then I felt sick about being mean to him, like having a hot knife in my stomach and the thing about him is that he forgave me, although when you think about it, it's not like he really had much of a choice.

Sean went out again, and Denzie rinsed her hair and it was drying, and it looked good, that was one thing, she did have really good hair, thick and shiny which was interesting because often very fat people have thin hair for some reason, like some part of them had to be thin and their hair got elected.

Then we heard Sean yelling because he's only allowed to play in the one courtyard where I can see him, and he knows the window is open so he just has to yell. The courtyard is surrounded by all the apartments in a u-shape with a fence on the other side where the street is, and the housing people have actually made an effort to make the place look not too bad by painting the doors different colours, and there is quite a bit of grass there, although this time of year it was still kind of brown from the winter and plus there was popsicle wrappers and old cigarette packages and empty potato chip bags and paper slushee cups around because nobody had picked them up which is pretty common in the courtyard for any time of year.

When Sean yelled, we saw two of Metro's finest, a woman, they look so tiny in the uniform and another guy, talking to Carlene's son and the man was holding his arm in an official looking and not too gentle way and they were leading him over to a cruiser and he looked like he was going to cry, but I guess they had come to the same conclusion I had about him, and Denzie got up and swayed towards the door and stuck her head out and yelled to Carlene in case Carlene's door was open but I could see Carlene running out the door into the courtyard because she had already seen it.

She was wearing a faded pink terrycloth bathrobe and a white T-shirt and you could see some of the blue veins in her legs that ended up in rundown slippers and her hair was sticking up all over the place and she went running up to the cops and started swearing at them, not that I could hear very well but I could tell they weren't talking about the weather and she looked madder than a bee, and the woman cop opened the back door of the cruiser and the man pushed Carlene's son in anyway, and then they both got in and drove away, with the woman driving no less, which I guess shows the steps women have made, and Carlene just stood there for a while, slowly drooping from her angry position into a sad and tired kind of position. The sun had given up entirely by then, which looked like it would suit her mood, even though it was warm and windy and the wind was pushing the popsicle wrappers and potato chip bags along the ground. Then she looked around, and of course everyone whose windows faced the courtyard was looking at her and so she straightened up and went inside again, and I made a note to drop by because even though I was right about the son it wasn't Carlene's fault, and besides, it's one thing to be speculating and another thing for something like this to happen and I almost felt a little bit like it was my fault, because I hadn't exactly been shy about expressing my views, although almost everybody else thought it anyway, so it wasn't like I was the one bringing it to anyone's attention.

Anyway, it was time to head down to the Price Chopper and pick up a few things so Sean would have something to eat, so I found my purse and sweater and Denzie packed up the hair stuff and out we went, and I made Sean come with me because even a nine-year-old shouldn't really be left, although sometimes I do if he's playing and he doesn't mind, but I didn't know what else was going to happen in the courtyard this morning and I didn't want any stray cops mistaking him for Carlene's son's helper or anything and placing him in a foster home quicker than you could say children's aid, and he was okay with it when I told him he could pick out some Kool-Aid packages.

I lost a little girl to the children's aid a few years ago, it's a long story and it's true I wasn't in very good shape then, although there was certainly no call to do anything that horrible and at the time it felt like I had somehow breathed in broken glass and the pieces had all settled in the middle of my chest and it hurt so much that even my boobs ached, and I had to lie completely still on the couch for four days waiting for the screaming in my head to stop. The worst is when I have dreams that it was all a mistake, I see her face, one of those skinny little faces with a pointed chin and straight, sandy hair and a pink sparkly hair band with a plastic rose on it that was her favourite thing, and she's got that piece of one of my old nightgowns that she used to rub on the bottom of her nose when she sucked her thumb, and she sees me and takes her thumb out of her mouth and starts to run down the hall of the agency towards me and a stab of hope screeches from my chest to the top of my head, except that for some reason instead of getting closer to me she's getting smaller and further away, and I can see that she's saying "muma, muma," which is what she used to call me, except no words are coming out, and I try to run after her but my legs have melted into the floor and my arms are glued to my sides, and I try and call her but my tongue has gotten so thick that it's filled up my whole mouth, and I start to break out in fear, sort of like sweat except it's cold and dry all around the back of my neck and arms and back, and I keep trying to run and call her but nothing happens, and then I wake up and I can tell you that there isn't a goddamn nightmare on the planet worse than this.

Anyway, sometimes I feel like I'm floating around the way you would in water or maybe like I was a balloon and there isn't anything that is kind of giving things a shape I can really grab onto but in the middle of all that one thing I'm always crystal clear on is that nobody is taking Sean away and I try to make sure of that by paying extra attention to details. Also by staying off welfare and working, because when you're on welfare a worker is more likely to drop in on you and decide that your floor isn't clean enough or that your parenting skills aren't up to par, and apprehend your kid as they say, because he's in need of protection, which as far as I can tell would more likely apply to most of the foster homes they send them to and all of the group homes.

Monday I went to the office, and Meyer was in as opposed to being in court. He had a long egg-shaped face, and his head was bald in the front and he could have done with a little more chin and forehead and a little less nose, but he made sure he had nice suits and a good tan, so he took care of himself and looked the best he could with what he was given. And even though he was getting a paunch, he jogged every morning because he was deathly afraid of having a heart attack, so it all seemed pretty firm. At least he looked kind of definite, which is a good thing in a lawyer, and also he had smooth manners, although they were the kind of manners that were smooth not because he was oily but because he was naturally the opposite of shy so that he could chat away with someone he had just met a second ago like they were his best friend, which helps in the lawyer business.

Meyer was in a good mood because he had played golf over the weekend and he had gotten a good score, and he said for about the tenth time, "What do ya think, Cheryl, think I should go pro?" which I knew he wasn't really serious about so I could ask him questions like "well, how much could you make?" without worrying about whether I might lose my job. Then in walks Carlene of all people, although if you think about it it made sense that she would need a lawyer, but how she got to Meyer I don't know, or at least without asking me. She had a legal aid certificate because her son, whose name was Blair of all things, which showed that she had high ideas for him that hadn't worked out well, or at least not yet, but her son was charged with trafficking so that was serious enough to get a certificate. We expressed surprise at seeing each other, and then Meyer took her in to his office, treating her with kid gloves the way he did with all his clients, which says something for him because they weren't the fanciest bunch although most were a little less down on their luck than Carlene, but just barely.

In fact, he was a good lawyer I think, although of course I had only seen him in court when Garnet was the subject of the proceedings, but he liked his files kept just perfect, all the letters in date order on a brass tack that split, a sheet on the left side that he would write down everything that he did except for the legal aid files where it was a block fee, and he was just generally very organized. He also had what he called a tickler system so that all the deadlines for filing things were recorded by me and then I would BF, meaning bring forward the files a few days before the deadlines so that he wouldn't miss any. This was something he told me was required by the Law Society because so many lawyers had screwed up, but Meyer would have done it anyway because he was that kind of guy. If I was going through one of those floaty kind of periods, all his rules and ways of doing everything made me feel less like I was seasick and gave me something to hold on to. He did a good job with Garnet, too, spoke in such a smooth way and without any ums and ahs, and made some good points about how Garnet couldn't possibly have done it, and then when he was found guilty, about how sorry Garnet was and how he was already rehabilitated. Luckily this last part was in front of another judge because they got an adjournment for a pre-sentence report, although in the end it didn't do Garnet all that much good, but let's face it, the evidence looked bad against him, and as Meyer used to say, a lawyer can't wave a magic wand over the situation.

Meyer's office was in an old building, a little rundown but his particular office was a real old lawyer's office, so even though it wasn't that big, it had brown wood all over it and one of those bannister things down one side which made it look very legal and helped to impress his clients a lot, that and his confidence. I think he had been there for a long time, although I had only been working for him for two years, but he seemed to have made his peace with doing the same thing for his whole life which frankly would have driven me bonkers, but he spent a lot of time telling me that he had a good life and mainly he was successful at least in convincing himself. Although you kind of wondered why he needed so much convincing.

Anyway, Carlene looked very nice, not at all the way she looked in the courtyard, partly because she had put on make-up and done her hair and put on some good-looking clothes, a long clingy dress which covered up her blue veins. Meyer took her past where I sat and into his office and after a few minutes I could hear her starting to cry. I knew enough from previous clients that trafficking often ended up with a jail term, although

I couldn't remember how long they were, but they weren't good, that I remembered, and I figured that's probably why she was crying. I kept on typing, even though it was disturbing hearing her cry, but a lot of disturbing stuff went in and out of that office, after all, that's when people are going to see a lawyer when they've got problems, take it from me, not many of them are there because they just won the lottery and need legal advice as to how to spend the money.

About half an hour later, out they came, Carlene with a reddish nose, not surprising under the circumstances, and Meyer told me to open a file and he gave me the certificate so I could send in the confirmation to Legal Aid, and he said good-bye to Carlene and I did too, and I tried to smile in a comforting way, although I don't know what comfort you can give someone whose son is facing what could be a longish jail term and judging from what I had seen, I suspected that they weren't going to have too much trouble proving a case, usually it turns out that one of the customers was an undercover cop, but she might as well keep her spirits up, what else can you do?

That night when I picked up Sean I told Denzie about the coincidence of Carlene coming to Meyer of all people, and she was interested, and at first I wouldn't tell her what I knew which wasn't too much, because everything that goes on in a lawyer's office is strictly and highly confidential. But she teased it out of me and I swore her to utter secrecy so as not to break confidentiality, and anyway, I figured everyone would know soon enough.

By this time Sean was getting antsy, he can only take so much of Denzie and me gabbing and he wanted to get back to our apartment and watch television so back we went.

The next day Meyer said that he understood that I knew Carlene, and I said yes, although not that well, but we had friends in common, and he asked me if I wanted to help with her case so of course I said yes. If it was a good year, Meyer had an articling student, but since it wasn't, he used me a bit like that and I was happy to do it. For one thing, he would sometimes let me borrow his car if I had to go to Markham or Brampton or Stouffville or someplace out of town. I didn't have a licence but I knew how to drive, and Meyer never asked, just assumed I had

one so it wasn't like I actually lied to him and I wanted to drive
so badly that I never brought the subject up myself. He had a
dark blue Toyota Camry but he wouldn't let me use it in the city
because he wasn't all that enthusiastic about lending it out, and
said that's what public transit was for.

Anyway, he asked me to go and Xerox some cases from the
law library attached to the courts which I had done before and
he had showed me how to find the cases from the string of letters
and numbers beside the names. While I was Xeroxing the
machine started flashing a jammed sign, and a call key operator
sign, and although I'm a key operator in our office what with
being the only secretary there, you needed the right key to open
it up and get out the jammed paper, so I called the librarian. She
said she would be there in a few minutes because she was in the
middle of something, and while I was waiting for her I read some
of the cases, and I'm telling you, things didn't look too good for
Blair, since they were trafficking cases I was reading. It seemed
like they had thrown out all the good excuses for the defendants
a long time ago.

That evening Denzie and I went to bingo at the rec centre and
Sean went too because they have a kids program on bingo nights
run by the family services where they do crafts. Sean likes it
because they sometimes do origami which is a clever Japanese
way of folding paper to make animals, and for some reason,
Sean happens to be very good at it, the origami champion of the
family services program you could say. Denzie took her bingo
bag which has her bingo markers, gum, her good luck charms,
scotch tape, and her diet pop because it's cheaper than buying it
there. Her good luck charms are all pinned to the bag, because
otherwise she might forget and leave them on the table at the
end. She has the kind of brain where she can scan thirty cards for
the number in the time it takes a normal person to look at five
or six cards, which makes it all the more of a shame that she
can't get ahead in life because of the fat thing. She has all these
systems too, like if it's a double bingo or a rotating "T" she
marks all the spaces that she doesn't need in advance in one
colour, and then marks the calls in another, and she tapes the
sheets of cards together so they don't slide around.

The caller was some dimwit from the community association who called real slowly, like we were all too stupid to know
where G 49 was. Every time someone won, and the numbers
were read off to check, she would announce "That's a good
bingo" in a surprised voice like it was the last thing in the world
that she had expected. As usual, Denzie won a lot of times, but
mostly what she won was more free games, which is what they
do to keep you going, and it doesn't seem like much of a prize
even if the proceeds are going to charity like they say although
I have my doubts about that, but Denzie didn't mind because it
meant she could play more, and as she says, it's entertainment.

About halfway through the evening, I went out to get some air
because they don't allow smoking inside if you can believe it,
not because of all the health stuff but because the rec centre's in
the basement of a Baptist church hall, and I saw the weirdest
thing. There was the Toyota Camry, and just as I was saying to
myself that there must be a lot of them in Toronto and not to
jump to conclusions, out got Carlene of all people and I saw
Meyer reaching over from the driver's side to say something to
her. They didn't see me because I was in a little peaked doorway
at the side of the church, and they were at the front, and they
kissed each other and then she went into the front door of the
hall and he drove off.

Well, I was pretty amazed, and I don't usually amaze all that
easily. It's true Carlene was good-looking, she didn't look old
enough to have an eighteen-year-old son but then she had gotten
started on that little project by accident at an early age. She
was naturally thin which made her look fashionable if she was
wearing the right clothes and she had thick, brownish-red hair and
white teeth, and dimples, and she could really act sweet the way
men like. So all in all it shouldn't have surprised me that much,
but it did. After all, as far as I knew they had just met the day
before, which was pretty short to be on kissing terms, and besides,
Meyer was a married man and a straight arrow, or at least that's
what I had thought before. In fact, part of me was a little miffed
because if he was going to start cheating on his wife, what was
wrong with me, here I had been available for the last few months
and continuing on for some time yet, and at various times in the

last two years, depending on Garnet's luck, and I didn't have blue veins. I figured what Garnet didn't know wouldn't hurt him, although he was sometimes suspicious and used to complain that he didn't have the temptations that I had what with him being in prison and not inclined the way you had to be if you were going to have sex in prison, although the truth was that the opportunities outside of prison weren't all that great either.

"Wonders will never cease," I said to Denzie when I went back to my spot beside her and told her all about it because I figured it couldn't be confidential if it was happening right out on the street. I had to tell her between games because she wasn't so good that she could watch thirty cards and listen to me, but she was impressed too when she was able to take it in. Towards the end of the night she won both the pack special and the mini-bonanza, so that was fifty bucks to the good, although you have to take away the money she spent on cards and markers.

Then I picked up Sean, who was in luck because they had done a new thing, instead of gluing popsicle sticks or whatever, they put plastic beads on little panels shaped like animals, and then the group leader had melted them together with an iron, and then you took them off the panel and you had a flat little animal. Sean had made a duck and a dinosaur so he was in a good mood and told us how hard the dinosaur was and even though Denzie was supposed to be ignoring him she was in such a good mood too from winning that she told him how sharp the dinosaur was, and then we walked back to our apartments, or Sean and I walked back and Denzie swayed back, and then we went to bed.

The next day I felt a little awkward around Meyer because of having seen Carlene and the kiss, but since he didn't know I had seen them only one of us felt awkward, which makes the awkwardness go away faster than if both people feel it. Also he was going to court so he was only in for about half an hour before he had to leave. I guess if he was sleeping with her he wasn't going to starting telling me all about it. Then I got to thinking about this a little more, because I didn't have much else to do and it seemed to me that Meyer wasn't supposed to be sleeping with a client, although I wasn't really sure.

Anyway, I figured it was none of my business, but that just shows you how much I knew about it, although maybe it would have been hard to predict what happened, even Denzie didn't.

After a month or so, Blair's trial came up and Meyer worked hard on it, I know he did because he had all the cases that I had Xeroxed highlighted in yellow marker. I offered to go and take notes just so I could see what happened but he said no, there was a court reporter and we needed someone to cover the phone. I could see he was nervous because he went to the bathroom twice before he left and kept on combing his hair and fixing his tie, like if all else failed, the judge might let him win just because his tie was so straight and perfect. He was gone all day which seemed long but wasn't really, it was just that I was in suspense. Part of my suspense was that Meyer had been so nervous that it was kind of catching, and I guess he wanted to do an extra good job because of sleeping with Carlene.

Along about 4:00 he came back to the office and he looked pretty bad, but he just said "lost" kind of short and went into his office and closed the door. Well, I was pretty shocked, and I felt terrible for Carlene, and the idea of this young kid going to jail seemed like a hell of a result for such a little thing, after all Blair was only selling to people that wanted to buy it, and really only so that he could skim off some and keep himself going, and what seemed like a kind of fairly average thing turned pretty ugly and I guess part of me had been holding on to the idea that it wouldn't happen. It was funny because it wasn't exactly the first time Meyer had lost a case, so I don't know why it got to me so much.

Anyway, life went on in the usual way, which is always a little surprising as well. I didn't see Meyer with Carlene again but it stood to reason that things might have cooled off between them in the circumstances.

About a month later, a man came in wearing a suit which wasn't that usual for our clientele, as Meyer called them. He gave me a card that said he was Paul Brankovic with the Law Society of Upper York which I took in to Meyer, and Meyer gave a jump like someone had slipped a lizard down the front of his shirt and it was heading for his balls and he was going to throw up. Then he kind of rearranged his face and his shoulders back to his usual confident style and went out and shook hands with Paul Brankovic and took him into his office himself. I hung around as close as I could to the door although I had to be careful because it had foggy glass in the top part so you could see that there was somebody there although not who it was, but who else was it going to be but me? I heard a little bit, a few words here and there when one of the voices went higher, and surprise, surprise, I heard Carlene's name. I figured as soon as I saw Law Society that this was what it was about because Meyer is pretty careful about the other stuff like the bring forward system. It seemed that Carlene had made a complaint to the Law Society for Meyer having slept with her, I guess she thought if she slept with him he would save Blair from jail and then she was mad because he went to jail anyway so she felt she had been tricked, and it turns out that a lawyer isn't supposed to be sleeping with a client which I had suspected. This also shows you Carlene didn't have a real grasp on the process, because if you were going to sleep with anyone to avoid your son going to jail it would have to be the judge, not the lawyer, which I could have told her at the time but she didn't consult me. Plus I don't know how you could figure out in advance who the judge was going to be. I guess she just figured that the only piece of the legal system that she could get her hands on was the lawyer, and so she better do whatever she could with him, and this was what she had done.

Not that Meyer was an innocent babe in all this. I guess Carlene just kind of happened along on some day when he hadn't got himself completely convinced that his life was wonderful and was looking for something else, and he kind of let her think that this would be a help to Blair by not saying otherwise. Although I figured he must have told her about the jail thing just to cover his butt, but maybe she hadn't really believed it would happen because I hadn't, and I wasn't even the mother, who's always going to be the most hopeful.

After the Law Society guy had left, Meyer spent a lot of time walking back and forth in his office, swearing really hard. I guess it was more serious than either of us had thought. It turned out that there had been a lot of trouble with this kind of thing, and it made lawyers look bad, or even worse, I should say,

When we got home, it was almost his bed-time but he was so excited about the beads I let him stay up for a bit, and he decided he was going to separate them so that all the greens were together, and all the reds were together, like that. I figured this was going to take him until he was thirty, and so I tried to explain to him that 4,000 beads were too many to do that.

"But, mum," he said. "There's two of us."

This was so kid-dumb optimistic that I couldn't think of anything to say, I was completely stumped because anyone that was going to take that kind of view, I wasn't going to be the one to break it to them, so I just got down beside him at the coffee table and started sorting little plastic beads like a goddamn idiot until I could think of something to say.

Then in the middle of this in walks Garnet, and there was a lot of screaming and yelling and jumping around. At first I thought maybe I'd just forgotten the date, like a bring forward file only it was BF Garnet, but then he said that he had gotten out early for good behaviour or something like that, and he was happy as a clam, and he grabbed me and gave me a little feel and grabbed Sean and wrestled him around a bit and just generally carried on. So we called a few people over and they brought some beer and somehow having a new person around made the rest of us sort of rise to the occasion and be more jokey, especially Garnet who was really a new-old person so you had all the advantages of feeling comfortable with him but also of him having new stories and ideas and his good parts impressing you again and also being pretty jokey himself, and so the party went on for a good few hours. Garnet also said that he'd met a guy who knew a guy, and it looked like he was going to be able to get a job in a packing plant that paid $12.00 an hour just for a general labourer so that was pretty good news too, although I'd believe it when I saw it. Around one in the morning everyone left and then we jumped into the sack, and it was like being starving and then getting to eat chocolate cake.

Unfortunately, the beer wore off about 3:00 in the morning, and I woke up and started worrying about the Meyer thing again and I couldn't get back to sleep. I got up and turned on the television and watched infomercials and played solitaire and smoked

lawyers not having a good reputation in the first place but being thought of as greedheads, and there had already been a messy inquiry on this topic so the Law Society was taking a hard line. Bad timing, I guess.

So then Meyer had to get himself a lawyer to defend himself from the Law Society which seemed sort of perfect and ridiculous at the same time. He spent a lot of time out at his lawyer's office and then one day he sat me down and asked me whether I would help him.

Of course I said sure, because I did want to help him, for starters I liked old Meyer and plus I couldn't see why jumping in the sack was so terrible, but mainly the problem was that I needed this job about as badly as you could need a job and if something happened to Meyer, Sean and I were likely going to end up on welfare, not a pretty thought, and one that made me start breathing too quickly like I couldn't get enough air, and the sweat start itching away in my armpits.

Anyway, I had to go to his lawyer's office whose name was James Blakely, and let me tell you this was no Meyer Kaplansky type building, this was a Bay Street office tower with sixty floors and an elevator so quiet and fast that you wondered if they were using rocket fuel, and the law firm had four floors all of its own and the reception area was almost all of one floor with blue grey couches and chairs and glass coffee tables and blue grey pictures on the wall and a receptionist that looked like she had just stepped off TV for a few moments and would be going back on shortly.

James Blakely was a tall guy with white, perfectly combed hair and a suit that put Meyer's to shame. You could tell it was top of the line because of how sharply it was cut and shaped and how soft the cloth looked, and I guess Meyer figured if he was going to beat this thing he needed one of the genuine article, downtown-type lawyers.

James Blakely took me into a meeting room that was painted in pink and grey instead of blue and grey and said that he was going to ask me the questions he would be asking me at Meyer's hearing so that I would understand what he was getting at, kind of like a rehearsal.

This seemed like a smart idea, and so he started firing away. A few times he suggested different ways to describe things from what I had said, and I was starting to get a little worried that I wouldn't be able to remember his suggestions and then I noticed that the questions had started referring to Carlene instead of Meyer. It started to seem like he wanted me to say that Carlene was a real nympho although he didn't put it quite like that, but that she slept around a lot and that she had put the moves on Meyer, rather than the other way around which is what she was claiming.

Well this took me back a little, because first of all Carlene may have gotten her share of the available hanky panky but it wasn't like she was running around ripping the clothes off every guy she met, and plus I didn't know who had put the moves on who as between her and Meyer, not having been sitting on one or the other's shoulder at the time.

I pointed this out to James Blakely, and he was nice about it and said that I shouldn't say anything that was untrue so I felt better, but that only lasted about twenty seconds because then I noticed that the way the questions were put ended up with me coming up with the same kind of answers but just hinting at them instead of outright saying them. Since they weren't outright lies, I didn't feel I could make the same objection but it worried me all the same, and that night I talked to Denzie about it.

"Jesus H.," she said, but then she told me about a couple of times that Carlene had slept with people I hadn't known about, and asked me who I figured had made the first move, and I said my guess was Carlene because of her wanting something and Meyer having been such a straight arrow up until then, and so Denzie said what was the problem then. The thing is that I knew she was trying to help me by saying it was okay to go along with Blakely because she knew that I needed the job and that if I had to go on welfare and if some worker decided I wasn't the perfect mother and took Sean away that I would probably cut my own head off. That might seem like quite a few ifs, but once it's happened to you before, it scares the shit out of you forever. Sometimes I think about Tracy, that was my little girl, and I get this feeling like there's a giant sad worm waking up inside me

and I have to be nice to it, and feed it, and trick it to
down again, and sometimes it takes days.

I kind of wondered about Denzie being on my sid
since she was a friend of Carlene's too, but she told m
didn't think Carlene should have made the complain
she wouldn't have done it if Meyer had been able to get
which just shows that that was her real complaint
shouldn't be putting it all on the sex. Well this was a go
but then I said that even so Meyer must have led her on
she was probably desperate at the time, which Meye
have known, so that wasn't right either and besides,
was right or wrong it didn't need me getting in there an
ing things the way the lawyer wanted me to and so I wa
a sweat about what I should do. Although I would ha
anything to keep Sean, I was kind of pissed that this was
had to do because I had a feeling that I was going to f
scum afterwards and here Carlene lived in the same build
everything. Plus maybe I would be able to find anoth
although it took me a long time to find this one, or maybe I
get a good worker and maybe she would think how I looke
Sean was okay, but then I thought about Sean not being
drugs and maybe them thinking he should be or that some
was wrong with how I looked after him that he was so sp
or that he shouldn't be living in an apartment with a man
had just gotten out of jail as Garnet would be soon. The he
was the next day so I didn't exactly have a lot of goddamn
to think about it either.

Sean was bugging me to go to Woolco because one of
other kids had told him they had the melting plastic beads t
like he had done at the family services program and it was o
late on Thursdays, and Denzie had laundry to do, so I said o
to going, but not okay to buying until we saw how much t
cost. Fortunately it turned out they were on sale, $6.99 for 4,c
beads in bulk which seemed liked a pretty good deal even thou
they were so tiny, and Sean was in seventh heaven which y
can't help feeling kind of taken by someone who can be so co
pletely every inch from one end to the other happy about son
stupid little beads.

my brains out, but nothing came to me. In the morning I dragged myself around because of being so tired, and snapped at Sean like he was the cause of all the problems, and he yelled at me and then he started to howl and then I felt like howling myself, and Garnet yelled at us for making noise because he was trying to sleep in. Anyway, we just had to plug along, so I rubbed Sean on the middle of his back to show that I was still with him even if I was grouchy and sent him off to school and put on my best outfit which was a turquoise skirt and yellow sweater, and put on make-up and blow dried my hair and put on my panty-hose and gold earrings, well not real gold, and just generally fussed with things as if I fixed myself up enough the answer would come to me, just pop out of the sleeves of the blouse or the hem of the skirt.

Well that didn't happen and so I ended up on the streetcar going towards the building where the hearing was going to be which was a very old building that had been cleaned up because it was so fancy, and it was surrounded by a fancy black iron fence. James Blakely had asked me to meet him and Meyer on the front steps and sure enough, there they were, Meyer looking extremely nervous like he had gone to the bathroom ten times and he smelled like a breath mint, and his usual confident style seemed to be the only thing holding him up and every so often you could get a glimpse of his real self just hanging on for dear life behind that. While the lawyer was finding out what room we would be in, Meyer said to me quietly that he really appreciated me doing this, and I liked that he would put himself on my level like that, although let's face it, the shoe was a bit on the other foot at that point, but we were both still in the habit of him being my boss.

The hearing room was average size but it had plaster curlicues on the ceiling and a table on a raised part and there were three lawyers there and you couldn't have made a mistake about that, although they looked more like James Blakely than Meyer, and there was Carlene and it looked like she had gotten her own lawyer too although maybe he was from the Law Society, but the room was just jam-packed with lawyers as far as I could tell.

Anyway Carlene got up and swore to tell the truth and her lawyer asked her questions and she said that she had gone to

Meyer about Blair and that Meyer had talked to her a little bit and she started to cry about Blair and then Meyer leaned over and starting kissing her and putting his hands on her thighs and then sliding them a little between her thighs and then suggested that they go somewhere to finish the discussion that had a bed and she was so upset about Blair, plus she felt she had to or Meyer wouldn't have taken the case and so they had gone out to the Holiday Inn which is a few blocks away.

When they got to the room, Meyer had kissed her again, and then unbuttoned her blouse and ran his fingers over her breasts and then things just kind of proceeded from there in the usual way.

At first she had me completely convinced and I was even getting kind of mad at Meyer for having taken advantage of her like that when she was so worried, but then I remembered that I was there when she had left and Meyer had just given me the file to open and the certificate and gone back into his office, although he had gone out a little later, so maybe he had met her there. But then I remembered that Carlene had been wearing a dress that day not a blouse, I remembered it because it was clingy, although I couldn't remember if the dress had buttons down the front because sometimes they do.

But then Meyer got up and said no such thing happened and that he had never laid a finger on her which I knew was not true either because I had seen him kiss her, and I started to feel like my head was going to burst like a melon, and I still couldn't decide what I should say, and all of a sudden it was my turn and there I was swearing to tell the truth and I had no goddamn idea what was going to come out of my mouth.

The lawyer started asking me questions and so I just answered them straight ahead because that was all I could concentrate on, even though I knew it would be coming out for Meyer because of the way he asked them. This didn't seem quite so bad by then, because it didn't seem like anybody there was being overly concerned about the facts, or at least anybody who had testified, and besides which I had a job with Meyer and there was nothing like that with Carlene. Actually I thought of these things afterwards, at the time it was all I could do just to answer the questions and keep breathing at the same time.

lawyers not having a good reputation in the first place but being thought of as greedheads, and there had already been a messy inquiry on this topic so the Law Society was taking a hard line. Bad timing, I guess.

So then Meyer had to get himself a lawyer to defend himself from the Law Society which seemed sort of perfect and ridiculous at the same time. He spent a lot of time out at his lawyer's office and then one day he sat me down and asked me whether I would help him.

Of course I said sure, because I did want to help him, for starters I liked old Meyer and plus I couldn't see why jumping in the sack was so terrible, but mainly the problem was that I needed this job about as badly as you could need a job and if something happened to Meyer, Sean and I were likely going to end up on welfare, not a pretty thought, and one that made me start breathing too quickly like I couldn't get enough air, and the sweat start itching away in my armpits.

Anyway, I had to go to his lawyer's office whose name was James Blakely, and let me tell you this was no Meyer Kaplansky type building, this was a Bay Street office tower with sixty floors and an elevator so quiet and fast that you wondered if they were using rocket fuel, and the law firm had four floors all of its own and the reception area was almost all of one floor with blue grey couches and chairs and glass coffee tables and blue grey pictures on the wall and a receptionist that looked like she had just stepped off TV for a few moments and would be going back on shortly.

James Blakely was a tall guy with white, perfectly combed hair and a suit that put Meyer's to shame. You could tell it was top of the line because of how sharply it was cut and shaped and how soft the cloth looked, and I guess Meyer figured if he was going to beat this thing he needed one of the genuine article, downtown-type lawyers.

James Blakely took me into a meeting room that was painted in pink and grey instead of blue and grey and said that he was going to ask me the questions he would be asking me at Meyer's hearing so that I would understand what he was getting at, kind of like a rehearsal.

This seemed like a smart idea, and so he started firing away. A few times he suggested different ways to describe things from what I had said, and I was starting to get a little worried that I wouldn't be able to remember his suggestions and then I noticed that the questions had started referring to Carlene instead of Meyer. It started to seem like he wanted me to say that Carlene was a real nympho although he didn't put it quite like that, but that she slept around a lot and that she had put the moves on Meyer, rather than the other way around which is what she was claiming.

Well this took me back a little, because first of all Carlene may have gotten her share of the available hanky panky but it wasn't like she was running around ripping the clothes off every guy she met, and plus I didn't know who had put the moves on who as between her and Meyer, not having been sitting on one or the other's shoulder at the time.

I pointed this out to James Blakely, and he was nice about it and said that I shouldn't say anything that was untrue so I felt better, but that only lasted about twenty seconds because then I noticed that the way the questions were put ended up with me coming up with the same kind of answers but just hinting at them instead of outright saying them. Since they weren't outright lies, I didn't feel I could make the same objection but it worried me all the same, and that night I talked to Denzie about it.

"Jesus H.," she said, but then she told me about a couple of times that Carlene had slept with people I hadn't known about, and asked me who I figured had made the first move, and I said my guess was Carlene because of her wanting something and Meyer having been such a straight arrow up until then, and so Denzie said what was the problem then. The thing is that I knew she was trying to help me by saying it was okay to go along with Blakely because she knew that I needed the job and that if I had to go on welfare and if some worker decided I wasn't the perfect mother and took Sean away that I would probably cut my own head off. That might seem like quite a few ifs, but once it's happened to you before, it scares the shit out of you forever. Sometimes I think about Tracy, that was my little girl, and I get this feeling like there's a giant sad worm waking up inside me and I have to be nice to it, and feed it, and trick it to get it to lie down again, and sometimes it takes days.

I kind of wondered about Denzie being on my side so much since she was a friend of Carlene's too, but she told me that she didn't think Carlene should have made the complaint because she wouldn't have done it if Meyer had been able to get Blair off, which just shows that that was her real complaint and she shouldn't be putting it all on the sex. Well this was a good point, but then I said that even so Meyer must have led her on a bit and she was probably desperate at the time, which Meyer should have known, so that wasn't right either and besides, whoever was right or wrong it didn't need me getting in there and twisting things the way the lawyer wanted me to and so I was still in a sweat about what I should do. Although I would have done anything to keep Sean, I was kind of pissed that this was what I had to do because I had a feeling that I was going to feel like scum afterwards and here Carlene lived in the same building and everything. Plus maybe I would be able to find another job, although it took me a long time to find this one, or maybe I would get a good worker and maybe she would think how I looked after Sean was okay, but then I thought about Sean not being on the drugs and maybe them thinking he should be or that something was wrong with how I looked after him that he was so speedy, or that he shouldn't be living in an apartment with a man who had just gotten out of jail as Garnet would be soon. The hearing was the next day so I didn't exactly have a lot of goddamn time to think about it either.

Sean was bugging me to go to Woolco because one of the other kids had told him they had the melting plastic beads there like he had done at the family services program and it was open late on Thursdays, and Denzie had laundry to do, so I said okay to going, but not okay to buying until we saw how much they cost. Fortunately it turned out they were on sale, $6.99 for 4,000 beads in bulk which seemed liked a pretty good deal even though they were so tiny, and Sean was in seventh heaven which you can't help feeling kind of taken by someone who can be so completely every inch from one end to the other happy about some stupid little beads.

When we got home, it was almost his bed-time but he was so excited about the beads I let him stay up for a bit, and he decided he was going to separate them so that all the greens were together, and all the reds were together, like that. I figured this was going to take him until he was thirty, and so I tried to explain to him that 4,000 beads were too many to do that.

"But, mum," he said. "There's two of us."

This was so kid-dumb optimistic that I couldn't think of anything to say, I was completely stumped because anyone that was going to take that kind of view, I wasn't going to be the one to break it to them, so I just got down beside him at the coffee table and started sorting little plastic beads like a goddamn idiot until I could think of something to say.

Then in the middle of this in walks Garnet, and there was a lot of screaming and yelling and jumping around. At first I thought maybe I'd just forgotten the date, like a bring forward file only it was BF Garnet, but then he said that he had gotten out early for good behaviour or something like that, and he was happy as a clam, and he grabbed me and gave me a little feel and grabbed Sean and wrestled him around a bit and just generally carried on. So we called a few people over and they brought some beer and somehow having a new person around made the rest of us sort of rise to the occasion and be more jokey, especially Garnet who was really a new-old person so you had all the advantages of feeling comfortable with him but also of him having new stories and ideas and his good parts impressing you again and also being pretty jokey himself, and so the party went on for a good few hours. Garnet also said that he'd met a guy who knew a guy, and it looked like he was going to be able to get a job in a packing plant that paid $12.00 an hour just for a general labourer so that was pretty good news too, although I'd believe it when I saw it. Around one in the morning everyone left and then we jumped into the sack, and it was like being starving and then getting to eat chocolate cake.

Unfortunately, the beer wore off about 3:00 in the morning, and I woke up and started worrying about the Meyer thing again and I couldn't get back to sleep. I got up and turned on the television and watched infomercials and played solitaire and smoked my brains out, but nothing came to me. In the morning I dragged myself around because of being so tired, and snapped at Sean like he was the cause of all the problems, and he yelled at me and then he started to howl and then I felt like howling myself, and Garnet yelled at us for making noise because he was trying to sleep in. Anyway, we just had to plug along, so I rubbed Sean on the middle of his back to show that I was still with him even if I was grouchy and sent him off to school and put on my best outfit which was a turquoise skirt and yellow sweater, and put on make-up and blow dried my hair and put on my panty-hose and gold earrings, well not real gold, and just generally fussed with things as if I fixed myself up enough the answer would come to me, just pop out of the sleeves of the blouse or the hem of the skirt.

Well that didn't happen and so I ended up on the streetcar going towards the building where the hearing was going to be which was a very old building that had been cleaned up because it was so fancy, and it was surrounded by a fancy black iron fence. James Blakely had asked me to meet him and Meyer on the front steps and sure enough, there they were, Meyer looking extremely nervous like he had gone to the bathroom ten times and he smelled like a breath mint, and his usual confident style seemed to be the only thing holding him up and every so often you could get a glimpse of his real self just hanging on for dear life behind that. While the lawyer was finding out what room we would be in, Meyer said to me quietly that he really appreciated me doing this, and I liked that he would put himself on my level like that, although let's face it, the shoe was a bit on the other foot at that point, but we were both still in the habit of him being my boss.

The hearing room was average size but it had plaster curlicues on the ceiling and a table on a raised part and there were three lawyers there and you couldn't have made a mistake about that, although they looked more like James Blakely than Meyer, and there was Carlene and it looked like she had gotten her own lawyer too although maybe he was from the Law Society, but the room was just jam-packed with lawyers as far as I could tell.

Anyway Carlene got up and swore to tell the truth and her lawyer asked her questions and she said that she had gone to

Meyer about Blair and that Meyer had talked to her a little bit and she started to cry about Blair and then Meyer leaned over and starting kissing her and putting his hands on her thighs and then sliding them a little between her thighs and then suggested that they go somewhere to finish the discussion that had a bed and she was so upset about Blair, plus she felt she had to or Meyer wouldn't have taken the case and so they had gone out to the Holiday Inn which is a few blocks away.

When they got to the room, Meyer had kissed her again, and then unbuttoned her blouse and ran his fingers over her breasts and then things just kind of proceeded from there in the usual way.

At first she had me completely convinced and I was even getting kind of mad at Meyer for having taken advantage of her like that when she was so worried, but then I remembered that I was there when she had left and Meyer had just given me the file to open and the certificate and gone back into his office, although he had gone out a little later, so maybe he had met her there. But then I remembered that Carlene had been wearing a dress that day not a blouse, I remembered it because it was clingy, although I couldn't remember if the dress had buttons down the front because sometimes they do.

But then Meyer got up and said no such thing happened and that he had never laid a finger on her which I knew was not true either because I had seen him kiss her, and I started to feel like my head was going to burst like a melon, and I still couldn't decide what I should say, and all of a sudden it was my turn and there I was swearing to tell the truth and I had no goddamn idea what was going to come out of my mouth.

The lawyer started asking me questions and so I just answered them straight ahead because that was all I could concentrate on, even though I knew it would be coming out for Meyer because of the way he asked them. This didn't seem quite so bad by then, because it didn't seem like anybody there was being overly concerned about the facts, or at least anybody who had testified, and besides which I had a job with Meyer and there was nothing like that with Carlene. Actually I thought of these things afterwards, at the time it was all I could do just to answer the questions and keep breathing at the same time.

Then Blakely and Carlene's lawyer each talked for quite a while, with Carlene's lawyer saying Meyer should be disbarred and Blakely saying nothing at all should happen to him, in fact he should get his legal costs paid, and they were pretty good because when one was talking I was perfectly convinced by him, and then when the other was talking I changed my mind completely to what he was saying, and I tell you I didn't envy the ones making the decision one goddamn little bit, and then I remembered that this was going to mean a lot to me, and that I should be rooting for Meyer.

The three lawyers at the front, the committee Blakely called them, excused themselves and said they were going to go and see if they could reach an oral decision which Blakely said meant right away, as opposed to sending it out in writing weeks later. We went and had coffee which wasn't a very social thing because Meyer was chewing his nails and the skin beside them to the point where I wondered if he might end up swallowing his whole hand and Blakely seemed sort of lost in thought, but I tried to chat a bit because of keeping Meyer's spirits up. I told Blakely that he had done a good job, which I've noticed people always like to hear regardless of how highly-placed they are, although Meyer just kind of nodded absently, and you could tell that Blakely would have liked it better if Meyer had said it, what with being a lawyer himself. Then we went back and hung around the room for another forty-five minutes and then one of the committee came back and said they needed more time.

By this time, Meyer was so tense he was practically rigid and one of his hangnails was bleeding. But there was nothing we could do but wait, so we went back down to the cafeteria and I had a butter tart and more coffee because Blakely was paying and I couldn't smoke because the whole place was non-smoking, and I had given up on talking, and then Blakely got a *Globe and Mail* and I got a *People* magazine, which he also paid for, and I sat and ate my butter tart which was a big one, and let the syrup slide around in my mouth slowly, and read about people who made more money in a day than I would probably make in my whole goddamn life, that's assuming I had a job, which didn't look too good at that moment. Blakely read the business section,

and then the sports, and then the foreign news, and then the
movie section, and then the comics and Meyer just sat and bit
his nails and tore his styro-foam coffee cup into pieces, except
that at one point he grabbed the movie section and read his
horoscope, and then grunted.

After a while of this, we went upstairs again to the curlicue
room and the committee was there and they said they had
reached a decision. Then there was another delay because
Carlene and her lawyer weren't there, so they sent somebody
down to see if they could find them, and it turned out they were
standing outside the side door, having a smoke, which if I'd
known about I would have gone with them.

So then we were all settled down again in out right seats, and
my head was buzzing a bit because of the butter tart and I
couldn't stop thinking about a cigarette, and the man in the
middle seat of the committee started talking about how important it was to uphold the standards of the profession, which I
thought was good to know that they had some because it wasn't
all that obvious, and then he went on about balancing this with
protecting the public interest but also being fair to Meyer, and
then he just went on and on some more, and all the time we were
on the edge of our seats to guess from what he was saying what
the decision was going to be, and after a while I started to think
that he was doing it on purpose to keep us in suspense, and I felt
like yelling at them to get a move on, and I could see that everyone in the room except the committee felt pretty much the same.

Finally, the middle guy stopped, took a few breaths, looked
at Meyer straight in the eyes like he had practised this before,
and said that they had concluded that Meyer had engaged in
sexual misconduct with a client, and that in balancing all the
factors, they would be recommending that he would be suspended for a year but not disbarred. I guess that was their way of
trying to split the decision so that Carlene and Meyer each got a
piece of it.

Then they stood up and walked out together, and Meyer
looked kind of stunned and Blakely took his arm and you could
see why he was a good lawyer because he took us out in the hall
and started telling us why this was really a win, and we should

be pleased that Meyer got off so light, but you could see that Meyer didn't agree, not surprising I guess.

By that time, I felt like if I didn't have a smoke I was going to start ripping the curlicues off the walls, so I told them I would meet them downstairs, because I figured Mr. Bay Street was going to need a little time to convince Meyer that this was all for the best. I mean, maybe the lawyers committee thought that was kind of coming up the middle, but what did they think Meyer was going to do for that year, not to mention me. The clients expect you to be there when they get arrested or need a divorce, and if you're not available they just go on to the next lawyer they hear about from their brother-in-law or whatever, and they don't come back, so picking up again is pretty hard. Not to mention there's the rent to pay on the office which doesn't make sense when you're not in it making money. All I could think about was "Oh God, what the hell am I going to do, oh shit, what the hell am I going to do, oh Christ," it kept running through my head like a song you can't get out of your system, and one thing was sure, neither Blakely or Meyer were interested in my problems.

I went outside and there was Carlene and her lawyer again, smoking away in this little courtyard kind of place, and they stopped talking when I got there. I said hello and they said hello, and then I lit up and stood a little apart from them out of politeness, but after a few minutes Carlene started drifting over, like it was sort of by accident.

"Happy now?" I said when she got to about a foot or two away.

"Not really," she said, looking at the end of her cigarette like it was the most interesting thing in the world.

Then we didn't say anything for a minute or two. It was still cloudy, and outside the weather had that tense in-between feeling, like you couldn't tell what it was going to do, and there were a bunch of these shiny blue-black birds swooping down and hopping around which Garnet says are grackles, although I don't know how the hell he knows, and there was a delivery truck backing up a little ways away on the street, and making that slow beeping noise that trucks make to warn you they're backing up.

Then she said "Have you ever seen so many goddamn lawyers," and I started to go "huunh, huunh, huunh," in a funny sobbing type way, it just came out of me, I couldn't help it I was so scared about my job and Sean, but she thought I was laughing and she started to laugh and then these sobby little pants that were coming out of me started turning into laughs too, or sort of crying laughing, and I couldn't stop, and she kept on too, and my chest and face started to ache and my eyes were all squinched up, and tears started to leak out of them, and then I really was laughing, so hard that I was afraid I was going to pee my pants, I was doubled over and I had to gasp between laughs because I didn't have any breath left, just splitting a gut and I was afraid my make-up was running but I couldn't stop, both of us laughing like there was no tomorrow, and her lawyer just stood there, looking at us like we had lost our goddamn minds.

TIMOTHY TAYLOR

Pope's Own

"**W**ell now," the man from Kinsale said, returning his pint glass to the dark wood bar. "I am to understand you have some knowledge of our Brothers."

There was a certain insinuation in the Irish cadence, Gillian thought, not that she would take issue. "I have an associate," she began, as neutral as possible.

"Do you then?"

"Chekov McGuigan."

She knew this would get his attention but that he wouldn't let on. And sure enough, the man from Kinsale scratched the edge of his jaw, silvery with afternoon beard, and murmured, "Ah, well then. McGuigan. Went to Canada didn't he?"

"Chekov said Brothers was the best washed-rind semi-soft in existence although, no offence, I'll believe that when I taste it. He said it was known locally as Pope's Own, that it was a closely guarded secret, that I might start looking in the Union Hall area, and he also mentioned your name."

"Did he say all those things now?"

Gillian sipped her Murphy's stout and decided to play silence. She had just dumped everything she knew on the bar between them, for one thing, but she also guessed there was going to be some peacocking around here before they got down to issues. Sometimes you just had to let the boys dance and jab for a while before they finally surrendered and told you how much, for how many, and when. This wasn't a lot different than a hundred (a thousand?) meetings she'd had with chief financial officers and

77

accountants and brokers and lawyers over the years, except this was not so much about money as it was about, well, cheese.

The barman came over. "Gillian Lacroix?"

"Mackin," she said firmly. Her maiden name never felt better.

"How they found you here I'll never know," the barman said, and pointed to a cream coloured dial phone at the end of the bar.

"I'm staying up the road," Gillian said. "I told one or two people before I left. Will you excuse me?"

"Of course," the man from Kinsale said.

"Yello," she said into the Transatlantic squelch.

It was Tremblay. She turned her back to the man from Kinsale and looked down the length of the panelled room towards the front door. Piggy's was dead empty. Odd to be in a bar when it was sunny out, even a bar with a relatively sunny name like Piggy's, but the streets of Union Hall were just as empty. Earlier that morning the boats had come in and there had been a slow motion flurry of people in front of the garage that served as fish processing plant and outdoor market. Gillian caught the tail end of it, bought some monkfish for dinner. By the time she'd walked up the hill to the house she was renting, made some calls and returned, it was like the small fishing port had been evacuated.

"How are you making out?" Tremblay asked. He was concerned, she thought, calling at 7:30 in the morning Pacific time. But Gillian's investment adviser had been expressing concern for her behaviour ever since the divorce, and she was getting more or less used to it.

"Tremblay," she said quietly. "I'm just sitting down with Mr. Clooney now."

"I let you go, but one thing," Tremblay said. "Something McGuigan was saying. I think we have ourselves another bidder here."

"Over there?"

"No, over there. In Dublin. He's a businessman, that's all I know."

It was bad news, but Gillian rolled with it. Chekov had described a pristinely beautiful piece of West Cork farm land with a large, well kept stone house and buildings, cheese making equipment, knowledgeable staff and a working herd of dairy cattle. It was a rare, complete package, and another bidder wasn't such a surprise.

The call was also well-timed. Gillian calculated that the phone had rung just as Clooney was about to puff himself up with how impossibly exclusive Brothers was, how not just any purchaser would do. Now as she got off the phone, Clooney would have to take a big breath and start all over again.

"Sorry," she said, sliding onto her stool.

Clooney had a little Murphy's stout cream on the edge of his trim mustache. Fifty-ish. Handsome in a tattersall shirt and sports coat way that remained boyish. He had a mess of black Irish hair she thought went nicely with the green-shouldered hills covered in shaggy goats and yellow broom. He opened his mouth to continue.

"Chekov says hello," Gillian interrupted. She imagined this like the left hook counter you throw just as your sparring partner telegraphs an overhand right.

"Does he? Well." Clooney accepted another pint of Murphy's without word or payment. "Was that him then?"

Gillian didn't answer, she watched instead as Clooney's left index finger dipped unconsciously into a vest pocket and withdrew a single bead of a rosary.

Why do they call it Pope's Own?

A religious man our Clooney, Chekov had said.

Fanatic?

No just Irish.

"May I do something?" Gillian said. And then without waiting for permission, she took a hanky from the sleeve of her sweater and very lightly wiped the Murphy's off the tip of Clooney's mustache. She didn't have to look over to know the barman caught that one.

Clooney suppressed a blush. It was hard to do, Gillian imagined, but she saw it bloom ever so slightly before being pinched off.

"I'm sorry," she said again. And in a way she was sorry, although she got the reaction she wanted. She was sorry, perhaps, to have deployed that kind of a feint even in service of this.

Clooney sighed. "Tell me about yourself," he said finally. "They'll want to know."

Nothing to tell really, Gillian thought. Nothing more than the standard investment banker turned quality-cheese importer story. Nothing to tell beyond the fact that not a single core feature of her life had survived the preceding two-year period beyond her sparring partner.

"You're hitting a bit harder girl," Maria told her a year before, shortly after the divorce was finalized.

"Sorry. I feel really loose."

Maria temped and was only in her twenties. They met at the boxercise class Gillian enrolled in before David moved out. She became more interested in the sport after the split. This was not entirely a matter of unresolved hostility, although there was a measure of that. Gillian thought it had more to do with reasserting authority over things, over herself.

Maria and Gillian hit it off. They decided to spring for private lessons together. First time in the ring with fight-weight gloves on, Gillian remembered that Maria put the instructor on his butt. They froze in a cock-eyed triangle, the two of them staring down at Franky. A trickle of purple blood emerged from his nose, and you could almost see the birds and stars and the little bombs with fuses swirling around his head.

Maria said: "Oh my god I am like . . ."

Franky scrambled to his feet, complimenting her through his mouth guard. "Thas'good. Thas'essackly it."

Over drinks later Maria said: "I caught him coming in, what can I say? The guy was moving like a sofa." Gillian thought of a stunned Franky sitting flush on his ass – it's always the punch you don't see coming – and she laughed so hard it actually hurt. Of course, she was out of practice laughing.

"You were management?" Maria said a little later. "Like your own office and everything?"

Gillian nodded and stopped smiling. That was then.

"What's with cheese? I have to ask."

Gillian looked at her younger friend. She felt sisterly, and she wondered a whole range of things in a single instant that seemed to wind up with the question: What suburban jerk was Maria dating at the moment?

"You know," Gillian said. "It just became really important to be in charge of my whole day. From morning to night. I answer to me."

"Well sure," Maria said, hands up like *you don't need to explain that*. "But you're gonna stay interested selling people Mozzarella?"

"Selling anything I can actually touch and smell," said Gillian. She might have added, anything the existence of which I can myself verify, but this was the harder part to explain to Maria. David being gone was more than a hole in her life; he made a blank spot she could not be sure had ever been full. The piece he removed came out of her present and – by transfiguring himself utterly, by rendering himself unknowable – David had expunged himself from the past as well. The operative word for the future became *tangibility*.

There was a period of chasmic anxiety attacks, but these eventually subsided and were replaced by the conviction that she must do something with her hands, something real and unimpeachably good. She quit her job. She cashed in the West Vancouver house and bought a tiny condo downtown and a piece of land up the valley with good out-buildings. She sourced the cattle, spec'd milking and cheese-making equipment, then ran into the administrative blockade known otherwise as the Milk Board. It seemed the cheese manufacturing industry in Canada – presumably while nobody was looking – had been tamped down hard under a grid of quotas and regulations and you pretty much had to commit civil disobedience to make and sell a batch of unpasteurized cow's milk Camembert.

She was forced to give up the whole idea, the closest to depression she had come through the entire preceding six months. Then her therapist found out through circuitous connections about the Ye Olde Cheese Shoppe. Thirty years in the business and Mr. Brian "Chekov" McGuigan was finally hanging up the slicer. A little dusty perhaps, a little prone to stodgy Stiltons in ceramic vases, but McGuigan's was situated nevertheless on a busy corner in fashionable Point Grey. Gillian thought: Martha

Stewart would buy cheese here if the place were redecorated to look like Dean & DeLucca's and if everything were expensive enough.

Her therapist was thrilled. "It's really great to be able to help. I mean, really help."

Gillian closed the deal with McGuigan personally. It tapped her out cash-wise. She had literally nothing left. But she was no longer in therapy, and standing in front of the Gillian Mackin Fine Cheese sign – copperplate lettering on a farm green background – Gillian thought she might never have been so aware of the potential for fulfilment.

Hardly recognize the place, Chekov McGuigan said, on hand at the opening,

It's all the customers, she said, bantering in the way they had adopted.

And it was true; business was good even without David's strained patronage. He was apparently selling more paintings a month now than he had sold in the six years they were married – paintings of the model he had been sleeping with, no less – and he was compensating by buying more cheese a month than he'd consumed in the same period. The facile selfishness of his quest for absolution notwithstanding, Gillian was grateful that he bought the expensive stuff: lait cru Pont Lévesque, an appellation-controlled Bleu de Gex that had to be coaxed out of a supplier in the Haute Jura, even the handmade gorgonzola-brie cross from the farm in upstate New York owned by Wolfgang Puck that came in at $67 a kilo without much margin.

I wouldn't bother with that one if I were you.

Why not?

Well it's a bit of a fake cheese isn't it? Gorgonzola-Brie. You'll be selling Cambonzola next.

I am selling Cambonzola, Chekov. Quite a lot of it actually.

Ever hear of farm cheese? Real small batch stuff. Comes alive in your mouth. These friends of yours would pay whatever you ask for it.

The last time she saw David he said: "Anything I can do for you here, I want you to ask."

"Well . . . thanks," Gillian said.

"I mean it. Things are good for me." He tried not to look too pleased. "New York and everything. I know you don't need money, I just . . ."

"I need," Gillian said, "that you not come here anymore."

It left her short of breath to have finally said it, but there was no doubt she caught him coming in. David's face went dreamy and confused, like Franky when Maria tagged him. "I only . . ." he said, clutching his paper bag full of expensive cheese as if that might hold him up. "I just . . ."

She stared at him and waited. There was simply no goddamn way she was obliged to explain herself. Bleed.

Don't be angry, Chekov said later. For yourself, don't be angry.

So that was the end of David. But it didn't matter anyway, she thought, because by then she had been given a nice write-up in a local food magazine and business was ticking along. It took a year to lay down the base, but Gillian Mackin Fine Cheese prospered and even began to pay Gillian Mackin a salary which she used to hire Maria.

And then it happened. A Thursday, she remembered, about a year and a half in. She was checking a delivery from the warehouse in France. Maria was up front. It was a good delivery, an overdue delivery. Gillian was standing with her clipboard, marking off all the colourful packages and boxes that she had pulled together from master cheese makers in the Jura, the Haute Savoie, in Normandy and Paris. Wheels upon wheels that she and Maria would now cut down to portions and sell inside four weeks. She could even pick Who for What. Who for the Crottins de Chavignol. Who for the downy soft-rinded Coulommiers. Who for the serious discs of Reblochon.

She imagined the pride of each of these cheese makers and the certain pleasure of each of her many customers. A pleasure that she facilitated, the cheese midwife. The thought filled her with sudden, sweeping anxiety she had not felt in some time, to think of all of these exquisite creations that she purchased and sold, that passed through her hands more or less unaffected, and which were then greedily consumed and gone to her forever.

Anything the existence of which I can myself verify, she thought. Her first impulse had been right, to make, to bring to life herself. That was verification. That was tangibility. And here she had been once again deflected – just as she had been during all her time with David – shunted to the banal and selfless periphery of the creative process.

Maria said. "Take a break already. You ever go to a Club Med?"

Well my dear . . . Chekov said to her when she tried to explain.

She cooked the monkfish in a bit of white wine. She made the most perfect potato pancake the world had ever seen. Then she carried her plate outside to eat dinner with the cows that speckled the green hills in all directions. Being halfway around the world was good in itself, but this was rapturously peaceful.

Clooney showed up early the next morning as agreed. He glanced quickly at the table on the lawn, now covered in dew, then back to her as she locked the door and approached him. On the driveway, hearing the gravel crunch underfoot, Gillian had a sudden awareness of her movement across the ground, of the microscopic trace mark she left on the great green back of Ireland. It was not uncomfortable, this sense of closing a distance between herself and Clooney, as his tweedy frame cast a long shadow in the light of a new day.

She climbed into his red Fiesta. Then, self-conscious about her own silence and the gyroscopic sensation that remained in her, she looked around the tight interior of the car and said: "Cosy."

"It'll get you there and back again," Clooney said, snugging the seatbelt around his waist.

"And to various undisclosed destinations," she said.

"Indeed."

"Your turn," Gillian said, as Clooney swung the Fiesta onto the narrow road. He accelerated quickly, shifting into second and then third, as they roared towards the crest of a hill, tall stone walls flying by very close on either side.

Clooney was a bit of a pioneer gourmand in these parts, it seemed, celebrating the culinary output of the country long before it was fashionable and for more years than he claimed to remember. Handmade pâté from farms in Kerry, walnut oil from Wicklow, cheese from every county in the Republic, all out of a tiny shop in Ireland's gourmet capital south of Cork City.

"For years only to foreigners," Clooney said. "Or restaurants where foreigners liked to eat. That was Kinsale."

"And now?"

"Well now even the Irish are fancying finer things," Clooney said, managing to sound disapproving of the national success story that he embodied. An odd gourmand, she thought. Country lanky, with the simple faith revealed by that unconscious finger to the vest pocket.

"So I was approved?" Gillian tried. They were skimming through the hills, deeper into the green and gold of West Cork. Towards Brothers.

"Well," Clooney said, a little dry. "You've made the short list."

"List?" Gillian said, feigning alarm. "How short?"

Clooney did not answer. In Skibbereen he shifted all the way down to first. The streets were clogged and sprouted from one another at odd angles. There were farm trucks parked on the sidewalk in front of the town hall. "Heart of famine country this," Clooney said. "But I suppose you've seen the television shows and know all about it."

"Why don't you buy Brothers?" she asked, when they were pulling out into the country again a few moments later.

"I'm not eligible," Clooney said. "I suppose I'm also too old for a new game entirely."

"Well look at me," Gillian said.

Clooney smiled. "I have already. I think you're very young indeed."

"What do you mean eligible?" she asked again.

Clooney didn't know whether he was allowed to answer this one or not, but he didn't seem ready to take a risk on her. Outside the countryside was spilling past, fragrant, verdant. She still felt light.

"Can we talk about the cheese?" she asked him. "Pope's Own from Brothers Farm?"

Clooney didn't say no.

"Washed-rind semi-soft?"

"It is that."

"Like anything I've tried?" Gillian asked.

"Perhaps a bit like a Morbier," Clooney said. "But different as well."

"And how is it I had never heard of Pope's Own before Chekov told me about it?" she pushed.

Clooney stopped the car on the shoulder just then, so close to a stone wall she couldn't have opened the car door. He produced a black kerchief from the glove compartment in front of her knees. "You won't have heard of it because it's never been for sale before," he said.

He raised the black handkerchief towards her eyes.

She tried to treat it lightly. "This is all very dramatic, isn't it?"

"I'm sorry," Clooney said, from quite close, his hands now behind her head. "But if you do not buy the farm, the seller does not wish its location revealed." He smelled just faintly of soap and bacon, not unpleasant in total. But even as he tied the kerchief in place so gently, Gillian had to fight a surging impulse to tear the thing from her eyes.

The car began to roll again. The breeze came through the window and her breathing slowed. They were on pavement for a short time, then on a rougher surface, perhaps gravel, whereupon she found herself shifting this way and that in her seat, once jostling to the right and rubbing shoulders with Clooney himself.

He wasn't telling her what he knew, Gillian thought. And that told her something else entirely.

Pope's Own? It sounds like a race horse.

Chekov put his hands flat together as he thought of it. There's nothing in the world quite like this cheese, he said finally. Golden paste like the sun on Derby morning. A trace of purple runs through the centre, like the blood of the Republic itself.

Why Pope's Own?

Chekov came out of his reverie. Because Brothers Farm is owned by the church at the moment, that's why. His balding holiness and a crimson gang of cardinals eat every wheel of it.

Gillian understood finally. How did that ever come about? She asked.

Chekov frowned as he thought about how to answer. I understand, he said finally, that Brothers was given to the church over

*thirty years ago by an elderly cheese-maker who had seen a
vision to the effect that this was what God wished of him.*

Crazy.

I shan't disagree with you on that score.

And why would the Vatican be selling Brothers now?

*Chekov looked disinterested suddenly. I can only imagine
they have their divinely inspired reasons.*

*So cheese aficionados from all over the world are descending
on West Cork for the first ever taste of . . .*

*It won't be like that at all. Chekov cut her off. They have a
man, Clooney. He will arrange a very quiet sale:*

And why me? Why not yourself?

*Just get to Clooney, Chekov said. Tell him only who you are
and that I have sent you.*

That's it?

*You might also try Matthew 13:45 on him. In a pinch, I
suppose. A religious man our Clooney. And then he recited it
for her.*

*It seems a little cheap. Gillian frowned. I can't say things I
don't believe.*

*Oh certainly you can, Chekov said. It feels good when you
stop.*

She jostled against Clooney as they rounded a bend. He joked
with her dryly: "Just another kilometre or so. Would you like
anything to read?"

She stayed in the jostle position, leaning a little on him. "I
might have drifted off," she lied.

They stopped a few minutes later. The tires had just changed
tone from the conversational scratch and ping of gravel to the
hollow rumble of a stone drive. She heard a gate close behind
them.

When the black kerchief came off, she was blinded. She
climbed out of the Fiesta, holding the door, and blinked into the
splintering halos of blue that fizzed on her retina – she had an
image of Franky on the mat, the two of them looking down at
him – and then her new surroundings slowly rose to her vision.

She was in a small courtyard in front of a tall house, stone
with blue wood shutters and a slate roof with many chimneys.

There were rose bushes flurrying over the lattices that had been built along the side walls. There were some farm trucks parked against a hedge opposite. A garden bordering a cobblestone drive, a narrow walkway that disappeared towards the farm yard. And rising behind the house in a broad, calm sweep, there was an expanse of green pasture that stretched up to the far ridge line.

When she pulled her eyes away from all of this she saw that there was another man there, standing with Clooney on the far side of the car.

"Meet Ferghal, our foreman," Clooney said. "Ferghal this is Miss Mackin."

She rounded the car to shake hands with Ferghal, who grinned widely. "Cheers. Yeah. God bless." He had a thatch of sandy hair and was wearing a white T-shirt with red suspenders, black wool pants and green rubber boots with the tops folded down.

"Just working the morning milk now," Ferghal said, motioning them to follow him. He led them past the courtyard, to the nearest building in the yard. And here, before their bags even came out of the car, they stood at the low doorway, and Gillian could see the large table vats where the milk was being coagulated over steam heat. Half a dozen women in gowns and hair nets bent silently to their various tasks, the hush reverential.

Clooney explained how it would work. Sunday, an envelope would arrive from Dublin with the other bid. That gave her all of today and tomorrow to inspect the property and the books. Ferghal and Clooney would be available for any information needed on the equipment, the buildings, the herd, or the cheese itself.

She put in a call to Tremblay first and got him out of bed. A Dublin real estate agent was what they needed, she told him, he might try using the Internet. Get some recent sale prices for a property of similar size with a large house in good condition, working farm attached. "Any kind of farm," Gillian said.

"Location?" Tremblay said, yawning.

"I don't know exactly, to tell you the truth. Somewhere in West Cork."

"By when?"

"Tomorrow, your noon?" she said. "Please and thank you."

"I'm assuming these monks of yours run a *profitable* cheese operation," he said then, awake enough to start worrying about her pressing tone of voice, about the impulsive quality of her request.

"They're not monks," Gillian said, finding again that Tremblay's attentiveness made her irritable. "Brothers is just the name of the farm. Brothers Farm. Pope's Own is the cheese."

Tremblay didn't care about any of this. He was waiting for his answer.

"I'm going through the books this morning," Gillian said, wanting off the phone.

Of course books were just paper on one level. Clooney spread out a plan of the property on the Brothers House dining room table and brought two hardbound black ledgers out of the next room. He left her with the words: "Well then, I imagine you'll want a few hours with all of this."

Which she emphatically did not. This might have been her old job, the mental framing of reality through the manipulation of financial results. She sat at the table, frozen above this brocade of written entries and blueprint lines and legal descriptions of the property, wanting only to look up from the pages and out the window to the fields beyond the rose bushes.

Really, she thought, what was there to say about a company that sold everything it made to the Vatican at a price negotiated thirty years before? Of course Brothers was losing money.

"All right, all right," Gillian said, finding Clooney outside washing the Fiesta. "I've had enough."

Clooney put down his rag. "So soon?" He looked genuinely disappointed.

"Not with all of this . . ." Gillian said, waving her arms around her, aware that he might have taken her to be disinterested in the farm itself, the cheese, the whole operation. "I only meant . . . with all that." She motioned back to the house.

Clooney scratched his chin. "I see," he said.

And so he found a pair of rubber boots for her in the Fiesta, and they walked for the rest of the day. From the big house up through the pasture to the ridge line at the north end of the property.

From there into the back meadow where the herd was grazing its way methodically towards an evening milking. From there they followed a small stream, to the low stone wall that marked the west side of the property. And this guided them south again to the creamery buildings, the paddock, the courtyard and the big house.

They had dinner in the big house. Ferghal had gone and they were in the hands of the Brothers' septuagenarian housekeeper Annie, who (if she was to be believed) cooked, cleaned, gardened, mowed the lawn, fixed the roof, and once chased off a prowler with a pair of hedge clippers. Annie had decided she liked Gillian.

She served them lamb chops and roasted potatoes, then sat watching them eat as if Gillian were someone whose arrival she had hoped for, anticipated for a long time.

After dinner Annie said only, "Well?" And Clooney nodded.

She disappeared behind the kitchen door, where Gillian heard the scraping of crockery, a brief clatter of silverware and then silence. They both stared at the door. When she re-emerged, Annie carried a white plate which she slid soundlessly onto the table.

"Mustn't muzzle the ox," Annie said.

Gillian stared down at the small triangular cheese, maybe seven inches a side. The rind was as orange as the sun had been that morning when she locked the house and turned to find Clooney out of the car, standing, watching her.

"Go ahead love," Annie said.

Gillian took the small knife and rotated the plate slowly. When the cheese was aligned with a corner facing her, she made two symmetrical cuts on either side of it, and gently pulled free a diamond of cheese. She turned it on one side to see more clearly.

It had the palest of yellow flesh, and horizontally through the centre of the paste ran a capillary of royal purple. It was a startling contrast, not only begging the question how the trace of purple had been introduced, but each highlighting the other: the yellow somehow a greater promise for the bloodlike residue, for the suggestion of prior despair.

"It's beautiful," she said.

"The sun on Easter morning and the blood of the Irish saints," Clooney said with a small smile.

"Is that what you think?" she asked him, cutting the piece into three smaller pieces. "Or is it the sun on Derby morning and the blood of the Republic."

Annie smiled and nodded. "Chekov," she said.

"And may I ask how he would have come to taste it?" Gillian asked, looking up at Clooney.

He raised his eyebrows in friendly exasperation, then stared down fixedly at the cut Pope's Own in front of them and said: "Will you be eating some of this blessed cheese, then?"

She put it on her tongue, squeezing it, chewing it almost gingerly. It was full and savoury, no sharpness or acridity, but tangy with the life that blossomed within it.

It comes alive, Chekov said. It will remind you in an instant of all that you have been.

I don't know if I like the sound of that, Gillian had answered.

You needn't like the sound of it at all, Chekov said.

She let the flavours swim through her for a moment. There was clover here, she thought, letting her eyes drift shut. There was the scent of broom and a faint saline back breeze. Was that earthy undertone the purple vein, she wondered. The flavours carried her aloft, to a point above the farm where all was visible and yet within her grasp. At once vertiginous and exhilarating. One might crash to earth from here or never touch down again.

When she opened her eyes again, she was not particularly surprised to find Clooney and Annie watching her carefully.

"Oh my," she said eventually. Embarrassed to find only those frail and grandmotherly words. "Oh my."

She followed Ferghal around the next day, squelching behind him in Clooney's pair of too-big wellies.

They took morning milk from half the herd and poured it steaming – still warm from the cows – into the table vats with the rennet. When it firmed into curds these were lightly cut with long thin knives, drained, then pressed gently into the triangular moulds filling each of them up halfway.

"All right then," Ferghal said. "You'll want to watch this part."

The gowned woman who was working with them produced a steel pail of purple paste. Gillian's eyebrows raised quizzically but the woman said nothing.

Ferghal answered: "Soot and port wine. To protect the surface."

"Soot?" Gillian asked. "As in ashes?"

He nodded, concentrating as the woman gently brushed the surface of the curds in the half-filled moulds.

They repeated the process with a late afternoon milking from the other half of the herd. After these curds were cut and drained, they were used to fill the moulds to the top, trapping the layer of purple ash in the centre.

"After about a week we salt them and transfer them to the curing house." Ferghal explained. "We'll wash the rinds with brine and brandy for a few weeks until they're nice and orange."

At the end of the second day she walked back through the Brothers pastures again, alone this time, and stood on the ridge line looking down at the farm. The cows had been released into the fields after the second milking, the seven employees from nearby towns were pulling out the front drive, driving slowly over the cattle guard. She could pick out Ferghal making his final rounds before shaking hands with Clooney at the front door and climbing into his small flatbed truck.

Above her the darkness was coming. Dropping down to enfold this farm and her. And she felt herself snugged down by the descending night, pinched between the air and the land and fused between them.

She called Tremblay after dinner from the old black and chrome phone in the main floor study. He was in an upbeat mood, the Dublin numbers having come back very high. "Bit of interest in West Cork at the moment," he said. "I'm afraid prices reflect it."

He told her. It was about twice what Gillian expected. She winced and looked out through the glass into the darkness. Her own reflection was superimposed over the silhouette of the ridge line, where the stars were just visible.

"You tried," Tremblay said. "That's the important thing."

"You think so?" Gillian said.

"To a degree, yes."

"To what degree, though?" Gillian asked. The comment had angered her.

"Gillian . . ."

"I want to know to what degree trying is the important thing. Is trying about half the value of doing something? Is it about a quarter the value?"

Tremblay listened patiently at the other end of the phone.

"Because I'm more of the opinion, at the moment, Tremblay, that it's about zero per cent of the value."

"Fine," Tremblay said. "Tell me where the money comes from and I'll get it to you."

"I could sell the property up the valley," she said.

"Bad idea," Tremblay said. "But it wouldn't be enough anyway."

"Bad idea?" Gillian said, gripping the phone tighter. "What do you mean bad idea?"

"Investing everything in Irish real estate? Is this the strategy we discussed? Anyway, it's not enough."

"Sell the West End condo."

"You have to live somewhere."

"I realize that," she said. "I could live here."

"Gillian . . ." he tried. "I think you're getting ahead of yourself."

"You have no idea where I am relative to myself," she said, irritated with this resistance. Always accommodating, always demurring to her, he chose this moment to carve a position on something.

"I won't help you run away," Tremblay was saying. He might well have said more after this, but those words obliterated whatever might have followed.

"Run away?" she said, incredulous.

"I know what's going on," Tremblay said. "What this really means. He was a bastard, all right? The world agrees that he was a bastard. That he deserves to be surpassed by you, for him to fail and for you to succeed . . ."

"You are completely wrong," Gillian said.

"I'm not," Tremblay said firmly. "You're falling for the oldest impulse in the book: flight. It's no more complicated than that really, you're going to run until nothing looks the same anymore and then that will prove to yourself somehow that you have changed, gone past him. But you won't have."

"Nonsense," Gillian said. They were both still on the line, and there were seconds that passed during which explanatory things might have been said, but all she could think of were the obstacles erecting themselves between her and what she had finally found. And as the thought surged, her hand slammed the phone down into the old chrome cradle.

Just don't be angry, Chekov said. For yourself, don't be angry.

How can I not be angry? Everything should be wiped clean just because he's buying $58 worth of expensive cheese he probably doesn't even eat? Makes me sick to look at him.

That's what grovelling looks like. I'm not suggesting you forgive David, only don't spoil it all for yourself by being angry.

He answered on the first ring. She didn't even say hello.

"What are you painting these days?" she asked him.

"Cheese?" David said. Then he laughed unnecessarily hard, his voice cracking with the manic pleasure of hearing from her. She supposed he might be thinking of a sunny future just then, a post-marital über-contentment during which he and his darling ex-wife would share friendly absolving banter over coffee, perhaps the odd fuck, so ran the purple vein of her insight clutching the phone in the study of Brothers House just then.

"I need to borrow money," she said.

She told him every detail, more than he wanted to know, no doubt, but she left him not one spare second to interrupt. She laid everything bare for this man who had himself a proclivity for laying things bare. Not caring. She told him about the farm up the valley, about the condo in town, the price of McGuigan's cheese shop, the value of the inventory. She told him about Chekov's tip, about Brothers, about the morning milk and the evening milk and the port-stained ash between. About the cobblestones on the main drive, the tended gardens, Annie and the women in their hair nets. About the sky pressing down on her like a lover on the ridge that evening, how it had pinched her to the earth and made her blood prickle in her veins. About – at the end of it all – what she had discovered and what, through her, it could become.

She wrote up the offer immediately after hanging up. And when she was finished she didn't think about anybody. Not about David or Tremblay or Clooney. Not even about Chekov. She walked the envelope down the hall to the last door on the right and slid it under, into the darkness beyond.

Gillian heard the front opening early the next morning, as a courier from Dublin dropped off the other envelope. But she didn't want to see Clooney until he had decided. She didn't want to see Clooney comparing her to some anonymous other.

She walked through the dairy instead. Watching the woman cutting the morning curds with those long tined knives. She watched the whole process as it unfolded again, thinking with pleasure of this gentle and perpetual repetition.

"What's your name?" She asked the woman who had applied the purple soot the day before. Now she was raking the curds, silently.

"Sal," she said, with a small smile.

They met in the front room as agreed. The sun streamed in off the meadow behind him.

"You were low," Clooney said.

She nodded, but couldn't bring herself to comprehend these words. "Low how?" she said.

Clooney sighed. "Lower than Dublin," he explained.

Over Clooney's shoulder she could see that the cattle had been released into the main pasture behind the house.

"I don't believe this," she said. "How close?"

"Does it matter?" Clooney said. "I have a duty."

"How close, goddamn it?" she said.

Clooney stared at her, a little sorrowfully.

"I'm sorry," she said.

"So am I," he answered.

She sat back in her chair, exhaled a long breath. "Who is Dublin? Who is this winner of Brothers Farm, maybe I could talk to him."

"Gillian," he said. The first time he'd used her first name. "You think I'd lie to you?"

She snapped at him. The man she needed in the whole process, the key to this whole thing and she snapped. "I don't take this personally," she said, sharp, voice raised.

"Oh no?" he said. "You're a bit like your friend Brian McGuigan in that department, I think."

She had to think who that was for a moment. Chekov. And then her mind was spinning forward already. "Who is the other bidder?" she asked.

Clooney squinted and thought.

"You can afford to tell me now, surely," she said.

He scratched the side of his jaw. "Colman McGuigan," he said.

She considered this, recalibrating her view of the situation. "Chekov's brother," she said eventually.

"The elder of two," Clooney said. "McGuigan the father willed Brothers Farm to the church some thirty years ago. It was to go back to one of the boys at a fair market price if ever one of them did wish to buy it. One of the boys, that is, or a designate."

"And you set them bidding against one another?"

"The McGuigan boys were born to bid against each other," Clooney said. "The surprising thing is that Chekov didn't come himself. He must think very highly of you to have sent you along instead."

"This is ridiculous," Gillian said.

"You might say so." And while Clooney sat there, comfortable in his chair, his index finger dipped unconsciously into his vest pocket. So instinctive was this impulse to reach for strength beyond. She didn't care that it was muscle memory at this point, she cared only that it was a telegraph. How dare this man, anyone for that matter, come wading in on her with a left hand at the waist, chin dangling.

Clooney rose slowly to his full height. Lanky at 50.

"You haven't passed the news along, yet," she said, setting up.

"I wanted to tell you first."

"The brothers," Gillian went on, keeping her eyes steadily on a spot in the middle of Clooney's chest. "I mean the McGuigan brothers. They're not believers are they?"

"Oh we're all believers in our own way I suppose," Clooney said.

"That's not so at all," she said. "Not true of Chekov. Not true of Colman McGuigan either. Chekov is a bitter ex-communist Republican and Colman is a successful businessman with his treasure stored up on earth. Isn't that true?"

Clooney appraised the comment. "Perhaps," he said.

"You think either of them understands Matthew 13:45?" Gillian said. And only now she let her eyes drift downwards, intending to play act sorrow and finding it right there, quite real in her throat and behind her chest.

Although she could no longer see him, she could hear that Clooney stopped moving.

"*Or again . . .*" Gillian said, and her cheeks flushed just a little as it occurred to her she might forget the verse, and she had to blot everything out briefly. The sound of the breeze, of cattle. The smell of straw and clover, of manure. The light of the country streaming in around them. She imagined herself channelling the scripture itself and the words then came easily:

"*Or again, the kingdom of heaven is like a merchant searching for fine pearls. When he has found a single pearl of great value, he goes and sells all his possessions and buys it.*"

You can hear someone listening.

As she thought back, Gillian knew she had never ever heard David or Tremblay or even Chekov listen to her as Clooney listened to her that day.

He listened so hard. Listened with everything in him to everything in her.

JESSICA JOHNSON

We Move Slowly

Matted and crusty, we move slowly, putting down one hoof at a time, careful not to scratch the hardwood. There seems to be so much body now – enough for two or more. Against the back of the couch, we stop to scratch our back, then on the sandpapery bricks around the fireplace, noticing how our coat is starting to hang shaggy in the places where we're rubbing off huge hanks of hair. Large and rubbery, our lips explore the lampshade, a doily or two, the wall-to-wall carpeting.

We go into the kitchen and slump down with our back against the refrigerator, forefeet sticking out in the air above our belly. Vast expanses of tile splay out whitely in every direction. We live in fear of marking up the floor or worse, of slipping and cracking open like the egg we dropped yesterday. The phone is off the hook, dangling to the floor from when the receiver rolled right off our hoof. This house was not made for yaks.

It's not what we expected; he merely dropped us off, showed us around the house and then said, *I think you'll be much happier here.* More firmly as he was about to drive away and we whimpered a little, not understanding, *Alecia, why do you have to be so difficult?*

His only warning: *I've bought you a house in the suburbs,* whatever those are; all we know is that we can't walk on these floors so we slide, using a blanket we found in the bedroom, hoping it doesn't belong to Alecia, whoever she is, perhaps another occupant of the house who lives in the basement and comes out when we're asleep, to fill the empty rooms against our absence. Or maybe we have seen her, as a disappearing figure standing behind us in the bathroom mirror. But when we peer in for a closer look we see only our own yellow watering eyes, a grizzled muzzle, mass of brown hair soft as a doll's.

In the emptiness of the house our breathing is comforting and real. A wet wheezing like a dentist's air suction straw. Only softer, and with a slight rattle, *GsGsGsGsGsGsGs*.

One night, when we've been in the house a few weeks, there's a knock at the door.

I'm out of sugar, the neighbour says. She hesitates, shifts her weight from leg to leg, then asks, *Could I borrow a cup of sugar?*

We don't have any, we say. *Unless you don't mind cubes?*

Oh no, she says, *I just had this craving to make cookies. But it's getting late to walk to the store.* She doesn't look so much like she is having a craving as that she wants to convey that she is having one. Her eyes roll and her arms gesture wildly, a little too wildly for this. If she were saying that a flash flood was coming and that we should all head for the high ground, it might be convincing.

We're going out soon, we say. *We can pick some up for you.*

Thank you so much, she says and we can see that she is trying to peer past us into the back of the house.

Arriving at the convenience store, we see a fat man dragging himself up over the curb and towards the door. We are entranced as he sweeps himself slowly down the aisles, a stopper in the flow of the convenience store traffic. We follow discreetly down the aisles as he picks things up and carefully puts them back, always with the labels facing out. At the cash register he puts down a Super Big Gulp, a pack of SnoBalls, and then, explicably, a Diet Coke, his hands shaking as he counts his money.

Sorry to hold you up, he says to the girl behind the counter.

Take your time, she says, focusing her eyes on the SnoBalls on the counter. She sucks rapidly three times on something in her mouth. We get a whiff of vanilla Tic Tac.

You have a good night now. He is suddenly smiling sweetly at the girl.

Oh I'll try, she says. Eyebrows plucked into defiant arches. Earrings dangly and glamorous.

The neighbour's house is dark everywhere when we get home, so we leave the sugar behind the screen door.

One night, when we're too restless to sleep, we go into the living room and carefully roll back the carpet with our front hooves. We pick out an album from the stack in the corner of the room. When the music comes on, we keep the beat in half-time, first kicking out our left legs, then our right. Little green and red lights spin across the pink sofa and the blue wing chairs, the dried flowers on the coffee table, the bricks of the fireplace. All the other houses on the street are dark, so our big picture window turns into a mirror.

In our reflection we see that a young woman is dancing behind us, mysteriously graceful, achingly young. It must be Alecia. We stop breathing for a second. Alecia's pubis juts out in the pink leotard she's wearing, and her skin is so pale we can see moles on her thighs through her tights. Her hair is sandy blond, of the kind that leaves her eyelashes short and stubby, lighter at the ends than at the tips. We look at her and want to coat her with frosting, or maybe a paper bag. We recognize that we are capable of doing her sudden violence – we, who wouldn't hurt a fly except to brush it off our back.

But we keep on dancing as we were before. There is nothing else to do, really, except go on.

The days, we spend rolling around in the sunny patch on the carpet, drinking Coca-Cola through a straw and re-reading old newspapers. Our eyes always settle on one ad in the 'personals' column; it's an ad we first read the day before he brought us here, a day when we didn't see him at all because he didn't come home. We remember roaming through different rooms, uneasy without knowing why, the moving truck in the driveway that never drove away but only sat, and we thought it must have come to the wrong house. *Middle-aged gentleman seeks two ladies, perhaps sisters or mother/daughter combo.* . . . We remember a time when this would have been funny; it reminds us of *him*, who used to read the papers and laugh. *Don't count on seeing me much anymore*, was one of the first things he'd said when things began to change. Now neither he nor the paper comes at all, but for a free local one called the *Liberal* filled with pictures of children and their pets, food on display in neat pyramids in the new grocery store, a hot dog day at the used car lot: 'Come have a weenie with Al Palladini,' reads the banner in the background. Now this same newspaper piles up around the house, bleached and yellowed by the sun of the front porch where it falls first, collecting webs and the husks of insects that have died.

It grows dark and the carpet turns cold. Regretfully, we heave ourselves to our feet, needing something to pass the hours until bedtime. Taking a tub of raspberry yogurt from the kitchen, we weigh our options. A movie might be nice, but hard to pick out when we consider the myriad titles in the video store, grouped in such misleading categories, WESTERN, also a kind of sandwich, THRILLERS, not really thrilling at all, RATED X, simply too abstract for our taste.

Inevitably, we go to the store and buy children's powdered pastel candy in long flexible tubes, a sucker in the shape of a human thumb, a small pink case containing more than fourteen metres of rolled-up chewing gum. The sugar overload immobilizes us until the following morning when we wake up shaky and ravenously hungry, too heavy to pull ourselves up, our chest like Plasticine, our heart feeling as though it has leadened and constricted and maybe even come to resemble what we have been told hearts look like: tightly clenched fists.

I'm having an Amway party, says a man standing on the doorstep one morning. *I was wondering if you'd like to come.*

An Amway party?

Yes. It's something I'm involved in that I'd like to share it with my friends and neighbours.

We shift on one leg. We don't know what to say.

Have you heard of network marketing before?

We shake our head.

It's the greatest opportunity for income growth you'll ever experience.

There's a pause, then we say, *We're not that concerned with income growth at this time.*

All right, he says. *That's fair enough. But Amway can do other things for you as well. It can turn you into a self-starter.*

We look at him.

You'll learn the discipline you need to run your own business.

Run a business! We say, incredulous.

You'd be surprised. Quite a few people from this neighbourhood have expressed an interest.

Well . . . it sounds complicated. We're probably not interested.

Here, he says. *Just take one of our pamphlets. And remember, the parties are also a great way to meet people.*

That idea so deliciously scary we run out into the backyard and do a number of high kicks in the air with our hind legs.

The summer moves on. We read the Amway pamphlet, but it seems very general in scope, and since the man hasn't returned we soon forget about it. Meanwhile, more and more mail arrives, which we pile up carefully by the front door, all of it addressed to Alecia. We become curious when we see that *he* writes to her, but we pile the letters by the front door mail slot. If only she could come to the front door one day, possibly with the intention of coming in for tea – everything could be discussed plainly and openly.

It is impossible to communicate with people one never sees . . . his name and hers are both included on a fancy postcard that arrives inviting them to a high school reunion. Required dress would be casual. We leave the invitation on the top of the pile where it's easy to spot.

We focus our attention on the series of flyers and promotional packages that have been coming in the mail addressed to Occupant. Apparently, our household has been selected from among a number of households to participate in market research surveys. We dutifully fill in every form to the best of our ability, hesitating on such puzzling entries as *Brand of shampoo most recently used?* . . . to which we can only circle, a little embarrassed without knowing why, *none*. The packages marked *For the lady of the house* are similarly puzzling, presenting a term we are barely familiar with. We look out the living room window and wonder if every other house on our street has a lady belonging to it, if perhaps we have one too but have misplaced it or not recognized it, tucked it out of the way beside the fireplace or under the couch, or worse, left it to rust and rot outside in the shed, unlabelled, misbegotten.

Lettuces sprout up in the garden, of their own volition. Almost immediately they begin to go to seed, reaching high with great stalks like small trees to tower over the plump zucchinis on the ground. Tomatoes burst open on their vines and insects gather in the split places to drink the juice that trickles out in the sun.

The nights are already growing shorter again when the Amway man comes back, this time carrying with him a small briefcase.

We're starting a second phase recruitment campaign. If you were ever interested in joining, now is the time, because we're offering benefits galore.

Benefits galore?

Round-trip airfare to Florida for our first-quarter top seller, plus our new members who sell to ten customers in their first month will all be invited to a special party.

What would we have to do?

We offer a starter package of merchandise. We'd set you an initial quota of $25 in sales per week. That works out to about two customers.

Cautiously we ask him, *And there will be a party?*

We sell two packages of bubble bath to the lady next door, and she gives us a dollar extra with no explanation, paying in cash and saying, *Keep the change*. None of the other neighbours on the street are as willing, however, so one evening we head for the convenience store, where we stand outside the door and stop people on their way in. In general, people are surprisingly receptive when approached, many of them less so when we show the brochure, but nevertheless we gain six more customers over the course of a few evenings.

We gain a sort of perspective on our clientele, given that many of them are alike. A series of women is always trickling by into the aesthetician's, which is beside the convenience store. We hear one of them say to her friend as they wait near the open door that she gets her nails done once a week; she considers this her time to herself. We, who have so little to do all the time, are mystified by one who spends her time to herself running an errand – for that is what we assume this is, a trip to have one's hooves serviced. We try to imagine what she does all the rest of the days and one image persists: The woman scurries around the neighbourhood, crossing the lawn between one house and the next with something small and dangling in her hands like the depilator we saw advertised as seen on TV, its thin wires trailing behind her. She uses this tool on people; it performs some kind of essential service that only she can do. Perhaps she has been trained in this from birth.

On the fourth or fifth night the fat man comes, pulling up on a bicycle that seems to be far too small for him, his legs sticking out at nearly right angles on either side. We haven't seen him all summer. He doesn't look at us but barges into the store, puffing, and we watch as he heads directly for the freezer to pick out two ice cream sandwiches. When he barges out again, head first but looking down, he gets on his bicycle and peddles furiously down the sidewalk. Only half a block away, his bicycle stops, stands still for a moment, and then crashes loudly to the ground on its right-hand side.

From somewhere inside us we hear a voice say, *Well? Pick it up then, Alecia. Why are you so clumsy?*

The man gets up and slowly rides away, wobbling. We look down at the brochure we are holding out, using one hoof like a wine tray: *Amway Favourites for Summer.* The hoof itself is brown with slightly chipped edges, its underneath cloven and textured like a tongue.

There is a sign at the end of the driveway that reads '4200 Block Fireworks Tonite!' We follow along the road, arriving at the edge of the schoolyard, where there is a sand pit near the grass. Men, bent over in the sand, try to insert sticks in it, gauging distance with spread forefinger and thumb, while off to the side women, some sitting on lawn chairs, hold clothing for the men and the children, who run back and forth holding little stars on sticks that they wave around.

We lumber around. We don't know where to sit.

A group of boys rides up on bicycles and they make some comments about the size of our ass, as if this will change anything about their lives or ours.

We go home. It is just dusk. We sit on the step and try to keep a numb brain, if only because we have no real conclusions to draw.

A sprinkler on the neighbour's lawn flops itself onto its side on the grass and writhes gracefully back and forth like a fish swimming across the lawn. It starts to scissor its way towards the house. A woman runs outside and tends to it, the arcs spraying confidently across the night air despite the way she wrestles. When she finally sets it back down the right way, it reverts to its old position, making geometric arcs in the sky, one after the other, wetting and re-wetting the same oval of lawn over and over. It occurs to us that everything, living or not, is wasting energy.

Darkness comes and we are still sitting on the front step. We hear bangs and whistles, and we look up: the street is exploding.

The man from Amway comes to call, carrying his briefcase and wearing his glasses. As always, he is mild-mannered. He sits with one ankle balanced on the knee of the other leg.

I have good news for you, he says, smiling a small smile. *Do you remember when I told you at the beginning that we offered round trip airfare to Florida to our top seller?*

Yes.

You are our top seller for this quarter. In fact, your sales figures are extremely high for all the regions. Quite startling, for a beginner.

We say modestly: *Well, we have quite a bit of spare time on our hands.*

No, he says, *don't bother with that*, and he cuts through the air with a choppy hand. *I have a proposition for you.* He leans forward. *We have positions available for people who are particularly motivated, and who have the potential to be great motivators of other people within our organization.*

Such as?

I've spoken to my superiors, and we believe you could do well at our training camp in Florida. People who graduate can go on to become motivational speakers within the organization, or instead may choose to bump up many levels in the marketing pyramid in order to take over an entire sales region. You would have to go wherever you were needed, of course.

And you think we have that potential?

Certainly, he says. *Your record, in what has always been documented as a difficult sales region, indicates that you are willing to face a challenge head on. Also, there's the fact you don't seem* (and here he looks kind) *to be tied down by a husband or family.*

Well, yes, we say. *But surely . . . we continue more slowly. It cannot have escaped your attention, what we are.*

He says, *This is a condition of which the organization is not unaware.* He looks at us openly, holding his hands together in a relaxed position between his knees. *But as you have shown, this is not something that in any way affects your ability to sell Amway . . . I myself would not consider it to be a deficiency.*

We sit reflecting. He stands.

I know you'll need a couple of days to think about it.

Yes, we say. *And thank you very much.*

He heads for the door.

We ask as he leaves, *Have you been to the training camp?*

No, he says, one hand on the knob. *I worked my way up the slow way.*

Are you happy with the way things went?

I am not unhappy, he says, pausing before going out the door. *Don't bother telling me that's not the same thing.*

∿

Once, there were seven zucchinis growing on a large vine in the tangle that is the back garden. Now, there are only five. We have watched their progress ever since they first appeared as tiny blossoms; now, these remaining ones are huge after a season of unfettered growth, as big as the arm of a man, so heavy and entrenched in dirt that we barely can roll them over with one nudge. And yet, their number is diminishing. We count them each morning. Five, then four.

We wait up, draw back the curtains to block our shadow as we walk through the different rooms in the house, stopping to pick up something here, to kick a closet door shut there. The house has acquired an abandoned feel. Little creatures jump up all over our legs when we walk in the living room. And the television screen is covered in a fine film of dust. There are smudges and smears we don't remember leaving on door frames and walls, breath spots on the bathroom mirror, little flecks on the windows. In the kitchen we see that despite our best efforts, the floor is covered in black scuff marks.

There was a garage sale today to mark the end of the summer, across the street, and we watched it from the window, saw people putting things out, others taking them away. All summer we have listened to these people's barbecues and cocktails around the pools in their backyard, caught snippets of conversation as they floated over the hedge: 'When are you and Shirley going up to the cottage, Nate?'; 'Not till August – her folks are coming in from Kingston for a week first.' The neighbours seem obsessively structured in the way they live their lives. They're always telling their children not to slam the back door, for instance, even if this means screaming at them to stop doing it through the kitchen window.

We cannot imagine spending a winter here, knowing that, however disappointing they may be, everyone around will disappear inside. We are already conscious of how short the days are getting, how the living room sun takes less and less time to move across the floor.

Standing at the kitchen sink to look out the window and into the garden we hear a small creak, then the sound of the back fence door opening. A lone figure comes into the back yard, carrying a basket.

The figure is neither tall nor short, dressed in a cotton shirt, pressed shorts, and leather sandals. She makes straight for the zucchini patch. In the light of the bug lamp we see her hair, curly and beige, sticking out around the visor she wears. Taking a big knife from her basket, she begins to saw at one of the great thick stalks, wiping from her forehead the juice that squirts up as she cuts.

We talk to her calmly through the screen window. *What are you doing?*

She starts and looks up. *Who is it?*

Those aren't your zucchinis.

The neighbour stops. Drops her knife to the ground. Meanwhile, we ease quietly through the back door. We confront her as she attempts to leave, startling her by appearing suddenly from behind the pea trellis.

Why didn't you just come to the door? we ask.

She looks away over our shoulder.

You should have asked us first.

She grabs her basket and runs past us down the side of the house. From the living room window we can see her struggling across the lawn, shaved skinny legs working up and down in the tall grass we've never bothered to cut, her pony tail flying out behind her as her basket jiggles, still hanging over one of her arms. When she gets to the fire hydrant she vaults neatly over it and disappears behind the hedges at the end of the street.

The alarm rings, for the first time. A rush of something unnameable courses through us. Only moments later, a car pulls up in the driveway and someone rings the doorbell. We answer it. *I'm your ride to the airport*, he says, and we see the air limo van parked in the driveway with several passengers already in the back seats. It is earlier than we expected, but it seems fitting, somehow: We look around. The kitchen is inert; it still smells of last night's dinner. In the living room, stillness reigns from the carpet to the sofa, the air hanging heavy with dust motes. The fireplace curtains are unwavering, still crusted with soot from whoever lived here before we came, who also let the smoke stains travel up the front of the bricks.

There is nothing more to do, so we lock the house and put the key in the mailbox, perhaps for the benefit of the people watching from the van. Then we take our scanty luggage down the front steps where the man picks it up. *All ready?* he asks.

Ready, we say, feeling as if even when we go, the house will carry on without us, folding and unfurling itself like the stale marshmallows we once tried to steam soft again in a double boiler, turning inside out the closets, mushrooming the floors and ceilings, billowing the rafters until something quite different will be created. From the outside, of course, it will always be the same red brick bungalow, bushes clustered around the windows threatening to grow over them like hands pressed over eyes, pine cones strewn sharply around the yard.

Going down the driveway we see things in the periphery, extra things that turn and flip where one wouldn't expect anything to be. A long time ago *he* asked us why we became a yak and we told him the truth, which is that we don't think we became one so much as one day we simply were one.

We follow the driver to the car. He stows our small suitcase in the back and indicates that we should get in the side door. Then he sits in the driver's seat and turns on the van, backing slowly out of the driveway past the bushes along the side. One of the other passengers, a woman with long dark curly hair, says a bit snootily to her blonde companion, *It's a nice neighbourhood, at least.*

The van reaches the end of the street. It signals and waits to turn right. Then we know we should look back now and so we do, to see her pressed up against the glass of the living room window, one hand half lifted up, fingers waving very slightly, Alecia.

KAREN SOLIE

Onion Calendar

The hobbies on my résumé were
sports and *trains*. No photo required, no time for an interview.
They were desperate, seeding done and Old Kambeitz useless
with stroke in his semi-private at Medicine Hat Regional four
months before retirement while kochia, flixweed, and nasty
foreign-born broadleafs muscled out of dormancy. The e-mail
came Friday. I spent Saturday in my parents' beige living room
watching the Canucks surrender the semis, cool Gibson's in my
hand, McLean missing a tricky lob on the stick side. By morning
I was gunning it south past strobing jackpine, feet on the floor,
one hand on the wheel, thermos of coffee beside me. My name
is late-'60s soap opera gender-neutral. They didn't know what
they were getting.

It was blowing hard my first morning on the job, blue hard-
pack sky dissolving to a brown haze of drifting topsoil along the
horizon. A bad sign. Dry spring. I parked my old Chev half-ton
on the gravel pad alongside the Pool office, the elevator less
than a decade old, testament to boom years of the late '80s.
Inside, the promise of a computer, humidifiers and dust filters,
new PVC conveyors. In the grey rutted yard a couple of farmers
leaned jawing and spitting on the hoods of jerry-rigged Fords.
Three clean little boys in primary coloured windbreakers were
left to the work of nailing a cat's tail to wooden struts of the
annex, cat yowling blue murder, wind throwing thistle down
sinkholed Railway Street. One of the boys had blond curls

tossing like clover. Vague stink of nuisance grounds to the south. I felt somewhat at home.

The metal door whanged shut a beat behind me before the men stamped in off the plank steps, a warp of clay dust woofing across speckled lino.

"What can I do for you?" I inquired officiously.

"Yeah. I guess we'd be wanting the agent," ventured the young one, elbowed, "about some, y'know, chemical."

"That'll be me. What do you need?"

A pause. Shotgun burst of gravel against the west wall. It was unseasonably warm. An El Niño year.

"Where's the agent?" broke the elder.

"That'll be me."

Incredulous grins of those attending yet another bonehead play.

I was the first and only female elevator agent in Enterprise, Saskatchewan. I know the job, have viable references earned from lackey summers under Spiritwood's Pioneer man, a couple of years after high school learning how to grade product and argue with farmers, putting in time at computer courses and WHMIS safety seminars, and years after that shovelling grain and pulling cars. This was before you had to have an ag degree or business diploma, before the Wheat Pool had to prove there weren't a bunch of hicks running the show. The guys up there knew me, perched on the five-ton's split vinyl seat from three years old, my dad and grandpa homestead grain men. I drove my first load in on the tail end of a growth spurt, 14th birthday, foot on the clutch, avoiding the baited mousetrap. The goddamn mouse squeaked out from under the seat with me waiting on the ramp. I eeked my boot off and the truck rolled back towards the line, men yawping, hauling ass, till I got my blushing act together a span from Peterson's International. Heard about that till the day I left.

Like most northern kids, my dreams led south. I grew sullen and sick of beards, bony birch, ice fog so dense it reflects shadows like a gyproc wall, the seasonal dances where bad local bands with no drummer struggled through "Mercury Blues" and "The Tennessee Waltz." On breaks we drank Strawberry Angel and Purple Jesus from jam jars in jacked-up Novas displaying confederate flags in their rear windows. We kept secrets everybody knew. There was an arena, a curling rink, a bar. No movies, no cable. A general lack of imagination, even for vandalism.

It was said that in the south chinooks blow warm in January and the power hardly ever goes out, that people shop in Montana and smuggle cheap Schlitz and Budweiser back from hockey weekends in Great Falls. Things would be different, I thought, that close to the border. Things would be happening. I couldn't wait, took a trip down my first weekend here, before I knew anyone. Rolling through greening sagebrushed ranchlands of Maple Creek, over the east end of the Cypress Hills, I was happy. Unfamiliar waving grasses and ditches full of brown-eyed susans bordered the Red Coat Trail. My fat rebuilt engine hummed a horsepower unimaginable to those first spooked flea-bitten Mounties conjuring hostile Indians out of heat mirages and slough willow.

America, The States, the U.S., the United States of America, I mused, accelerating, weighted to asphalt by a walletload of foreign money. I'd heard you could drink on the road down there, wished I'd brought something, even one beer. It was my first time across. I expected more. The Secondary 233 splits Big Sky Country's flat face like a grey scar. There were cows, crackerbox houses of trigger-happy militiamen settling on treeless yards. Signs at barbed-wire gates read TRESPASSERS WILL BE SHOT and THIS PROPERTY PROTECTED BY SMITH AND WESSON. More cows.

I found Havre behaving as if someone had driven a stake through its heart. A couple of shifty-eyed burger joints, parallel rows of peeling bungalows, a few bars with neon Coors signs sputtering in a weirdly vacant noon and the same old wind. I bought a Spark-O-Matic tape deck and had it installed at the Peavey Mart, anchor to the one gasping mall, and drove back the same day, declaring nothing. The young border guard was from Shaunavon and crazy to pass the time.

"Sometimes I don't talk to anybody for hours," he said. "I dream about trunkloads of guns and hash. Caught some doofus from Swift Current bringing back duffel bags full of fireworks.

I read off 'fireworks' from my duty list and a little kid in the backseat clapped a hand over his mouth and started bawling. The wife flinched. A flinch says it all. We look for the flinch. But that was last year. That's been about it."

I haven't been back since. I guess you could say disappointment in general over Saskatchewan.

It's been almost a year now. I'm lurching into lengthening daylight with sugar in my tank, having lost all heart for Enterprise. And I'm not the only one. Occasionally a man will pay up his insurance, drive out to a high spot overlooking a willow slough with its redtail hawks and opera of green frogs and stick a shotgun under his chin. Two since I've been here. The weather wears you down. Watching the sky is a spectator sport. *Nothing but empties*, the old guys sigh at yet another promising storm turning tail rising ozonated wind south, east, west, north, anywhere but here.

It's not like this was unexpected. We're midway through a dry cycle: seven good years, seven bad. But hope for rain is a dark, dark spell. Farmers will put seed in spring fields drifting to dunes around them, sit out on the porch at dusk with a Pilsner watching topsoil lift off towards Manitoba, and be back out there at dawn. Despite the knowledge of cycles, Farmer's Almanac and meteorological data, every New Year's Day all across the heartland we build our onion calendars. Bottles of Canadian Club and Silent Sam pushed aside, 12 halves are hollowed and salt poured into the teary bowls. Each represents a month. After 24 hours, the salt in some onions is wet, some dry. Wet salt, wet month. Results are marked on new gratis Credit Union or Esso calendars. It's a bit of a joke. But later, wet salt marking another month of dry heat and drift stings our eyes, gets stuck in our throats. We sweat it out.

There've been a few bad years, what with the Crow Rate long gone, free trade weaseling around to bite us in the ass, prices bottoming out. I was the last straw. A lot of farmers consider a woman agent a step down from complete automation. One after the other, as trucks lined up on the ramp and out the yard, I fought over shrivelled feed-quality specimens they swore were

No. 1 high protein red, top dollar. *There's no arguing with a woman. I'm taking orders from a goddamned girl.* I've heard them mutter this. Over and over.

I know what I'm doing, I've choked, treacherous eyes hot, throat closing. They crave my tears like chocolate. *I know what I'm doing*, I've told myself later at my leaning rented house crying in front of *MASH* reruns, the rug an orange shag fog. At times I've felt like that little Oz character – utterly misunderstood and unappreciated, I think – behind the scenes pulling levers and punching buttons on my Pentium-powered IBM. I pick information like apples from the Web. At any one time I've had nearly 900 producer files at my disposal, can in seconds secure enough fertilizer to make one holy hell of a bomb, enough to blow the rural municipality of Big Stick sky high. I've amassed herbicides and pesticides bearing sweetly beneficent names like Horizon and Refine in quantities to destroy the western water table forever.

You'd think these powers of acquisition would've rendered me indispensable, even given me the upper hand. But when I pinned up memos all over town last spring regarding the ineffectiveness of a certain killer mix, I was ignored. And when the fresh-faced chemical rep came down from Regina with his ag degree and spiff Gap khakis, they bought gallons of the stuff, spread it thick as corn syrup over field and fallow. Weeds sucked up the scalding sauce like mother's milk. By June wild oats with stalks like bamboo were waving prehistorically, heads heavy with the promise of future generations, tiny sawflies leaping happily hither and yon in the canopy above slowly strangling grain. It's hung years on the face of the young rep. He's been hounded mercilessly, his cellphone a pox to him.

The strange thing is, I like the job. During harvest hot air is close with sweetgrass and clover. The nut smell of grain spilling wide and red-gold through the floor grate into the pit puts me in mind of beer and bread. Good solid things. Like work. Heartfelt heartsore labour. In operation, at capacity, the building sounds like all elements in motion: wash of water, fire hiss, wind through long grasses, sink and shift of earth. All this in the measured shake of the separator, the flashing scalper, grain rushing up stainless steel legs and flowing into 18 bins that hang above me heavy as thunderheads, and my beating heart at the centre of this gathering. I don't even mind the dust and chaff, though when coughing up honey-coloured phlegm I've thought about the black lungs of West Virginia coal miners, how work's illnesses root in the body's groundwaters and take purchase there.

My way to refine, my horizon, has been a pack of Player's king-size and Grasshopper wheat ale. In the hotel beverage room, with its red terrycloth tabletops, black painted interior and bohunk jukebox, I drink local beer as a matter of principle. I've sold their raffle tickets, volunteered and moderated, joined the ladies softball team. Playing left field, I scooped a hot grounder skittering wildly over gopher holes to nail the snotty blond daughter of Assiniboine's pharmacist cold at second to preserve a one-run lead. I've been queen of at least one beer garden.

But ancient laws govern how people move about the few square miles of their Canaan. Crack a new deck and on the first card are the rules: Rules For Playing Stud Poker, for Hearts, for War. Discard all jokers. I am new here and newness is suspicious. New People have strange ideas, try to instigate drama clubs and choir practices. It was the same back home. Our new high school math teacher was very nearly run out of town for trying to introduce basketball into the phys.ed curriculum. We were a volleyball school. New People are new for generations.

I was way behind and working Saturday, my seventeen-year-old so-called second man snowed in out east with some moon-faced Ukrainian relatives. It was early January and 20 below with the kind of mythic prairie wind chill that prompts concerned radio voices to offer a Mission Impossible countdown to how little time it takes exposed skin to freeze. *This organism will destruct in 30 seconds.* At four p.m., evening was moving in. The red and green of Christmas lights splashed on the deepening blue of snow mirrored quilted clouds lit from beneath by a big orange sun. A cold carnival. I finished shovelling the tracks and climbed the ladder to the first hopper car, hoping to load at least a couple before quitting for the night. Clambering and skittering on the slippery steel, reefing on the recalcitrant lid, I saw two figures lurch out of the shadows of my elevator. They were lugging hockey gear, barking out quasi-conversation in a familiar low halting accent of Teutonic ancestry and post-game beer buzz. *Go on*, I muttered. *Pass by.* But they stumbled into the shelter of the car, sank swearing on two old railway ties and fished cans of Canadian from the guts of their bags.

"*Fuck* it's cold. Need some help there little lady?" sneered the young farmer, the town mouthpiece I'd met on my first morning here. The other was a local pothead hell-bent on driving his ailing father's hardware store into the ground. He snickered like some stunned cartoon. "No thanks," I yelled down, banking, after a moment's consideration, on civility. They conferred. "Come down for a beer," shouted Mouthpiece. Light was failing and the wind was picking up. It was hopeless up there, frozen solid and tight, my fingers numbing. I could have taken them into the warm office, drank their beer and locked up around seven. Anyone else would have. But I couldn't. It felt like admitting something. I whacked away dumbly.

"What're you too *good* for us now?" Mouthpiece stood, eyes narrowed. The line was drawn. It was getting hard to see. The evening star disappeared above a bank of cloud moving in fast from the west. I should've gone down, should've taken a dive. Pothead spied an opening. "I'll betcha she's a dyke," he yodelled. "I'll bet she's a fucking *lesbian*." They laughed. And then they stopped, picked up their sticks. I was hooked to a safety harness mounted on the elevator. If you fall off a car, it's supposed to act like a seatbelt, catch and hold you inches from the ground. "Wonder if this thing works," said Mouthpiece. "Let's just see about that," he grunted, trying to hook the blade of his stick over the belt, becoming more serious with each jump. "Yeah!" grunted Pothead, getting into the spirit, "Yeah! Yeah!" I was trying to hold the belt away and unhook it from the small of my back at the same time, panicking now, fingers dead meat. I shook my gloves off and they blew away like birds. I don't know if I was hooked, or if I slipped, but I went down hard, fast, head hitting the empty car. *Gong.* I laid there, blood from my nose sinking into ice, swollen eyes on the two who stood now with their sticks in the snow like 10-year-olds. "Shit," said Pothead, backing up and giggling, the retard. Mouthpiece lingered, mouth opening and closing. "Fuck. Are you . . .?" Nothing. They grabbed their stuff and buggered off, leaving me like a broken window.

I lay there awhile and held the spine of the train that caught me, thinking of millions of moving parts working in sync to propel an unlikely vehicle over equally unlikely terrain. Each to its function. Watching a multi-engine surge across a high-level trestle, the odd bolt ricocheting through a half-mile of struts, is like witnessing a miracle. I stuck my fingers in my mouth to warm them before climbing down. I tasted it then. Underneath the salt of my blood and skin was something other. I held my right hand under my down jacket for a bit, laid it flat on the black ice, licked my palm. It was rain from ocean-born clouds filtered through giant cedars and creaking firs, spicy fog shrouding the Vancouver grain terminal I had seen only on calendars. All the airborne coastal waters that cling and freeze as the train sways through the Hope Ridge, Rogers Pass, the saw-tooth Kootenays.

Walking home, I remembered friends of my parents who'd visited their daughter, or maybe a son, anyway a lawyer now, in Victoria. "Everyone has at least one fireplace," they crowed. "I don't think they ever have to dust and there are *no bugs*. We didn't wear jackets once while we were there." "You can't trust those west coast people far as you can throw 'em," my dad said later. But that's just how he is. He doesn't care about daffodils and cherry blossoms in February, or how you can walk down the street and pick fruit off the trees.

That night I opened a bottle of Canadian Club I'd been saving since Christmas. And with snow blowing through the window frames and under the door, my rug growing uglier by the second, I made an onion calendar. When I got up the next morning I had a pretty good shiner. But my nose wasn't broken and the salt was wet 8 months out of 12. I spent the next day at the office looking through Tourism Vancouver's website. *The average temperature on the south coast is between 10 and 20 degrees. Vancouver is home to a host of different ethnic communities. Colourful festivals take place throughout the year.* Everyone does well, gets along. That Monday, I faxed my notice to the Wheat Pool.

No one's said much about my eye. "You should see the other guy," I laugh, when they do. Once in a while here some woman will walk into a wall. I'm no snitch. But it doesn't matter. I never fit in, and by all indications my job is becoming obsolete, what with the consolidation of handling into huge new concrete terminals rising 10 grey storeys above the flatland. They're hideous, but that's progress. I'm all for it. I've read that some homespun housewives with too much time on their hands have organized a group to try to preserve old elevators. Never mind that occasionally one of these "Prairie Icons" will go off like a rocket in a grain dust explosion, leaving someone to bury a pair of boots. Don't get me wrong. It's sad when another is torn down, when the school goes and one more town sinks back into dust. That doesn't mean I have to go down with the ship.

My linens are dull, pillows clotted with dirt. Everything hinged is gritty and seized. I'm leaving all of it, and have sold the truck. Tomorrow, I will hop the bus in Medicine Hat and ride smooth Trans Canada pavement alongside the main line all the way to the delta, to where rain clouds gather against broad sides of mountains. At the very edge of the continent my skin will soften and plump. I'll wear heels and dresses to work, my fingernails clean. Though I may miss the glittering concerts of meadowlarks, there are new names of birds to learn. And in an immaculate crystal tower high above the salt heart and branched lungs of the city, there will be days when I don't think at all of indifferent freighters bearing hard kernels of another season out into the open water of the Pacific.

TIMOTHY TAYLOR

Doves of Townsend

"Doves of Townsend, good morning."

This is me, answering the phone at the shop. After which I frequently end up explaining the inherited family name. Sometimes (I admit) tired of telling the real story, I'll make something up. "There's a flock of doves found in Townsend, my dad's hometown," I'll start. Then I finish the story by saying the birds hunt as a pack and kill cats, or that they bring good luck if you catch one and pull out a tail feather. The mood of the story rides up and down on the sine wave of my menstrual cycle.

The truth is plain. My father came from Townsend and he was a fanatical collector. Knives, as it happens, but it could have been anything. Magpie, hoarder, packrat, whatever you want to call him, I had long understood him to be obsessive-compulsive within certain categories. His suicide note read: *I fear I have covered the full length of this blade.* But at auctions, where he lived the happy parts of his life, he held up his wooden paddle and said his last name so the auctioneer would know who was bidding. "Dove," he'd say, eyes never leaving whatever dagger, cleaver, oiseau or machete had captivated him. And then – in case there was another Dove in the room – he'd say it again, louder: "Doves of Townsend."

So, here I am: "Doves of Townsend?"

It was two months ago, Alexander Galbraithe calling. He wanted a set of chrome 1940s ashtrays, the ones with the DC-3 doing the flypast over the cigar butts. I've known Mr. Galbraithe since I was a child. When my father started Doves of Townsend as an extension of his own collecting (a very bad idea I came to think), Mr. Galbraithe was one of his first steady buyers. I assume he stayed with me out of allegiance or sympathy, since after Dad's death I sold off the knife collection quickly and resolved never to replace it.

"Clare?" he said. "Are you familiar with the airplane ones?"

I knew he was talking about the famous deco ashtray since none of the other things he collects – coach clocks, cigar cutters, Iranian block-print textiles, even knives as far as I know – come in an aeroplane model.

"Pedestal or tabletop?" I asked him. "Illuminated?"

We began to work out the specs.

"Real?" I asked, breathing a little into the phone. "Or fake?"

Mr. Galbraithe didn't laugh often, although he found many things funny. What he did, instead, was roll his massive balding head back an inch or two, squint slightly and crinkle his cheeks. When he was done, he'd roll his head back to its normal position and resume where he left off.

This is what he did now. I could tell over the phone. And when he returned he said, "Clare. My dear. Really."

It pays to be straight on this real-fake question. There's no point looking for something real, something authentic and old and possibly rare, if the client has no preference. My some-times-boyfriend Tiko used to send art directors my way from time to time, and all they cared about was that an object look good on camera. Some collectors, on the other hand, collect fakes. So go figure.

What's bad, clearly, is to get fake when you're after real. Most dealers will learn this the hard way even if they resist being obsessive collectors themselves. Me, for example. I was just starting out. Dad had been gone a year, and I overcame all the good sense I had and bought a set of *les Frères* locking steak knifes. I literally saw them in a shop window, stopped on the sidewalk – reconsidering everything I had resolved after my father slipped somewhere beyond reach, after he did what he did – then went in and bought them. Of course, I knew the famous French maker produced knives that were rare and beautiful, knives with a four-inch hand-forged blade folding into a black pear-wood handle with silver inlay and locking in place with a tiny gold clasp in the shape of a dove. I knew the *les Frères* dove had meant something special to my father, among all his knives. These were the first I had seen since his death and, for that instant, I was host to a perfectly synchronous collector's impulse.

What this lapse taught me was never to buy a thing merely because it is rare and beautiful and you are able to construe some tangled family significance. What I didn't know then was the number of *les Frères* reproduction steak knives that had been made over the years by Spanish, Korean and other manufacturers. When I learned this, which was soon enough, I sold my Taiwanese fakes for about one-twentieth what I paid for them. To Mr. Galbraithe, in fact, who rescued me. Tried to pay much more than they were worth, but I wouldn't let him.

"You see the clasp here, Clare?" he explained very kindly. "The reproduction clasps are stamped flat from stainless steel, then gold-plated. A real *les Frères* has a hammered dove figurine, sculpted in three dimensions, in 18-karat gold."

"Fake," I said, shaking my head. "I should have known."

"But now you have seen it," he said, putting a large hand weightlessly on my shoulder. "I am quite sure you won't miss it again."

He was a huge presence, six-and-a-half feet tall; God knows how many pounds. In his other hand, the knife looked like an antique folding toothpick I'd once seen at auction. Mr. Galbraithe always leaned a little forward when we spoke, canted just so, careful to hear and understand everything that I said. He wore dark, heavy double-breasted suits and two-tone black and white shoes. Tiko met him once and referred to him thereafter as Sidney Greenstreet, although he looked nothing like that. He brought to mind the force of gravity, yes, but not the crushing pressure of it. Instead, he made me think of the way some large things elegantly defy it. I've looked at suspension bridges the way I looked at Mr. Galbraithe.

He folded the fake *les Frères* into his palm, first popping the gold-plated clasp with his thumb, then clicking shut the blade with his fingers. Then he wrote me a cheque using a large black fountain pen. In the nineteenth century, I thought on occasion, I could have ended up marrying the widowed Mr. Galbraithe despite the thirty-year age difference.

"You have an eye for the fine line," Mr. Galbraithe said to me another time, admiring a more successful purchase. I thought the words left unsaid were something like: *but be careful, so did your father.*

He wanted the ashtrays for his office, he explained.

"Of course," I said. He'd been a pilot at one time. During the war, the Second I suppose. He kept a suite of offices out near the airport, and when we talked on the phone I could hear the jets taking off and landing.

I began a fairly typical search: local, then national dealers. Then American. Surprisingly, I turned up only a few singles, none in fine condition and none illuminated. I searched the Internet and found a few more, but I couldn't tell what condition they were in and I didn't know the dealer.

I phoned Mr. Galbraithe back.

"Where are they?" he asked.

I told him it was Los Angeles. It wouldn't have been the first time he'd sent me off to inspect something. He flew me to Boston once to look over a case lot of clocks. He expressed deep trust in my judgement and reacted with gratitude, but not much surprise, when I produced exactly what he was looking for, time after time.

This didn't seem worth it, frankly. "Let's leave it for a while," I said. "Something will turn up."

He asked about local dealers, and I told him I'd long exhausted those options.

"Yes, yes. Of course you have. . . ." A jet was coming in for a landing just then. "What about the flea markets and what have you?"

It was an unusual suggestion from him. Everything in the entire flea market might be worth as much as one of his coach clocks on a good Saturday. It was, in my view (which I kept to myself), a vast sea of junk.

I phoned Tiko on Saturday, got him in bed. He said: "Baby . . . what time is it?"

I told him, and then described my plans for the day. "Chances of success are very slim, but it might be fun."

"What's Greenstreet want in a flea market?" he said, yawning and stretching. I could hear the sheets sliding over him, slipping off his chest, down his stomach. But when I asked him again, he said only: "I can't, I'm going skiing."

Work is work. I went down without him.

The flea market was held every weekend in a massive wooden warehouse in the industrial part of the city near the railway tracks. It's the kind of neighbourhood where the streets collude to form gigantic shallow ponds during the rainy season and an unlikely number of shopping carts spend their final days.

I paid my sixty-five-cent cover charge, took a big breath and went into the main hall. I didn't go there often enough for its vastness and futility not to strike me again. Here there were hundreds of independent dealers set up at folding tables, which stretched in their rows far back into the gloom, the warehouse air smelling of boiled hot dogs and vinegar, body odour, cat litter. The aisles sluggish with people. The vendors pessimistic.

I let myself drift with the currents of this sea, eyes down as I passed the tables, trolling through cheap, newish merchandise that would be of no interest to any collector now or in the foreseeable future. Acres of airport novels, CDs suspiciously unboxed, video games, socket wrench sets, Ren and Stimpy T-shirts and boxes of paper clips or batteries or ballpoint pens that presumably fell off the back of a truck somewhere. And scattered among these tables the personal collections, which for their madness and desperation held an increment more promise of delivering the unexpected. These were the tables heaped with costume jewellery, constellations of twinkling, unwearable rhinestone earrings, pendants, tiaras. Tables with shallow glass cases stuffed full of coins, or stamps, military medals, old wristwatches, brazenly ugly cufflinks and spent cigarette lighters. Tables stacked dangerously high, any item on top of any other, a collection of large-format Japanese glamour magazines balancing on a pyramid of teak salad bowls, fondue sets and a condiment tray in the shape of a dachshund. A glass fishing float, purple. A collection of faded teacups, none Royal Doulton, most chipped, worth no more or less than the fifty cents marked on masking tape and stuck to each handle.

I imagined Mr. Galbraithe here, however unlikely. He would hover at each table just briefly, I thought. He would ask questions with respect, his eye scanning, sorting and cataloguing in an instant the incomprehensible rubble pulled together by these other collectors.

I was getting on towards the back of the warehouse by this point, having seen nothing of real interest. Here the black creosote-soaked timbers rose to a distant roof, netted under with sheets of small mesh to keep the pigeons from roosting there. It had only worked to keep them in, judging from the six or seven mummified birds lying suspended in the net. But it made me think of one of the Doves of Townsend stories I used to tell, the one about the doves living in the rafters of the Townsend railway station. And that thought brought me back to where I was, what I was supposed to be doing. I closed my mouth and looked down.

I was standing near a group of tables, a personal collection although no person was apparent. The mounds of junk on some of the tables had been covered over in orange tarps. A sign read The Shickey Shack, scrawled in crayon on a piece of two-by-four nailed to an upright. There were stacks of magazines – years' worth of something called *American Rifleman* – which I leafed through, not curious about the content but about the person who would buy such a collection. Who might collect it in the first place.

There were other books, adhering to a military theme. Many dozen drinking glasses, no two the same. A large quartz polar bear with zirconium eyes, and a stack of room-service silverware from the Hotel Vancouver. I picked some of these up, wondering if the dull clang of the worn plate cover against the warped plate would call forward someone from behind one of these piles.

Under the plate cover, in the middle of the service platter, there was a butterfly.

It startled me enough that I took a step back from the table before I realized that it was dead, entombed in a clear plastic silver-dollar-sized coin case. I put the plate cover aside and picked up the butterfly, forced to smile.

It was fixed neatly to a square of Styrofoam cut to fit the box. The front wings were burnt orange darkening to coffee-brown at the tips. The back wings were white, covered with a lacy grey pattern, impossibly complex. The two brittle antennae curled away to tiny clublike tips. It was an exquisite thing, quivering on its pin as I rolled the box in my fingers.

Looking around the table with renewed interest, I saw there were several more. A few were strewn among the hotel silverware, others dropped carelessly through the boxes of magazines and among the books. I pulled together a small pile of cases, a dozen or fifteen specimens, each one different. And before I even looked at them closely I began to sift through the junk on the rest of the table. In a beer mug marked "Oktoberfest 1988" I found another six. There was an old naval officer's cap sitting upside down at the very back of the table. I leaned as far as I could, got it by the rim and felt immediately that it was heavy with many more.

Large and small. Of more colours than I knew. None of the boxes labelled, although the names wouldn't have meant much to me. A tiny one with rounded dark khaki wings. One with notched brown wings and a pronounced nose. Another lacy pattern, this one brown and orange, fading to light brown on white like a melting snowbank. A large, regal yellow one with black trailing pieces like counterweights on each wing. And a dull grey, mothlike creature, which up close was not grey at all but a shimmering, luminescent blue. I stacked and restacked the boxes in small piles as I browsed, at first by size but then by wing shape and colour, arranging the boxes in a spectrum from the blacks and dark browns to the palest gold and shining white.

There was still nobody around, nobody to answer the questions that were forming. Where from? Significance of? Even, how much? It didn't occur to me then that I had no buyer in mind for these. That I had no personal need for what appeared to be dozens of dead butterflies that were probably worth nothing in the first place. Still, I had become curious and interested, imagining that if I didn't buy them somebody else might only for the delicate, colourful improbability of them being there.

"Very strange," I said aloud, shaking my head and picking up a case that held a black butterfly with blood-red stains in the centre of each forward wing.

At which point a small, rusty voice from nowhere said: "The purpose of butterflies will not be found. . . ."

I was startled a second time. In fact I think I yelped.

The voice started again: "The purpose of butterflies will not be found . . . in the few flowers they may inadvertently pollinate." And then the man got up from where he had been sitting on a milk crate, and stepped out from behind one of the tables tented in orange tarp.

"I'm sorry?" I said, hand on my throat.

He stood looking down at his own merchandise without curiosity. "From a book," he said. "A butterfly book. William Howe."

"Oh yes?" I said.

"Nor in the numbers of parasitic wasps they may support," he carried on, his voice building up to an insistent scrape. "And to peer beneath a microscope at their dissected fragments will in no way elucidate the reason for their being."

He stopped and thought.

"Where are they from?" I asked, but he didn't hear me. He had grizzled sideburns that tapered to points and wore a chocolate-milk-coloured thigh-length leather jacket, green gabardine flood pants with two-inch cuffs. His blue wool socks collapsed casually to the top of the arch of his chisel-toed black loafers. If it weren't for the missing front teeth and his age, I thought he could have stepped from a Prada ad. Past hip though, not knowingly funky. Just poor.

He was reciting the last line again, to himself. ". . . *their dissected fragments will in no way elucidate the reason for their being*. . . ." Then his voice rose to full volume again as he remembered the remaining lines: "Their purpose is their beauty and the beauty they bring into the lives of those of us who have paused long enough from the cares of the world to listen to their fascinating story."

He nodded once, satisfied with his recitation, then returned behind the table and produced a heavy, crumbling encyclopaedia of a book. "*On Butterflies and Moths. William H. Howe.*"

It crossed my mind that the book was probably worth something. It was full of colour plates that could be removed and sold individually. I took the book in my hands, ignoring the fact that I didn't deal prints, that I didn't know them or their buyers particularly well.

"Twenty dollars," the man said, looking away, across the warehouse. Adhering to flea market convention by communicating a dry certainty that I would not buy.

"It's beautiful," I said, my hand drifting across the brocade pattern on the binding. And then I heard myself ask: "And the collection?"

"This is a Tiger Swallowtail," he said, not answering, but picking up the large yellow butterfly with black tails on its wings. I took it from him and admired it. "And this," he said, tapping another box on the table. "Ringlet. Here's a Pearly Eye. Pine White here. This guy's a Little Wood Satyr."

"A what?" I asked, incredulous. He repeated himself, handing me a case holding a tiny butterfly, less than an inch across, with dark green-brown wings, spots like eyes, each rimmed in ghostly white.

"You like them?" he asked. "There's a collector's log here too. . . ." And reaching again into a box behind the table, he took out a spiral-bound notebook, the precise journal kept by the original collector. On its pages, in achingly tidy rows and columns, had been recorded the capture data for each butterfly: date, place (latitude, longitude and altitude), time, prevailing weather, vegetation and topography of the habitat, full species name. And so I read that the butterfly known as the Postman was to lepidopterists the *Heliconius melpomene* of the family *Nymphalidae*. And that the Postman in this collection had been found in a tangle of brush at the edge of a tropical forest not far from the Orinoco River, some day's drive south of San Tomé in

Venezuela. When netted, the notes went on, this particular Postman had been feeding near passion vines.

I had never thought about butterflies before. Not the species, nor the thing that might be collected. Although for a few seconds I imagined them wall-mounted, a dozen in a frame. And the loose ones, this Postman included, scattered in their little clear boxes across my desk for me to pick up and handle, to admire from time to time while working.

"Buck apiece," the man said, jarring me from my thoughts. "There's sixty-two of them. Seventy bucks and I'll throw in the book, the collector's log and this too."

He brought out the killing jar and held it up for me to admire. But I was already coming out of it. The price had startled me awake, having the reverse effect of the hydrocyanic acid gas that the man was explaining to me emanated from the plaster of paris at the bottom of the killing jar and put a butterfly painlessly, permanently to sleep. In an instant, by being so affordable, so not-exorbitant, the seventy-dollar price tag reminded me that this was exactly the kind of thing you can spend an unhappy lifetime picking up at auctions and flea markets, dollar by dollar, day by day without purpose or analysis until you need a bigger warehouse, a bigger line of credit. Until you wake up one morning – like this butterfly collector undoubtedly did – riding alone across the vast and lonely landscape to which you have been driven, the only place wide enough, unpeopled enough that it will accommodate the obsession you have allowed to spread tangled within you.

"They're very pretty," I said, clearing my throat.

"Not what you're looking for though," he said, shaking his head, just short of disgust.

"No," I said, although it wasn't clear even to me whether I was disagreeing or agreeing with him.

"Didn't think so," he said. "A gift maybe?" And he hoisted the quartz polar bear, with effort. It appeared to weigh twenty or thirty pounds.

I remembered then what I had come looking for, and blurted it out in one ragged breath, as if eager to convince him that I did have a purpose. When I was finished, he laughed out loud.

"Airplane ashtrays?" he said, the immensity of the world's foolishness revealed to him in full. "Those shiny things like from the movies?"

"I suppose," I said.

"Little whirly bits and lights?"

"Yes," I said, weakly.

1940s chrome-and-slag-glass DC-3 pedestal ashtrays. He pulled back the orange tarp on one of the covered tables and there they were. Filthy, but they cleaned up well. Back at the shop, a week later after I had the wiring fixed, the propellers turned and all the little windows on the airplanes lit up. One in this condition would have been rare. A matching set of four from something called the Long Island Flying Club was without question a very good find.

I delivered them to Alexander Galbraithe's office myself. I didn't remember the last time I had been as excited about finding something exactly right. But there I was, heart beating lightly, quickly. I had the ashtrays on a flatbed mover's dolly, covered in a white sheet. He would know immediately what they were; he would react with his usual low-key appreciation, but he would know they were perfect.

His secretary let me into his office with an expectant smile. He came out from behind his broad mahogany desk, glided across the room-sized Tabriz to take my hand, gently, raised it to his lips like he had so many times before, always somewhere between chivalry and self-deprecation.

"Clare. My dear."

I was grinning like an idiot. "Check this out," I said, as I sometimes do, becoming a teenager around him. I was pointing at the dolly, the sheet tented across the four objects underneath. His eyes went round. His eyebrows lifted high. When he pulled back the sheet, he actually drew in a breath, theatrically, and stared at them for several seconds, touching one lightly with his fingertips in disbelief. "Incredible," he said, finally. "Did you. . . ." And here he spun very slowly on one foot to face me. "Did you go to Los Angeles?"

He knew I hadn't; it had been his suggestion I go to the flea market in the first place. And with this thought I registered Mr.

Galbraithe's unusual surprise at my having performed just as I always did.

"No," I said. "I didn't."

"Well where then, my dear girl?" he asked. Which was about when I decided he was faking it.

"Um . . ." I said, stumbling on the answer, because now, not only was I transfixed by the thought that he had set the whole thing up, my mind was also sweeping across the history of his patronage. After my father's suicide he had never pressed, only been nearby. I knew where to find him, and I confess I looked from time to time. Not just to find for him his various objects of desire, I talked boys to him once. I told him a sad story, early-Tiko no doubt, before I had come to accept the limits of what that relationship was all about. Mr. Galbraithe had taken me out for a drink at the Wedgewood. I was talking between sips of a crantini. He was holding a gimlet judiciously between his index finger and his thumb, sitting forward in the wingback lounge chair that was too small for his full frame, listening, listening always. I think he said: "Well. Clare. It may be no reassurance . . . but let me say this. There are certain types of unkindness that will bleed out of a young man as he matures."

"The flea market," I said, finally answering his question. "I found them at the flea market, just as you suggested."

Sure enough, his face flattened with recognition. And his eyes did squint, and his cheeks did crinkle, and his bald head did roll back in silent recognition. But I wasn't seeing the humour in any of this.

I didn't say anything else. It felt impossible. I worried a range of things at once. Mutually assured embarrassment. That it was too late to unwind anything that had been done. That unwanted favours can't be graciously accepted or easily rejected. That I didn't know what I thought of the favour anyway. He defied gravity, Mr. Galbraithe did. He hovered without effort, a teacup in his hand now. He listened as I mechanically told of the flea market. He laughed silently at my description of the place, its strange topography and population, the very terrain over which he had walked himself to plant something in my path.

I charged him what I'd paid The Shickey Shack, claiming that I paid much less. He objected and used the opportunity to counsel me on profit margins until his secretary removed my teacup from my hand. I had my coat on again and was actually in the elevator, the doors sliding shut.

Tiko took me to dinner, a surprise. He was back from a shoot in Whistler that had taken much longer than expected and he took me to the Alibi Room. New, hip, sexy, full of film types.

I told him about the flea market, at least most of the story. I left out the butterflies, not sure why. But I told him about finding the ashtrays. I told him about the strange feeling I had that Mr. Galbraithe must have known they were there. Must have put them there for me to find.

Tiko didn't understand. I told the story three ways before he finally said: "You mean he goes to the flea market, gives the guy these ashtrays, then sends you there to find them?"

From a nearby table a woman's indignant words wafted over: *If he thinks I'm coming back from New York for a ten-minute short . . . well. . . .*

"It's an incredible coincidence," I said. "These things are hard to find. Impossible to find at a flea market."

"Why though?" Tiko said, frowning.

"Because they're rare," I said.

"Not that." He was angry. "Why do it? Is it, like, a test?"

I hadn't really thought of that.

"Is he making fun of you? Having some kind of sport?"

I hadn't thought of that either.

"They're all total nut cases," Tiko said then, his nose wrinkling with distaste for my clientele. "Greenstreet's no different, just fatter."

Our peach consommé arrived just then, and Tiko ordered decaf espressos from a waiter who was almost embarrassingly eager to please. From the corner of my eye, I could see the woman with the indignant voice looking our direction.

Tiko looked somewhere beyond beautiful, as always. There were times I thought the only descriptor of his good looks was the word *ridiculous*. His eyes were brilliant green, his hair dark, thick, perfectly unkempt. His jawline descended like an executive order from his cheekbones.

He had work in Montreal, he told me. A perfume ad.

"Will you miss acting?" I asked him, when the espressos arrived.

"It's still acting," he said. "I wouldn't actually wear Yves St Laurent."

We kissed in the elevator going up to my place. I liked to touch his face, to trace it with my fingers. In the apartment, the blinds were up and the mercury glow from the street lights was awash over everything. He undressed me in the living room, led me by the hand to the bedroom, pushed me down onto the bed before taking his own clothes off. He stood over me, stripped off his jacket, then his shirt, unbuckled his belt very slowly. It was borderline Chippendale, but still sexy. I would have liked him to sleep there, wake up with me. But the fact that he had to leave, had to catch a flight in the morning, the fact of his rough kiss, the wool of his overcoat brushing my breasts and his scarf falling to the pillow beside my head . . . all this stayed somehow romantic.

He said, just before he left: "Lying there . . . you are so beautiful."

Weeks passed. Mr. Galbraithe left a message, which he had never done before. He said: "Clare. I am very fond of them. Thank you again."

"Doves of Townsend?"

The caller identified himself as an art director.

"Tiko says. . . ." The art director spoke like he was waiting to hear an echo. ". . . that no *matter* . . . how obscure the item . . . and no *matter* . . . how much craziness you have to wade through in its pursuit . . . you, Clare, always find The Object of Desire."

"When did you talk to Tiko?" I asked him.

"He told me about your airplane things," the art director said.

"Oh yes," I said, but I have to admit I was distracted thinking about where Tiko was at the moment. Montreal? Or back in Whistler?

"You know, women. . . ." The art director seemed to be holding the phone away from his head. "Women are *made* . . . to find *things*. I believe."

"What?" I said.

"Well certainly you are." And here I imagined that the art director leaned back in his ergonomic chair and kicked his feet up on a glass desk mounted on the backs of two giant black ceramic elephants. Cracked the micro-blinds with the tips of his fingers to peer into the parking lot. "You see, in old times . . . very old times . . . Jurassic Park-type old times . . . women found the thing . . . and then men killed the thing. There was this . . . division of labour."

I agreed to go down and see him anyway. He had a film on the go, an unhappy director. They had a character, he explained. "He needs a little *je ne sais quoi*."

And no, he didn't know where Tiko was.

The art director's office turned out to be brightly lit, swatches and tile samples lying around. I was right about the blinds and the chair, but the resting place for the art director's pink-bunny-slipper-clad feet was actually a massive ball-and-claw partner's desk.

"Come in," he called across the room. The art director had flowing black hair, a large, thin nose and wore contacts the colour of a Bombay Sapphire gin bottle. He brought to mind a bust of one of the bad Caesars. "Coffee?"

"Sure, thanks." I took in his room, then his slippers as they disappeared off the desk and reappeared on the parquet hardwood, padding across to the espresso machine in the kitchenette.

"Cappuccino, espresso, flavouring?"

"Black," I said.

"Americano is it?" the art director answered, delighted with whatever this revealed, humming now as he burped out the espresso into old Wedgewood cups. A discontinued pattern. Kimono, I thought.

"So?" he said, handing me the cup. It was Kimono.

"So," I answered. "Tell me about this character."

He nodded, then lifted the coffee cup to his lips, pinky quivering erect. "All business," he observed, as if he found women a bit useless to work with normally. "Male. Thirties. A loser I'm afraid. Tight for money."

They needed something for his apartment, it seemed. Something that would make a subconscious comment on the character's head, his heart and history. "We tried boxing posters, to emphasize his physicality," the art director said. "But in the rushes it came out too Sean Penn."

"So who is this guy?" I asked. Part of me always became impatient with these types of clients, although they paid well. "What does this man do in the film?"

I should have known better. Scripts are state secrets and all the art director gave me was: "Travis Bickle in Kafka's *Metamorphosis*."

I wanted to laugh, but didn't.

No family, no interest in girls.

"Metamorphosis?" I asked.

"Yes," the art director explained. "Because he is one thing, then changes into another thing. A very dramatic, colourful change."

I was thinking of the stages, which I tried to remember while sipping my coffee. Egg, larva, pupa, adult. The last stage brief, a moment of beauty. The struggle to emerge followed by that instant of first flight.

"Say . . ." I said, as the idea fluttered into my head, bursting into the fullness of what it could be.

Perhaps the most appealing aspect of the idea was the way that something I had been tricked into finding could be used to lead me on towards my own discovery. That by resisting the collector's impulse, I had yet been rewarded.

I went to the flea market the following Saturday, first thing in the morning. I took an enthusiastic breath of the fragrant air inside the turnstile and jogged the length of the warehouse to The Shickey Shack. He didn't let on that he recognized me. But they were still there, the butterflies scattered once again without order across his tables. The naval officer's cap had been refilled. The black butterfly with the blood-red stains sat at the very edge of the table, and I picked this up first, failing to suppress a small smile of recognition.

"The Postman," he said wearily.

"This is the Postman?" I said, remembering the name.

He cracked a look up at me. "There's sixty-two in total," he said.

I asked him how much, casually.

"Some people think they're worthless," the man said, scratching his head. "Buncha dead bugs, know what I mean? But to the right person, these are priceless."

We talked back and forth a bit, and I admit faking much greater knowledge of the collection than I had. I said it was on the small side, with a common assortment of specimens, although in pretty good shape. He saw right through me, apparently, and upped his quote to a hundred and fifty dollars for everything, the specimens, the William Howe book, the collector's log and the killing jar, which he pulled out and proceeded to explain all over again.

I held onto them for a week before phoning the art director. I left them scattered on my desk. I used the book and the log to figure out their names. Part of me also knew that this drove up the drama value of the delivery. I even wrapped them for maximum impact on opening. I kept the books and the killing jar – the art director wouldn't be interested in those – but loaded all the butterflies carefully into a small wooden crate, wrapped the box in heavy brown waxed paper, then tied it up with butcher's twine. It might have been shipped in from the Amazon Basin.

"Good God," the art director said, staring at the elaborate package. And when it was open, there was an instant when the small clear boxes spilled onto the table, and it seemed that the butterflies had escaped, that they had been released and would now fly away, each to its own home.

"Remarkable," the art director said. Shifting his pale blue, faintly distrusting gaze onto me. "Quite remarkable."

When he asked how much, I suggested he make me an offer. I hadn't thought this strategy over and I had never used it before. But without thinking, it came out: "These are worthless or priceless, depending on how you look at it. What are they worth to you?"

Spending somebody else's money, this did not strike him as disingenuous.

"How about a thousand?" he said finally.

I hadn't heard from Tiko in almost three weeks, not the longest stretch by any degree, just a disappearance of striking similarity to many others. The kiss. The final words. "So beautiful." The sound of the door closing behind him.

I phoned his agent and learned only that he was "out East." I wasn't at a good place on the sine wave. "A lot of things are out East," I snapped, and hung up.

It made me think dismally of my father, I confess. There came a day following his death – day 111, day 147, I don't remember – but there was one day different from every other day that he had been gone. It was the day I woke up not envisioning his absence as a separation, a distance that might be somehow closed through my efforts. Instead, that day, I woke up knowing the space between my father and me to be measureless, just as the time that stretched ahead of me into the unwritten future.

I thought of this, and then of phoning Alexander Galbraithe. Something that hadn't occurred to me in several weeks and an impulse I quickly suppressed.

I went to the flea market that weekend, no reason, no objective. No Object of Desire for me to find or miss. I just rolled with the uneasy crowds. I bought the purple glass fishing float. Fifteen dollars bargained down to ten. Why negotiate? I couldn't say.

I walked by The Shickey Shack but didn't stop. The American Riflemen were still there, ditto the quartz polar bears. My man was nowhere to be seen, but I knew he was on his milk crate, head in his hands, socks collapsed around his tired ankles.

Past The Shickey Shack were the darkest corners of the warehouse, such undesirable real estate apparently that not all the tables were in use. Here is where the new worthless junk and the madly compiled personal junk gave way to the utterly unsellable junk. Headless golf clubs, TVs with cracked screens, torn couches, bent bicycles. These were the people selling anything they could lift and carry here, their own things. These were the people burning furniture to stay warm, selling organs, consuming themselves.

At a table against the very back wall I stood and inspected a computer with foreign characters on the keys, no English. A skinny man in a faded grey suit offered to demonstrate. He turned it on, typed in the password – the name of his father, I wondered, a favourite drink or food from home – then flashed up the various programs, all written over with the same language. He finished the demo with a winning smile. I made a sympathetic face. We both shrugged.

I turned away from the table and left the flea market. Out past the pessimistic vendors, cutting through the sluggish crowds, under the dead hanging pigeons, through the turnstile and into a light afternoon rain. Driving unnecessarily fast across town, it occurred to me that the skinny man had only one potential flea market buyer for his computer: himself. And he already owned one. There was a painful irony in his linkage to that thing from his home, his past, a painful emblematic power in his attempt to sever the connection.

I found myself stopped in front of a well-known antique dealer on Granville Street. Not a place I used often anymore. The woman at the counter recognized me, but could not place my name. When I gave her my card, she nodded immediately and said: "Yes of course, Doves of Townsend. I knew your father."

She had more knives to choose from than I could bear to consider. And in all of these, she had one set of *les Frères*.

They were in a square black wooden box, with a very worn blue satin lining. The knives themselves were immaculate, like something gifted with eternal youth, forever fresh as the mundane world aged around them. A set of two *les Frères* steak knives, the black pear-wood inlaid handle at once familiar. I picked one up, turning it over in my hands. Letting my fingers ride over the sculpted, golden dove figurine. Three dimensional, very real. It released smoothly under my thumb, the blade unsheathing, extending, locking rigidly in place. Still very sharp, I noticed.

Sharp enough to cut flesh.

And then I was crying at the glass counter of an expensive antique store on Granville Street. Weeping. Inconsolable, although the woman did not try. She only stood at a distance, respectful of my grief. I suppose she didn't have to share it to sense that it came from memory. From lives already lived.

It was my idea to go to dinner. It's just possible, thinking about it now, he might never have called me again. Let it go finally, released to the future.

So I phoned him. A jet roared in the background.

There is a French bistro downtown, dark but comfortable, the food hearty in the Parisian style. Walls covered with photographs of famous people, some who had visited the restaurant. Others who could not have, but who one might imagine spending an evening here. Jack Johnson. Carl Sandburg.

I knew this to be one of his guilty pleasures. A quiet table at this bistro, a companion. *Steak Frites* and a bottle of Burgundy.

I arrived first and took a seat in the corner I had reserved, at a small table covered with a thick white cloth. I sat with my back to the wall, under a photograph of Sigmund Freud, enjoying a clear view of the restaurant and the door.

When he came in, the maitre d' bowed just slightly at the waist, and they exchanged a few words. Then he turned into the room, spotted me, and began his weightless navigation through the tables. The *Queen Mary* approaching the jetty, all double-breasted grace and size.

"Clare. My dear." His lips floated down to my hand. Then to my cheek. He smelled just faintly of soap. Of wool and oak.

I kept my surprise until the main course arrived, the filet a delicate island in a pool of dark demi-glaze. The pile of potato-straw *frite* a cloud at one corner of the plate. Seven pomegranate seeds and a spray of snow-pea pods providing balance.

The waiter produced steak knives, and when he had gone, Alex held up his glass and said: "Santé."

We touched glasses, sipped.

"Now wait," I said. And I pulled out the black box from the seat beside me and slid it across the table to him.

This time, his surprise was genuine and warranted. He untied the red ribbon I had tied around it, and when it was open he looked down at the knives for some time without touching them. "Oh my, oh my," he said. And when he did finally take one of the knives in his hand, he only held it, unopened, touching the clasp.

"Real," I said.

"Oh quite, yes," he said. And he looked at me with a small smile.

We walked afterwards. I held his arm, which meant reaching up just slightly. It was cold but clear now, and we walked from the restaurant all the way down to the water, then along the sea wall as far as English Bay. A boat churned past, heading to berth in False Creek. There was phosphorescence in the water. We talked only a little. Alex held the box of knives tightly under his other arm, as if they made him very proud.

At the beach houses we turned out onto the sand, and found a log to sit on. It was enormous. He helped me up onto it, then sat himself, his black-and-white shoes comfortably reaching the sand.

Neither of us said anything for some time.

"They're very beautiful, Clare. Thank you."

"You've been good to me," I said, not looking at him. "And I appreciate it."

"I am devoted to the Doves of Townsend," he answered. "For a long time, yes?"

"Doves," I said, holding up an imaginary bidding paddle and speaking with what had been my father's imperial cadence. "Doves of Townsend."

Alex smiled at the memory. "A name for which you once gave me a very colourful, if not entirely truthful explanation."

"Did I?" I asked, not remembering immediately.

"Oh yes," he said. "You told me that in Townsend there were doves that lived their entire lives in the rafters of the train station. When they died, you told me, they would fall onto the trains and be carted off throughout the countryside. The opposite of homing pigeons, I think you said."

"Gosh," I said. "Did I tell you that really?"

"I think perhaps you were in a black mood that day," he said.

"Quite possible," I answered. "Although it could have been worse." And then I told him how I had remembered this story in the flea market, looking up at the pigeons that had been caught and suspended after death.

He cocked his head at me. "Where you found my *les Frères*, perhaps?"

I let the corner of my mouth twitch into a small smirk. "I'm not that lucky," I said. "Not twice." But I told him where I had bought them, and how I got there after an unusual trip to the flea market. "Just wandering around without objective," I said. "Very unlike me."

His soft eyes were resting on my face, my hair. "That can't always be bad," he said. "Wandering without objective, that is."

It wasn't, and I admitted it.

"You know?" he said, exhaling a tiny breath of resolve. "I left you a gift there once."

"A gift?" I feigned surprise.

"Yes," he said, looking out at the sea. "I left you something there that I wanted you to find. Something I wanted you to find by accident."

I didn't say anything.

"Aren't you going to ask me what it was?" For all his immense weightlessness, I could feel him next to me now. I could feel his gaze on me, on my skin.

I turned on the log, shifting to face him. "What it was?" I said.

"I thought you might wonder."

I put a hand gently on his arm. "I didn't know when I first found them that they were a gift," I said. "But I figured it out once I got to your office."

He looked back at me curiously, processing this.

"The ashtrays," I said, squeezing his arm.

I wondered if I had embarrassed him by knowing about it, if I had spoiled the kindness he had shown. But he didn't say anything right away. He slipped his fingers into his jacket pocket for what I expected to be one of his cigars, and brought his hand out closed around something small.

"Ashtrays." He said the word like he had just learned what it meant.

"I don't mind, Alex," I said. "Maybe I was a little angry at the time, but I'm not now."

"The airplane ashtrays," he said again. "I'm fond of them." I nodded.

"They look very handsome in my office," he went on. "I receive compliments daily."

"I'm glad," I said.

"But I wouldn't give them as a gift," he said. And he shook his head slowly, thinking of how improbable this would be. "Not to you. Besides, would they really be a gift if you didn't keep them?"

I was still nodding for some reason but I wasn't certain.

Alexander Galbraithe opened his large hand. My eyes were drawn immediately to the middle of his palm.

It was a small clear plastic box. In it, I recognized the fragile stamp of colour. The blood-red spots on black wings, the tendril antennae with their clublike tips.

I took the single butterfly from him, staring down at the case, hearing the sound of their wings as they exploded from the box, released back to their grasslands, their forests, their mignonette, mustard or passion vine, each to their own corner of the world.

"Oh no," I said.

He had no doubt I would find them. That once there I would search the place thoroughly, ask questions. "I was confident they would haunt even you." But he smiled as he said this.

One of the sixty-three, he kept. There had been two Postmen in the collection. And with that one, pressed from his large palm down into my own, he considered the gift given. And I accepted it.

And yes, sometime later I did track down my art director and I did ask if I might buy the others back, but he couldn't find them. "What do you mean, can't find them?" I didn't get angry. I kept my cool.

They hadn't been sold he was certain. They hadn't been thrown out that he recalled. He thought that the prop master might have returned them to the antique store where they had rented the furniture.

Did he remember the name of this store? Well . . . he could find out and get back to me.

"Surely you can find some more?" he said. "How's Tiko?"

"Probably not," I answered. "And I have no idea, respectively."

Alex laughed silently when I told him. He said: "I don't mind that someone else will have discovered them, found them beautiful."

"They are beautiful," I said, still wishing, wishing. "I could have kept them so easily, they made me want them."

"Clare. Dearest," he said, his warm hand on the side of my face. "Of course they did. Their purpose is their beauty. It's what they're for."

I still have the books and the killing jar. The Postman I keep on my desk as I imagined the others would have been kept. From time to time I imagine them out there, want them to return, and then I may spend a week or two looking in shops, asking around. No one has ever seen them, and I know that the more time passes the further away from me they will have flown.

I went into a shop once, idle, directionless on a Saturday. I asked about my butterflies. Described them: a collection maybe, in small plastic cases? The proprietor considered this very carefully, then produced a stuffed toad and asked me if I wanted that instead.

It doesn't matter. The Postman, where I am now, is very real. It sits there on the corner of my desk, and every day it tells me a fascinating story.

R.M. VAUGHAN

Swan Street

Because she is nine years and several months old, and she can count to 1,000 without stopping, and remembers all the words to new songs after only three tries, and because she knows, in detail, where babies come from, Lucinda Wallace prefers not to hold her mother's hand in the middle of the afternoon on the first day of summer vacation.

Mrs. Wallace, a modern parent, keeps herself soberly outside of her daughter's original logic.

"Lulu, hold Mommy's hand," she whispers.

"It's too hot," Lucinda lies, and, proving the point, she skips into the shade underneath the green-piped awning advertising Burlaw's Dress and Shoe.

Mrs. Wallace never insists with her children, never pleads or bribes. She merely waits them out.

Lucinda, the last-born, pities other children her age. She grins at the teary, red-faced arias they must perform for the littlest, most forgettable permissions – trophies Lucinda can have for, literally, a smile.

"She's my best friend," Mrs. Wallace tells suspicious parents before she hands over the goods.

"My best little girlfriend."

In a pinch, Lucinda can mimic her mother perfectly, even on the telephone. In the Wallace family, power is like tap water or light switches or the downstairs den – nobody has to ask to use it.

Lucinda clears the dark front of Burlaw's in three long jumps, stops to reset the pinwheel knot on the top of her head with two quick tugs, and grandly holds the front door of Kinner's Candy and Novelty open for her mother. She does not look behind her, she knows her mother's pace.

And so does the tenant in apartment 504 of the Waterside Hotel.

With Parasol Street to the right and Swan Street parallel, meeting in a busy T beneath his only window, the tenant has a clear view of the shopping district, the back door of City Hall, and the lake end of Swan.

There used to be a fat maple just under his window, cluttering his view, but when the tree produced no new leaves by May, the city men came and cut it down.

The dry sap spell is an old and reliable farmer's notion. A handful of cat's blood, a brown candle, a mumbled verse before a new moon. Buds fail to appear, and no bird will nest in the crooks.

Now the tenant watches with leisure as Lucinda roughly jostles her mother's packages for a Scotch mint. A delightful child, this one, full of kicks and agitation. The top of her head is a golden pentagram.

Mrs. Wallace pauses at Adelson's Delicatessen, remembering to buy cream and a pale cheese. She wishes she had brought a light scarf, the back of her neck is cold.

Lucinda watches pigeons jab and bully each other off the roof of the Waterside Hotel. Her mouth is slick with mint sugar.

"Lulu, you're tearing the bag."

Lucinda nods and takes another mint. Her fingers are green and webbed with icing.

"Mother, how old will you be when you die?"

Mrs. Wallace absently turns up her collar with both hands. She tells herself: cream, cheese, sausage, buttermilk.

Lucinda is already inside, picking out a caramel sugar stick. Adelson Sr. is patting her cheeks. She is a good girl, overall.

On the rooftop of the Waterside Hotel, a fat hen pigeon cranks its blue, oily head over the ledge. Something is not right, not in order.

The pigeon is not meant to understand that the hard, bright seed she discovered on a windowsill and swallowed an hour ago is actually a slice of broken soda bottle, and that she will die. But the pigeon does know comfort from distress.

The pigeon looks down with its watery left eye and sees an old man in a window.

The old man is hairless, except for his eyebrows, which are long and wispy and curled upward at the ends. The old man's skull is mapped with curious green rashes, shaped like constellations. He is thin, twig thin. Where his legs meet, a pouch of fat collects.

The pigeon feels something inside itself come undone, turn bloody, then falls to the sidewalk. The other pigeons shake their wings in embarrassed disapproval. The tenant waits.

"Don't touch it, Lucinda. The poor thing. Lucinda, stay with Mommy. It might bite you."

"Why can't it fly away?"

"Disease, dear. Stay back. Poor birdy."

The tenant watches and listens. Inside his mouth, he makes a tiny clicking sound. The sharp point of his tongue flicks along the tops of his lead-coloured teeth until his mouth is bloody and music fills his head. We know no instruments to match such chords.

Lucinda is surprised by her own tears. Lucinda never cries, except when she bumps her knee. Mrs. Wallace holds her daughter close to her thigh. The child's head is scalding hot.

"Lulu, now, now. You'll stain Mommy's dress."

Lucinda wipes her forehead against her mother's leg. Her sweat darkens a gathering of cotton pleats. Starch dissolves, the pleating's vertical lines bend and smudge. From a distance, the lines resemble a star.

Below Lucinda, the pigeon's legs begin to jerk and kick. Instinct tells the bird that it is vulnerable on its back, that the hovering shapes can crush it with a single, heavy step, press in its chest with their towering weight. The pigeon flaps itself upright and spins onto the street.

Go, the tenant says to Lucinda, who can and cannot hear him. Catch it, catch the pretty bird. Help the birdy, save the birdy.

Lucinda runs behind the pigeon. Her fat arms stretch low over the street, reaching for the pigeon's wings.

From the high driver's seat of any car, only the top of Lucinda's head is visible. She is no more distraction than a passing cloud.

Mrs. Wallace is larger prey. She is frightened, but not alert. On the street, she is a blue whip of fabric, a stumbling mass, a pair of too-slow legs, a trapped scream.

Because Mrs. Wallace is a mother, she cannot choose her actions. We know this because no woman would elect to throw her body under a moving automobile.

In the silence that swells and echoes behind her, Lucinda corners the pigeon on a cement step and watches it bleed. The pigeon does not return her gaze.

The coroner's report is succinct and unremarkable, but for one point.

In clear typing, anyone may read that Mrs. Wallace gave chase to her daughter. Further down, it is reported that Mrs. Wallace died due to injuries sustained. In conclusion, the recording coroner's sincere belief is that Mrs. Wallace met her death instantly, and suffered no pain.

Lucinda Wallace, age nine years, was discovered by a constable on the adjacent sidewalk. The child did not appear to have witnessed the accident. Lucinda Wallace was escorted to the back room of Adelson's Deli, where Adelson Sr. gave her a glass of water and a candy sucker. Mr. Adelson observed the child attempting to bite off her tongue.

JOHN LAVERY

The Premier's New Pyjamas

I was dreaming about a man wearing boxing gloves as red and thick as kidneys.

That is to say, I was writing a speech for the premier about a boxer who was being inducted into the State of Missouri Sports Hall of Fame. An excellent American who, as it happened, was not only born in one of Canada's ten provinces, but had even lived the first three years of his life there.

The premier of the province in question was, therefore, invited to Saint Louis to attend the induction dinner and, of course, to say a few hundred words.

Which I, the premier's speech writer, was in the process of preparing.

It was not yet seven in the morning. I had been working for some time, I started before five usually, writing myself hoarse even before the daily tide of press releases, letters, toasts and endorsements submerged the stony beach of my discursive reason.

Each item was a dream. Thirty seconds after writing it, I could not remember a single word. If I remember the dream about the Saint Louis boxer's kidney-gloves, it is because I was roused in the middle of writing it by a tintamarre of people stamping and singing their way down the corridor outside my door.

I opened the door. A young woman made a sour face at me as she passed by. She had a sleeping bag draped across her shoulders. They all had sleeping bags, or blankets and pillows, they were all wearing Mountie hats with toy provincial flags poked into the points, they were clacking their thermos bottles, or their foil plates, or their folding garden chairs. I closed the door, turned, and there he was.

The premier.

"I can't be here," he said.

And I, my surprise undermining my generally dependable sense of fawning deference, "How did *you* get in?"

"Ahhhh," he said, a gleam in his voice. And then, "The place is crawling with students. I can't be here. Have you got your car parked downstairs?"

Early '70s, by the way. A meagre time, in my estimation. Deceitful. Inept. The assassinators, after a string of glorious successes, had managed only to disable as motionless a target as George Wallace. And the student movement was still staging sit-ins, still straining drily for attention.

"Yes," I said. "Sir."

"Prepare to leave. I'll be back in a matter of minutes, no more."

He pressed his thumb into the wall then, there was a muted click, and a concealed door opened. He looked at me without the trace of a smile, raised his eyebrows slyly once, and disappeared through the doorway. I found the button he had pressed; the door clicked open, I closed it again, opened it, stuck my head through into the penumbra where a dim, carpeted staircase descended indolently, and closed the door again, my throat thick already with dreams of sexual encounters.

When the premier reappeared, he was wearing a wig with sideburns, a false moustache, and a pair of black-rimmed glasses with rectangular lenses.

"Ready?" he said. And down the carpeted staircase we went, along a turning, footlit corridor to a heavy door which the premier shouldered open cautiously. The standard spring-time sunlight ricocheted off the chrome of the cars parked in the lot outside, skimmed past us sideways, and disappeared down the corridor.

"What kind of car do you drive?" he whispered.

"A Sprite."

He nodded knowingly, it not being permitted for the premier to admit ignorance on any topic whatsoever.

"Lead the way," he said. "Don't hurry."

He was a little excited fitting himself into my car, which was very small. He wriggled and huffed. The seat springs cursed under their breath.

"We'll take the Algord Road," he said.

And so we did. The sky was stuffed with several atmospheres of blue. The leaves on the poplars lining the road applauded as we passed by. There was adventure in the premier's presence, so close beside me, the thick, vegetable odour of sleep still clinging to the beard he had not shaved.

"Have you had breakfast?" he said.

"Not really, no."

So we stopped to eat, and after the waitress had brought the coffee, the premier pulled a flask out of his jacket pocket. He topped up first mine, then his own cup.

"Ever live in a comic strip before?" he said.

"You mean the moustache and glasses? You don't look so comical."

He raised his eyebrows in doubt.

"If anything you look more like a premier."

"Speech writer," he said, snorting. And then, assuming his disguise extended to me, which perhaps it did, "Have you ever travelled incognito before?"

"Wale now," said I, talking Texas, "ever' day."

I am homosexual. Was, I suppose. McCorkingdale, my constant and best, my prickly companion, my bippy, bowsprit and organ of non-reproduction, McC. stays to himself pretty much now. I ain't gay. I go back far too far. Just good and queer.

Gays are great, but. Gay families like with kids and all? Yikes. I always thought families were horrible things full of perfumed hatred and fragrant jealousy, even when they weren't full of screaming and tears.

I thought, no doubt ingenuously, that gentlemen preferred men, that homosexual relationships were, therefore, as fugitive as tenderness, unetched by snarling, or snooping, or teaming up.

I thought that joy, by nature, is more joyous in the closet than parading in the streets. No?

At any rate, I was, in my time, a subversive. Nobody knew me. I cultivated the vocabulary, the humours of men, so I could navigate among them, hail them, listen to the clatter of their winches, the creaking of their hulls. All men. Square, squeamish, dainty or crude, bad-breathing, flaccid or beau. Their handshakes thrilled me, their queer jokes made me laugh and laugh, me and McC.

Which, out of so many, were, like me, the fairies with their wings tied down? Which were the sleight of heart men? Which? This simple question informed all: all my meetings, jostlings, left me deliciously perplexed, expectant, irrationally so. If I suspected my interlocutor of giving me so much as the ghost of a look, I was stiflingly happy. I shot off immediately a box of many-coloured flares hoping to see at least one reflected in his eye. I seldom did.

Oh, I studied physiognomy hard under every kind of light and dark, but I never really learned to spot another queer.

I had fairly good ideas, of course.

I had a fairly good idea about the premier.

He ate a little toast with his jam, the premier did. The jam he fed himself by the tablespoonful, directly from the jar. He ordered me another coffee, slipped me his flask, and went off to phone. Twenty minutes later, he came skulking back, tapping his leg with a rolled up newspaper.

"Ready?" he said.

We walked together to the cash, he looking nervously at the floor, I fumbling for my wallet.

Outside he said, "I don't have any money with me. I don't usually carry any."

"No problem."

"I don't have a driver's licence either." And then, reasserting no doubt his exceptional identity, "I do have my will. It's folded in seven and taped to my thigh."

"I'll drive carefully anyway."

And drive we did. The new cornfields, planted as systematically as a doll's scalp, parted for us endlessly. Far back floated the white clusters of buildings that would in another ten weeks be hidden by the deepening crops.

"It is on days like these," said the premier, his false moustache bobbing, "that I most enjoy being the central administrative figure of this province. If I could, I would take every school child for a drive down this road, and many others like it."

"May I point out," said I, "that it is the school children, the university-age children, who are undermining your administrative program. Who do not apparently believe in the defining principles of our society. Or any other society known to man."

"But," said the premier, "that is what I find so exciting. It is not true to say the students do not accept our society. They want something, yes. But they also think they can get it. Doesn't our society define success as finding a way to get what you want? I like people who want. I want them."

I want them. The words sniffed at McCorkingdale like the shiny nose-leather of a substantial dog. "The students," I said, reddening, "don't know what it is to want. They've gotten too used to getting."

"As you say, children who get make adults who want."

"I said that?"

"Adults though, unlike children, have to keep thinking up things to want to get themselves. Lack of necessity is the father of creativity. Hoo, I've read so many of your speeches, I'm starting to sound like you."

There was, of course, nothing I could say to this.

It is not without bemusement that I report my part in this conversation. I did, in fact, support the students to a considerable extent. Note, however, that the vast majority of my verbal production tumbled into existence through the mouths of others. Always distorted. If not by the speaker's grafting his own lexis onto mine, then by faulty microphones, by the sound of saliva mixing with trout inside the mouths of eating listeners, by the wind. So that I did not often pay attention to the distortions of my voice when it tumbled out of my own mouth. In any case, the premier, by now, was on another tack.

"Myrtleville," he said. "A remarkable town. The deciduous treeline cuts right through here. You can see it perfectly from the air, poplar and aspen on the south, conifers on the north. Look! Some of the white pines are four hundred years old. We should pay a visit to Alfie Gallant. His farm is off Markham Road, just past the creamery."

Alfie Gallant. Unbeatable. Every January, a hundred or so short-headed snowshoers raced headlong some thirty-three miles up the frozen Massapatawquish River to a clearing, built a fire there only large enough to make tea and raced right back again. Frostbite was part of the fun. And Alfie Gallant was unbeatable.

"Every year," said the premier, "as I stand at the finish line, I'm afraid Alfie will win again. I think to myself, this will be the year when, at last, he'll turn into the braggart. And every year he manages to contain his barn-sized ego inside his half-way smile. His farmer's smile. When the rain falls, at last."

I was flattered that he was talking to me in this way, not as speech writer, but as apprentice say, conveying to me the nature of his province, the province of his own government-high ego.

"And every year," he said, "I'm afraid Alfie will not be first."

On and on we drove, the premier dozing, knees wedged against the dashboard, head tilted back, glasses over his forehead.

"When I was a student," he muttered, "I didn't have the slightest idea what I wanted to do. I knew a lot of things I didn't want to do, so I eliminated all those – the list got longer and, longer, until all that was left was premier. You?"

You? The question licked at me hesitantly, seeking encouragement.

"Me?" I said. "Oh I eliminated premier right off the bat."

And he, yawning, "Wise man."

"Are you going to sleep now?"

"Might."

"Do you want me just to keep driving then till we get to Paraguay?"

"You can if you like. Or you can stop at Eleanor's."

"Eleanor's is a restaurant somewhere? A motel?"

"No, Eleanor is my mother. Eleanor's is where she lives."

"My, my, my," she said, "what are *you* doing here?"

She was a short woman, Eleanor was, humorously short beside her tall son. The undercurl of her dry hair brushed her shoulders when she turned her head. Her skin was grainy from long hours spent not so much in the sun, as in the open. She wore a shirtwaist dress, the lowest buttons left undone to reveal her legs, sturdy and balanced, the strong calves curved like overturned dinghies.

Striking legs. McCorkingdale, self-willed as ever, craned to catch a glimpse.

"A horde of university students," said the premier, "are crawling over my desk at this very moment. Haven't you heard?"

"Yes." Her voice was as husky as her skin. "I also heard somewhere that you were the central administrative figure of this province and that your place was, therefore, in the capital city. I may have misheard."

"You may have. I am, in fact, the premier."

"Ah," pausing, looking into his eyes. "And this gentleman is . . .?"

"Mr. Watson. No, no. Mr. Gilfillan. What was I thinking of to make me say Watson? Mr. Gilfillan. My speech writer."

"Aaaahhhh. You'll be able to deliver a speech in the kitchen then."

"Or the greenhouse, or the lava-tree, wherever. The bedroom if you like."

"I think I may have had enough bedroom speeches for one lifetime. Unless . . . Are you particularly good at bedroom speeches Mr. Wa . . .?"

"Gilfillan," said the premier quickly.

"I'm sorry. Mr. Gilfillan. Mr. Gilfillan looks like he has been driving a car for several hours and would like something to eat. Come." She hooked her arm into mine. "Tell me how it is you manage to make my son sound as though he had learned something at school, and not simply studied law."

Watson. What was he thinking of to make him say Watson? Oh I knew, I knew. The sly puss-'n-boots. I trembled with the familiar ebullience. The frothy darkness pushed itself into my eyes, I could hear my hand knock once and once only, could feel them all breathing.

"My son, you see," continued Eleanor, leading us into a well-appointed kitchen with a thickset, not to say corpulent, wooden table, blazing with varnish, "my son is of the old school, the Old King Cole school. He believes political leaders should give the impression that good God himself inflated their little lungs at birth, licked his thumb and touched it to their forehead, that they should be dignified, up-beat, meat pie with gravy? . . . be alright? . . . conniving, bursting with probity and hot air, and entirely without talent. Or children. Surely a man in such a position could arrange to have children. A daughter-in-law I don't require. But children, grandchildren . . ."

Watson's. My dear Watson's. Although it may have been a slip. He did not, perhaps, know about Watson's.

"He does not," she went on, "seem to be aware," no, he knew, he did, he was sitting on the table now eating olives, "that while he doubtless makes a rare prime rib of a minister, dolled up in his shimmering eye-talian civvies," holding the pits in his hand, My Dear Watson's, where you went down to the men's room, the oven door clanging shut, "it does not last forever, his body is increasingly ovoid, his nose is getting puffier and puffier with long drinks and circumlocution," the premier squeezing his nose to see if it were swollen, his good humour attenuated with consternation, "one must eventually *do* something with one's life, mustn't one, what point is there in history scratching its head to remember a name that no one else does, except me, and who is to remember me, except he," the gravy caramelizing on the stove, Eleanor's pebbly voice glinting across the table, and I, I was dreaming about Watson's, an Englishy pub with leatherette seats, pictures of London in the rain at night, waiters in Sherlock Holmes hats, My Dear Watson's to the heavy-smelling blackguards of queerdom, down you went to the men's room, you did not go in mind you, you went past it to the next door, your hand trembling as you knocked lightly once and once only, the door no sooner open than the darkness behind it sucked you inside, you could see nothing but you could hear the humid, lupine breathing of a dozen men, not a word, not a word, but the pulse in your neck like a trapped insect, you were taken hold of then, you were hoisted over the heads of the dozen men, you floated on their quick, unhurried, invading hands pulling your clothes away, you dipped and rolled, but they would not put you down, you shuddered and arched on their palping, kissing hands, you were drowning in your own, you were awful, awful, and they would not put you down, you merely woke up alone, if you were me, in your corner, ill with exhaustion, naked, sticky, your underwear still stopping your mouth, your genitals aching, until someone knocked lightly once and once only, the door opened wide enough only for a hand to reach in and turn on the lights.

"Goodness, Mr. Gilfillan," said Eleanor, "do you always eat like three horses?"

You were in a storeroom, there were huge jars of mustard, of instant gravy powder, tubs of shortening, a bundle of clothes smelling of fabric softener was thrown in to you quickly, and the door was closed.

"And are you always as quiet as a carp?"

Is there, thought I, any way to shut this woman up?

"Well now," said the premier, "the students, like everyone else in the province, think I'm on my way to Saint Louis, and to get me to come back quick, they will have to all go quietly home. Of this they have been made abundantly aware. Now as I see it the boy students will not sleep tonight for agonizing over the accessability of the sweet bodies breathing beside them, the girls will not sleep for being constantly on the alert to yank the boys' hands out of their sleeping bags, there will be those of course, very likely a plurality, who will not sleep for finding the parliament building too exotic a location to resist, they will all, tomorrow, be tired and testy and faced with the cold thought that fun is fun, but to get what they want they need me."

"Premiers," said Eleanor, "like to feel needed."

"I think," said the premier, "one night should do it. Two at the most. Feel like staying a night or two, Derek?"

Derek was me.

"I'm sure," said Eleanor, "Mr. Gilfillan has better things to do with his days. Has he clothes with him? Pyjamas?"

"I bought half a dozen pairs of new pyjamas the last time I was here," said the premier. "I haven't even opened half of them. I'll put a box on the bed. So."

He finished his coffee standing up, waved, and was gone.

There was a moment, a band of silence. And then Eleanor swept her arm across the table in front of her, bowl and plate, utensils, glass and place mat all sent soaring, rushing up to the ceiling where they floated and circled with the unbearable slowness of ships in a sea port seen from the air. Until the tears welling up in her lower lids compelled her at last to blink, and down crashed the dishes onto the red-tiled floor, the place mat gliding obliquely into the sink.

"Shhhh!" she hissed at me fiercely. "Listen. You can still hear his footsteps climbing the stairs."

I confess I could not. I can not fathom the ability of women to hear the faintest sounds in their houses. She sputtered and fustigated, my astonished ears heard the word "faggot" squeak out of the side of her mouth like a breathy note from a cold flute. She took, from out of the cupboard under the sink, a dustpan and whisk.

"Let me do that for you," I said, getting up smartly.

"Over my dead body!" she snapped.

I do not remember the bedroom well. There were a lot of wooden things, there were magazines and Chivas. The bedspread I do remember. It was as green as green, and served as a field for the sleek black and gold box lying on it casually.

I drank and waited. The intense, country silence clung to me, moved when I moved. I waited. And drank.

Until I could no longer put it off. Undress I must. Open the box I must, I must. Open the box I did.

The black and gold box, which was empty.

The sly puss-'n-boots.

I lay in the dark, dressed only in the premier's new pyjamas, shivering between the glossy sheets, awaiting his majesty's silk-draped flesh to enter by some secret door and have at me, I was twisting with sex, I was tired, tired, I had driven too far, I had eaten too much, the whiskey was turning to acid in my intestines, and Eleanor insisted on dancing over me, Eleanor, dancing over my dead body, her shirtwaist dress knifing through the night so close to my face, snicking at my nose, her stoney legs opening in silence, opening to reveal the crown of his-majesty-to-be, I lay shaking between the sheet-metal sheets, I wanted to sleep, only to sleep, but the premier was coming, and I could not stop crying.

The door opened. The tiger leapt.

McCorkingdale stood hard to attention.

In poked a head.

Enter, enter, murmured McCorkingdale. Bring on the body politic.

But it was not the premier.

"Sleep well?" said Eleanor.

"Sleep? What time is it?" said I, instantly awake, rolling onto my side to hide McC.

"Ten past seven. Did you find the pyjamas?"

"Ahh, yes."

She sat on the edge of the bed, sending a ripple through the mattress that made McC. tingle. She looked vaguely in the direction of the window.

"He left during the night," she said.

"Who did?"

"He did. With his cabinet chief and the minister of transports of delight."

"Pardon me?"

"His pals."

"Oh. When did all this take place?"

"Two-thirty. Three."

"I didn't hear anything," I said, piqued, foolishly.

She turned towards me then.

"You're a very good speech writer, Mr. Derek Gilfillan." She placed her palm on the bed beside me. McCorkingdale, fascinated, strained towards her.

I thought, for a moment, that it was snowing in the bedroom.

"Goodness," she said. But it was not snow that was falling. She had a freckle on her colourless lip. It was dust perhaps. Particles of dust swollen with light, it may have been that.

"You are not very substantial for a man who eats like three horses." Sequins or spangles or tiny Venetian coins.

"He's a bit of a murderer in his way," she said. "I know." Venetian chocolate coins tossed into the sunlight from the Rialto bridge. "We have only one life," she said, "but one life that is wrapped in so many existences. It's good to get murdered every now and then, to kill off an outer existence or two. They get dry and papery and peel away, and then we are a little closer at least to our life. Of course we are also white and juicy and ready for more murder." Or words, palatal glides and fricatives for all I know, or seeds perhaps, dandelions. "Nothing murders like not being loved very much. But then, when you are not loved, you are not anyone. So you can become . . . anyone. Every big ambition begins with a small murder." Or meteorites, quite possibly meteorites, but they were not actually falling. "Look at all these bourgeois silverfish who sleep with their windows locked and never dare try manslaughter unless it is brought to them by Kellogg's. Bfff." It was the light slowly turning that made them appear to fall. "Look at them with their precious existences interlarded with bulletproof foam. Bfff." A parti-coloured particular ray shot occasionally into my eye. "You are not one of them, Derek." They were floating, they must have been, because they did not accumulate on the floor, it was the light slowly turning, it was the light that accumulated. "The three horses you eat like have wings," said Eleanor, her hand on my knee, her palping, kissing words washing like smoke over McCorkingdale, turning the particulate air into solid light, I could not see for it all, I could not breathe, I was awful, awful, is there not, I pleaded, *any* way to shut this woman up?

So we got out of bed, we did. McCorkingdale and I.

"Mmn," said Eleanor, "Very nice. The pj's. Just your colour."

"Eleanor," I said, dressing, "you're very good at speeches. Very. I write his. That's all. Sometimes he even reads them. I do his press releases. I answer his letters, of which, by the way, an astonishing number are from women, of a confessional nature, often intimate, usually intelligent. I enjoy it. I forget everything thirty seconds afterwards. Everything."

I drove back then, and as I did so, I heard Eleanor's words over and over, felt McCorkingdale rise towards her husky voice.

And when I arrived, there were squads of cleaners in the otherwise empty corridors. I slid my key into the knob of my office door, but before I had time to turn it, the door was opened from the inside.

"You made good time," whispered the premier. He slid one of his prestigious buttocks onto the edge of my desk, drank coffee, high-octane presumably, from a paper cup. Anita Devlin, the student leader, quite high-octane herself with her hair as straight as water and her mouth full of braces, was reading intently in my chair.

"You knew I was on my way?"

"Eleanor phoned to say you were coming. She keeps tabs on us all." He leaned toward me. "She called the papers," he murmured, strong with coffee and cologne, "in the middle of the night. Pretended to be one of the neighbours. Said I'd been seen at her house."

"Are you sure?"

"Of course. She told me. We'd have been better off staying at Alfie Gallant's, eh. You are to come any time, by the way, and not wait for me to invite you."

"Miss Devlin!" he said then. Miss Devlin looked up, high matters in her eyes, entirely, I would say, under the premier's power. "I'd like you to meet my speech writer, Derek Gilfillan. Hot awful good on his good days. Look at this. It's the dinner speech I was to give tonight in Saint Louis."

"What are the drawings in the margin?" said Miss D. "They look like kidneys."

"Kidneys?" said I.

"Now that you're here, Derek," said the premier, "we'll give you your office back."

He pressed his thumb into the wall then, there was a muted click, and the concealed door opened.

"Oohh," said Miss D., duly sarcastic, duly impressed, "secret passages and all."

The premier guided her past him into the dim, carpeted penumbra.

"Eh!" he said suddenly.

"What's up?" said I.

"The pyjamas."

"The pyjamas?"

"I was going to leave a box of new pyjamas on the bed for you, wasn't I?"

"You did."

"I did?"

"There was a box."

"There was. Eleanor must have put it there for you then. Good for her. What *would* we do without Eleanor." He looked at me without the trace of a smile, raised his eyebrows slyly once, and disappeared through the doorway.

Jilted I was. Murdered. Just as Eleanor said. Jilted, jealous. But in love, in love.

"Faggot!" I squeaked out of the side of my mouth, to prove it. McC. was feeling forgotten. Weren't you, McC.? But what do you know about love?

"*Faggot!*" Joyously.

A one-word speech of course. A curt dream.

ANDREW SMITH

Sightseeing

"W hy do they call it Goat Island?" Margo asked.

The woman looked at Margo. They were standing in January sunshine at the Niagara Falls viewing area called Table Rock, their backs to the gift shop and restaurant. The woman had appeared while Margo was uneasily eyeing an ice-encrusted stone wall and wrought-iron railing, built to protect people from tumbling headlong into Niagara Falls.

Margo had visited this exact spot four or five times before, but she'd mistakenly remembered the wall as being solid stone, and much higher. She'd forgotten that sections of sinuously curved wrought-iron railing rested on top of the wall, which was actually quite low; the wall and railing together were no more than five feet high.

It was typical of Margo to think something was different than she knew it to be. As a child one thing at which she'd been particularly adept – the only thing, according to her mother – was inventing stories. As she grew older she hadn't been able to kick the habit; she changed facts to suit her purposes, consequently she often misremembered events or places. A high wall, difficult to scale, is what she believed she'd find at Niagara Falls, not this flimsy railing.

Margo grudgingly acknowledged that the railing did make for better viewing. On this glinting, winter afternoon she could clearly see, between icy, iron tendrils and decorative metal leaves, the living, green brow of Niagara Falls that curved away towards snow-laden trees on the shore of Goat Island. Sturdy masonry posts at intervals of six or eight feet held the railings in place. Nevertheless the whole thing seemed to Margo distressingly ineffective. The woman was a welcome distraction.

"It's over there, you see," Margo pointed. "It says, Goat Island – on the sign – that flat area beyond the Canadian section of the Falls," Margo said. "Do you think it's inhabited by goats?"

Despite the winter chill a huddle of Japanese tourists, most with cameras held up to their faces, hovered by the railing fifty yards or more downstream. Margo and the woman were the only visitors at Table Rock. Apart from the boy, of course. He'd arrived at the same time as the woman, leading Margo to assume that they were together – a nephew perhaps. Margo, the woman and the boy stood, a little apart from each other, a few short strides from the railing.

The woman had a square jaw, and a determined mouth – she was taller than average. Impressive was the word that sprang to Margo's mind when she first glanced at the woman. She was intrigued by two laugh lines that bracketed the woman's mouth. Parentheses around a potential smile were how they appeared to Margo.

The woman turned to look in the direction Margo was pointing. Silver hairs glinted among blonde in the dry winter sunlight. At the woman's throat Margo could see a delicate, gold chain. She was wearing a crisp white and pink striped shirt under a dark blue, quilted jacket.

"I'm not so sure. Perhaps, once, there might have been goats," the woman said. "But I'm not from here so I don't like to say."

She turned towards Margo.

Margo's eye was distracted momentarily by a purple bruise spreading down the boy's left wrist and onto the back of his gloveless hand.

Margo didn't give the boy a thought when she saw him edge towards the railing, but she must have noticed his eyes as they darted from the expanse of falling water to the faces of the women. Afterwards, when she was asked to estimate the boy's age, Margo, searching for a number of years to pin on him, recalled his eyes quite clearly. She saw in her own mind's eye the tic in the boy's eyelid.

Margo detected an accent in the woman's voice. "Are you German?"

"No, from Holland," the woman replied.

"What a coincidence. I was living in Amsterdam until just recently," Margo told her. "I'm English, actually, but I live in Canada now."

"I am from near Rotterdam," the woman said, still looking at Margo's face.

Margo turned her head slightly and gazed towards Goat Island. She lifted her sunglasses and propped them above her hairline. She stared at the turbulent rapids above the Falls. Her eyes followed the river as it surged towards the cliff's edge.

"Yes, I'm a musician. You probably know that Amsterdam has some very good recording studios, everybody records in Amsterdam sooner or later," Margo told the woman. "Spice Girls, Rolling Stones, everybody. There's a lot of work for musicians so I lived there for a time."

Margo had been forced to study piano as a child – a talent for music was one of the many things that had been expected of her – but she'd been bored by the tedium of practice and then terrified by the vehemence of the piano teacher's exasperation with her. Margo's story of her career as a musician was a lie.

Margo glanced at the Dutch woman, who stared back at Margo. Margo was stricken by a hollow feeling in some indeterminate part of herself. Maybe the woman didn't find her interesting despite her story. She searched the woman's eyes for some positive effect of her untruth. The woman's pupils were velvety brown and unblinking, her face was perfectly still.

"Did you learn Dutch in Amsterdam?" she asked Margo.

As Margo answered she was aware of cold air brushing the surface of her lips, and of muscles moving inside them.

"Oh, no. I think it's a very difficult language for English-speaking people to learn," said Margo.

"Yes, this is true. Also most of us speak good English."

"Yes, absolutely," Margo said.

Margo felt safe in agreeing that the Dutch often spoke English well because the fact was that she had actually spent some recent time in Holland. She often started her stories with a kernel of truth; embellishment is how she considered the rest of it.

A few months earlier she'd met a man in a Toronto bar who was on holiday from Amsterdam. He seemed to like her. He was entertained by her yarns, not seeming to take them too seriously. Margo saw a lot of him. After his return she found herself missing him. She bought an airline ticket on a whim, and surprised the man with a visit. He welcomed her warmly. During the day, when he was out working – in a recording studio – Margo was happy to wander, anonymous, a stranger in a foreign city. Sometimes she spent whole, peaceful days in the man's attic apartment, contented under the eaves of a narrow house whose tiny windows afforded a view of a sparkling canal.

A week or so after arriving in Holland it became obvious that the man was falling for her. She was thrilled but couldn't quite believe it. She'd been led to believe since an early age that there was nothing remotely interesting about her. Margo was unaware that the man could see more of her than she could herself. He was able to dismiss the carefully crafted layers of showy veneer that she arranged around herself because he sensed a solidity beneath them. Margo, however, felt the pressure of maintaining the façade of a person with whom she thought the man had fallen in love.

When Margo finally admitted to herself that she too was in love her anxiety intensified. She felt increasingly self-conscious in his presence, she could only enjoy her emotions when she was alone under the sloping ceilings of the apartment, surrounded by the man's possessions and dreaming of their life together. She was afraid that, even if she could act naturally and be herself – whatever that meant – the man would find her dull.

Eventually she couldn't take it any more, she stole away one day when the man was at work. She told herself all the way across the Atlantic that it was for the best. But in the couple of months since her return she'd thought constantly of the man, the attic apartment, and the view of the sparkling canal.

"It's cold," the woman said, watching Margo's eyes. "As impressive as this is," her eyes glanced towards the Falls, "I think I'll leave."

Margo held her gaze. Out of the corner of her eye she glimpsed the boy standing by the railing, shivering in the cool winter air.

"You don't feel the cold?" the woman asked.

"I'm accustomed to it," said Margo.

"Ah, yes, of course," said the woman. "Goodbye, then."

"Goodbye."

The Dutch woman hesitated, watching Margo's face, before turning to leave. Margo fixed her gaze on the railing ahead. Any comfort taken from the impression she might have given of herself evaporated into the freezing spray of the Falls.

It was this exact moment that the boy chose to climb, sure-footed despite the ice, onto the top of one of the stone posts. Using the low wall and wrought-iron railing as footholds, he scrambled onto the masonry post directly in front of Margo. He jumped without hesitation. His leap from the top of the wall seemed effortless, one might have thought the frozen stones were elastic as a trampoline.

Margo didn't move. She stared at the top of the masonry post, at the place where the boy had stood. No, not stood, there'd been no delay. The boy had accomplished his suicide – it was certain that he would be dead, he'd plunged into the thundering, frigid water of Niagara Falls – in one fluid series of movements, not pausing. The only evidence of the passage of time was the change in the position of a seagull that had flown ten or fifteen yards through the mist that spewed from the Falls. The boy's self-destruction had taken less than three seconds, from pavement to waterfall.

Margo heard the Dutch woman's cry of "Gadver!" but didn't look in her direction, she continued to stare at the top of the stone post. All Margo could think of was the efficiency of the boy's actions. At the same time she remembered her piano teacher's saliva hitting her young face, shrapnel from a final explosion of exasperation. She didn't respond to the slight pain caused by the strong grip of the Dutch woman's hand around her upper left arm. However Margo did flinch at the memory of her mother's unremitting stare of disappointment and disdain, when, having read the piano teacher's damning letter, she finally looked up at Margo.

"There will be the problem now of my passport," the woman said.

They were sitting. Margo and the woman – Irene Rietsma, Margo had overheard her tell her name to the police – at a table in the restaurant upstairs from the gift shop into which they had gone to report the boy's leap. The only person in any position of authority had been the woman working at the cash desk. Margo saw no alternative but to join the end of a line-up of Japanese who were waiting to pay for their souvenirs, tea towels, ashtrays and postcards, each carrying a crudely rendered depiction of Niagara Falls. Margo's assumption of a relationship between Irene Rietsma and the boy had been wrong, he was unknown to her. Nevertheless it was Irene who elbowed her way, towering over disgruntled tourists, to reach the cash desk so she could make their story known.

"Has your passport expired, Irene?" asked Margo.

The restaurant was empty, it was four o'clock in the afternoon. A policeman had had no trouble placing them at one of a line of empty tables next to large windows overlooking the Falls. The policeman had said a few words to a drowsy waitress. The giving of their accounts of the boy's suicide to the matter-of-fact policeman had diminished the horror of it. Both women felt calmer, yet saddened. Before leaving, the policeman had asked for ID and told them to wait.

Irene applied pale pink lipstick with the help of a small mirror. Then she turned her attention to the view outside. After a few seconds she looked at Margo.

"It's the question of gender. I am a transsexual," she answered. "My passport states that I was once male, it's often a cause of concern for the bureaucracy."

"I see," said Margo, thoughts of the boy and suicide were thrust aside by Irene's astonishing statement. Margo immediately assumed – as she would – that Irene was telling a colossal and wonderful lie. She was impressed. Irene held Margo's gaze, her clear blue eyes steady and unblinking. Something about her stare suggested to Margo that perhaps there was no pretense. She considered Irene's bone structure, thought about the register of her voice. Irene was clearly telling the truth. She had once been a man.

Margo glanced down at the tablecloth. Irene interpreted Margo's downcast eyes as a sign of confusion, or perhaps animosity. Irene looked away, returning her gaze to the view outside, giving Margo time to come to terms with whatever emotions she might be experiencing. She stared at frosty trees glinting in the sunlight on Goat Island where spray from the Falls had frozen on lower branches.

Irene would have been surprised to know that Margo had lowered her eyes because she was overwhelmed by flattery. The fact that Irene had confided in her without any trickery on Margo's part delighted Margo. The sociability that she always hoped would result from her stories had arrived quite spontaneously. Margo was overjoyed, flushed with the warmth of what she considered to be true intimacy.

Margo glanced at Irene's hand where it lay on the table. She considered the thickness of Irene's wrist where it disappeared into the crisp pink and white striped sleeve of her blouse. Margo strained to think of something to say, anything to maintain the closeness she felt had been established by Irene's confession.

"I'm so glad you told me," Margo said. "You see I have a brother, Ben." Margo lied, she was an only child. "I really can't talk to most people about him but I'm sure you'll understand."

"What do you mean?" asked Irene, looking at Margo.

"Well, I first thought there was something odd . . . no, not odd, that's a terrible thing to say. Unusual, that's what I meant. I thought there was something unusual about him when I found him trying on one of my sundresses when we were kids."

Irene continued to look at Margo, saying nothing. Instead of the knowing smile Margo had hoped for she thought she saw a flicker of annoyance in Irene's eyes.

"Anyway, to cut a long story short," an expression Margo often employed when she sensed things weren't going as well as anticipated, "I told him as far as I was concerned he could wear whatever he wants. He often wears women's clothes now; we even go on shopping expeditions together. He's a gas, you'd love him."

Irene stared at Margo for several seconds. Margo tried a smile but Irene's expression didn't change.

Eventually Irene said, "I'll give you the benefit of the doubt and assume that you told me this story in an attempt to somehow reassure me, to make me feel comfortable. However I need no reassurance, I'm perfectly comfortable as I am." She turned her gaze away from Margo. "Also if you had any experience whatsoever you'd know that I have very little in common with your brother."

Margo was filled with anguish. "Look, I'm awfully sorry. The last thing I wanted to do was offend you. I don't know what came over me, I'm. . . ."

"I think perhaps you'd better stop now before you make matters worse," said Irene.

"I'm really sorry," blurted Margo.

Irene sighed. "Apology accepted," she said. In the awkward silence that followed Irene sat contemplating the scene outside. Margo glanced at her, hoping for a softening of expression. She couldn't help examining Irene's plucked eyebrows, her eyelids with their hint of blue eyeshadow. She immediately hated herself for noticing them. Eventually Irene turned her attention from the view outside to look back at Margo. Margo glanced away. She pretended to look around for the waitress.

"Look, we're forced to sit here until that poker-faced policeman returns," said Irene, "so let's talk about something – anything."

When Margo turned to look at Irene she remembered the expression "an open face," which had always puzzled her. Irene's face, Margo realized, was "open." There wasn't a cunning line: her eyes held no hint of artifice. "OK," said Margo, smiling. The glow of fellowship returned.

"Tell me about your time as a musician in Amsterdam. What Dutch words did you learn?" Irene asked.

The glow retreated, Margo's smile disappeared. "I told you I didn't learn Dutch."

"You must have picked up something," Irene insisted.

"Perhaps *jenever*, the gin everybody drinks? Or the name of a place? *Scheveningen*! It's impossible for most foreigners to say *Scheveningen*, so we ask them to try. To tease them."

"I didn't learn a word," said Margo. "Sorry."

"Ahh," said Irene.

Margo looked around again for the waitress.

"Such a young person. I wonder why?" said Irene.

"Pardon?" said Margo. Irene, deep in thought, said nothing.

It took Margo a moment to understand. "Oh, you mean the boy," she said, thankful for a change in the direction of conversation, despite the subject.

From their seats they could plainly see the spot from which the boy had jumped.

"He was bruised," said Margo. "Literally, I mean. He had a bruise on his wrist."

"It's ridiculous," said Irene. "Now I'm feeling the anger." She snorted.

"You fight, you fight like hell. And then, in front of your eyes, somebody throws their life away."

"Excuse me," Margo called to the waitress.

She asked if she might have a cup of tea. Irene ordered coffee.

"You English like tea," said Irene. "It is a restorative, no? In times like this, times of stress."

"I suppose it is . . . I hadn't thought, I mean, of the stress."

Having delivered their tea and coffee the waitress shuffled into the darkness at the back of the café leaving Margo and Irene to look out of the windows, waiting for their drinks to cool.

"He gave no sign," Irene said, "I hardly noticed him, I was thinking of you."

"Of me?" asked Margo.

"Of you, yes. About our conversation."

"Ah," said Margo.

The lower the afternoon sun sank the yellower it shone. Out of the window Irene and Margo could see frost-encrusted rocks turning the colour of vanilla ice-cream along the near shore of the river. Irene's mention of their earlier conversation had panicked Margo. She struggled to think of something to say that would draw attention away from herself.

"Do you think the . . . the problem with your passport is why the policeman is taking so long?" asked Margo, turning to look at Irene.

"Perhaps," said Irene, still staring out of the window.

Margo couldn't help thinking about the squareness of Irene's jaw, the sturdiness of her neck muscles.

"I hope you don't mind me asking," asked Margo. "Your change, your . . ." Margo hesitated.

"It's OK. I'm glad you asked," said Irene, switching her gaze from the scene outside to Margo. "Would it be enough to say that I had no option?"

"I don't quite understand."

"I could no longer appear to the world or myself as something I wasn't," said Irene. "How's that?"

"You mean you thought you were a woman."

"I was, I am, a woman."

Margo glanced at the swelling of breasts under Irene's pink and white striped shirt.

"But you were born a man?"

"Correction. I was born with the body of a man."

"It seems such a drastic step – the surgery and everything."

"I didn't give it a second thought, it was necessary so that the rest of the world could see me as I saw myself," said Irene.

Margo sipped her tea. Something in Irene's words brought to mind Adam and Eve in the Garden of Eden. Was it lack of modesty? It couldn't be innocence, surely the opposite should apply to Irene. Margo cradled her teacup between her hands and gazed into it.

At last she said, "But it must be incredible to have had such a clear impression of yourself, of exactly how you wanted the world to see you . . . especially when it was so different to how you were."

"Different to how I appeared, you mean. How we appear is often not how we are, don't you think? I was lucky, my mistaken appearance, my male countenance, was so obviously not me. And I was fortunate to be able to do something about it."

Irene lifted her coffee cup as if to drink, but, instead, held it in front of her. She continued to look at Margo.

Margo noticed that the pink of Irene's nail varnish matched the colour of her lipstick. "Well, all I can say is it must be marvellous to know yourself that well," Margo said.

"Mine was rather an obvious case. But all of us have unwanted attributes, characteristics imposed upon us – usually family members are the guilty parties. We adopt them unwittingly. Consequently we often appear – and behave – differently than we truly are, or would wish. Only the lucky ones realize this." Irene took a sip of her coffee.

Margo was dismayed to find that Irene's tone annoyed her. She was alarmed because it was her experience that intimacy, if it existed at all, fled in the face of disagreement. But Margo's idea of disagreement had been formed by her mother's inarticulate glares, her "tut tuts," her oblique yet barbed comments. She'd never thrown Margo a bone of a specific accusation to gnaw on, a definite criticism that might indicate areas for improvement. Instead, her mother's unexplained yet obvious distaste for her daughter left Margo feeling worthless and isolated. However – like mother, like daughter – instead of confronting Irene about her smug tone Margo asked, in a suitably sceptical tone of voice, "Don't tell me you've never had moments of doubt?"

Irene glanced at Margo.

"It's recommended one lives as a woman for some time before the operation – just to be certain," she said. "I remember when I was in the limbo stage, I'd been taking hormones for a year-and-a-half, I had small breasts and I'd grown my hair long, but I hadn't yet had surgery. All I wore during that time was a loose sweatshirt and jeans. I flew somewhere, it doesn't matter where. At the airport security I froze, not knowing if I should approach the male or the female guard to be frisked. When the woman called me to her it was all I could do to stop myself from hugging her. After that I could have wielded the knife myself."

"What a wonderful story," muttered Margo, her annoyance with Irene forgotten. She almost wished she had a penis that *she* could despise!

Irene lifted her coffee cup to her lips, "But, as I've said, mine is rather a drastic case." She swallowed a mouthful of coffee. "I'm sure there's something about yourself that you would consider important? An expression of who you really are?" Irene raised her carefully shaped eyebrows inquiringly.

"Of course, all kinds of things," muttered Margo. She took the teaspoon that was resting on her saucer and made a performance out of vigorously stirring her half-drunk cup of tea. She considered saying something like, "I adore modern jazz," or she could insist that French food was her "absolute favourite cuisine." But she stirred her tea and said nothing.

Irene examined Margo's face and her hair, looked down at Margo's hands. At last she turned to gaze out of the window. "As desperate as I was I never doubted I'd eventually be able to be myself," said Irene. "I was never so hopeless as this poor boy."

Margo struggled to suppress another prick of irritation at what she saw as Irene's superior manner. "Doesn't everyone consider suicide at some time or another?" asked Margo.

"Never, not me. Not suicide," said Irene. "Have you?"

Margo hadn't anticipated the question being thrown back at her. She was suddenly struck by the silence of the restaurant. Out of the corner of her eye she caught the movement of the river and the Falls, but they were rendered soundless by thick layers of glass window. Margo felt lost, wondering at what point during the conversation she'd found it impossible to lie.

She decided to act nonchalant, yet worldly. "Of course. I've even tried it. . . . a couple of times," she said.

"How?" asked Irene.

"The first time was with pills."

Irene leant forward, her breasts rested on the edge of the table, hands clasped in front of her.

"And this time the boy he, how do you say, it's a poker term I think, he aced you? Or maybe it's tennis," said Irene.

"What on earth do you mean?" Margo asked.

"That's why I turned around to take another look. Not at the Falls, but at you. To see if I could tell what it was about you that made me feel uneasy. Then, when I saw your expression of, how do you say – chagrin – when the boy jumped. I knew you weren't here for the view only."

"Chagrin?" Margo echoed. If asked she'd have found it difficult to explain why she felt stirrings of anger towards Irene. She felt exposed. Why should she be the one to feel like a fraud? If she hadn't been told by the policeman to stay, Margo thought, she'd march out right now, leave this Irene person to her – or his – own devices! "You speak English so well," she said, sarcastically. "I'm sure I haven't a clue what *chagrin* means."

"Disappointment at failure," replied Irene. "Especially in the light of another's success."

Margo panicked at a thickening sensation in her throat. "Ridiculous," she gasped. If challenged she'd claim her choking was the effect of stale air in the restaurant.

Irene reached her fingers across the tablecloth towards Margo's hand. "To fail at suicide is not such a bad thing, no?"

Margo slid her hand under the table, watched her two hands clutch each other in the privacy of her lap. The women sat motionless. Thousands of tons of water surged silently over the Falls. It wasn't until Irene finally withdrew her outstretched hand that Margo realized how much she'd wanted to grasp it.

Irene pulled herself upright. "Tell me, where were you born?" she asked.

Margo looked up, she considered the velvety quality of Irene's brown eyes for so long that she almost forgot the question. She looked away, out of the window. A seagull was gliding with motionless wings in ever-decreasing circles above the Falls. The wrought-iron railing appeared even more insubstantial from where they were sitting. The green brow of the Falls glistened. The water was mesmerizing, but Margo tore her eyes away, forced herself to look Irene in the eye.

"I wasn't born in England," Margo said.

"But you said you were English?"

"My mother was English. She married a Canadian, my father. They met in London but then moved to Canada, he worked for the family business, a law firm. I was born here, in Toronto. I was sent to boarding school in England at age seven. I stayed until I was eighteen."

"So young to leave one's parents. I suppose they thought it would be better for you, a good education and all that."

"No. My mother couldn't stand to have a daughter around her who talked with an 'American' accent, so I was sent away to lose it."

"She was probably jealous," said Irene.

"Jealous," gasped Margo.

"Sure. Parents are, you know. She probably envied your youth, your lack of inhibition perhaps, that sort of thing."

Margo was astonished, it had never occurred to her that her mother might envy her.

"But I think you sound Canadian, no?" asked Irene.

"I don't know how I sound, I guess I'm a bit of a chameleon. I pick up whatever accent I'm surrounded by."

"This is OK for chameleons but rather confusing for a young woman, don't you think? Do you think of yourself as Canadian or English?" asked Irene.

"I don't think of myself as anything particularly."

"Oh, but you must!" said Irene.

Until then Margo had always thought "must" was the worst possible thing anybody could ever say to her. She looked out of the window savouring the concern that Irene had managed to inject into the words "you must." The sun was slipping down the sky, and the rapids above the Falls had taken on a coppery sheen. The colour of the falling water had darkened to jade. Margo sat quietly for several minutes, aware of Irene watching her. Their silence was interrupted by the voice of the policeman.

"I'm sorry for keeping you waiting for so long," he said. "You're both free to go now."

He handed Irene her passport. He gave Margo her driving licence. "We may call on you for the inquest," he said to Margo and smiled. "Since you live so close."

"Sure," said Margo, and attempted a smile in return.

"You might like to know that we've established an identity. A coat with a letter in one of the pockets was found on a nearby bench. It belonged to the . . ." he hesitated and glanced at Irene. ". . . to the young man."

"Well, I should be going," he said. "Enjoy the rest of your coffee."

He turned on his heel and took several steps.

"Just a second," Irene called out. The policeman stopped.

"If you have any information about the young man I think it would be helpful for my friend," she indicated with her head in Margo's direction, "and I to know something of him."

"Friend!" thought Margo.

The policeman turned and stepped towards them. "Well, I can't tell you his name, of course, but I suppose there's no harm in telling you that he'd run away from a half-way house. It's the usual story – abuse, removal from the parental home, foster homes, and so it goes. He had a record, a little fraud, nothing very ambitious. It's unlikely that anyone will miss him. Good night." He walked briskly away.

As he'd been talking the sun had disappeared completely. Now the sky was turquoise at the western horizon, changing quickly to dark blue and then to indigo in the east. Margo cradled her tea-cup in both hands.

"Idiot," said Irene scathingly. "He had it wrong about the coffee too."

"What?"

"He told us to enjoy our coffee, but you are drinking tea."

"Yes, I suppose he did," said Margo. Now that she was free to go she discovered she was reluctant to leave.

"It didn't occur to you to tell him?"

"No. I didn't give it a thought," replied Margo.

"People make assumptions. Sometimes it's understandable, but I think it better to correct them if they make the wrong ones."

"About whether one is a coffee or a tea drinker?" asked Margo.

"It seems a small thing, but sometimes the small things are the most telling," said Irene.

"It's true, I am a tea-drinker," Margo said. "I suppose it means something."

"Not herbal tea either. Proper English tea with milk and sugar. It says a lot."

Margo could see lights appearing in the buildings on the other side of the Niagara River gorge. She drained her tea cup.

The drowsy waitress had woken up and was noisily setting up tables for next day's lunch. If this was a hint for them to leave, Irene and Margo were oblivious to it.

"Where do you live?" Irene asked.

"In Toronto."

"With your parents?"

"God, no."

"Did you like English boarding school?"

"I hated it but in our family one doesn't make a fuss."

"Oh, but making a fuss can be so satisfying," said Irene, her eyes shining with mock mischief. Margo couldn't stop herself from laughing.

"What do you do for a job?" asked Irene.

Margo stopped laughing abruptly. The question stung. From somewhere deep she remembered being slapped across the face.

"I told you, I'm a musician."

"Of course, of course, forgive me. I don't usually forget such things," said Irene. She reached across and laid her hand on top of Margo's. Margo's reaction was to pull her hand away, she was glad when she managed to suppress the impulse. "It's just that I'm sure there are all kinds of things you could do if you wanted to, with your education, and good looks. I'm sure our young policeman thought you attractive."

Margo, reassured, smiled weakly and looked again towards the lights on the other side of the river.

"How do you feel about men, Irene?" asked Margo, and suddenly, unexpectedly, felt gleeful – to be sitting around talking about men with a friend!

Irene gave Margo's knuckles a soft pat as she removed her hand. "I enjoy their attention, it makes me feel more feminine," replied Irene. "However sex has not really been my preoccupation. But don't misunderstand me. I have as much the body of a woman as modern science can allow, which is considerable. To all intents and purposes I am anatomically like a woman who has undergone a hysterectomy. I can have orgasms, my erogenous zones retain their sensitivity."

"You sound like a medical text book," said Margo, and smiled.

"Perhaps that's because genitals and hormones only interest

me insofar as I wanted mine changed to match my true gender," replied Irene.

She drained the last of her coffee.

"Why do you think the city of Paris, and all ships are referred to as 'she'?" asked Irene, eyes wide with delight, even though she'd posed the question a thousand times before.

Irene and Margo could have left the building by way of an exit at the rear, which would have been more convenient for the car park where they'd both left cars, Margo's rusty Honda and Irene's gleaming rental. However they went out of the front doors, through which they'd entered, placing them in the exact location where they first met.

Once outside, they paused. The roar of the Falls drowned all other sounds.

Margo looked towards the wall, she could see the outline of wrought-iron railing against star-studded sky. It was hard to remember the shock when she'd discovered, earlier in the day, the existence of the railing, twisted and slippery yet such an effective stepladder. Unlike the boy, she hadn't anticipated – or welcomed – its convenience.

"Did we imagine it?" asked Irene. In the light falling from the windows behind them Margo could see steam drifting from Irene's mouth, warm breath colliding with freezing air.

Margo remembered the boy's eyes, she saw them as clearly as when he was standing in front of her, poised by the railing. Margo recognised the damaged expression that permeated his irises. She was reminded of crushed, blue petals in the pale palms of her hands – a bunch of violets her Sunday school teacher had handed out one Mother's Day. The flowers were intended as a gift for the children to give to their mothers but Margo had squeezed the life out of hers on her way home. She'd thrown the strangled flowers in the gutter outside the house.

Frigid spray pricked the women's faces. Margo shuddered with grief – grief for the flowers, grief for the boy, grief for a mother she'd never had. "God, no," Margo said. "We didn't imagine it."

She turned abruptly and walked quickly around the building to the rear. Irene caught up with her at the curb, where they waited for some cars to pass so they could cross the road to the parking lot.

"Are you OK to drive?" asked Irene.

"Why didn't they build a better wall. It's ridiculous, so ineffective. It's Niagara Falls, for Christ's sake."

"You can't blame this," said Irene. "The wall is only ineffective, as you put it, in the face of desperation such as his."

Margo looked around, stared into the darkness towards where they'd been. "After all, you didn't disappear, did you?" asked Irene.

Irene took Margo's arm in hers, and gently turned her away from the Falls to face the road again. Margo was instantly reminded of local women in the English town where she'd gone to boarding school. She remembered how she'd often watched, enviously, while a woman, standing at a roadside curb, would hook her hand through the arm of her companion so that they could both cross safely to the other side of the street.

"Why don't you come and visit me in Holland sometime. Perhaps you could revisit your old haunts."

Margo turned her head to look at Irene, she couldn't remember being so close to another person's face in her entire life. "Haunts?" she asked. She thought of the man in Amsterdam, his attic apartment, and the view of the sparkling canal. She remembered the warmth that emanated from his body in bed as she lay next to him.

"In Amsterdam. Perhaps you could get work again as a musician."

Margo averted her eyes. She looked across the road, beyond the steady stream of cars, to the curb on the other side. "I'm not a musician," she said. "I never was."

"Ahh," said Irene. After a moment's silence she tightened her hold on Margo's arm. "Come anyway," she said.

"Honestly?" asked Margo, daring to look into Irene's eyes.

"Of course, you can stay as long as you like," said Irene, and Margo watched the laugh lines that bracketed Irene's lips soften and deepen as she smiled at Margo. At that moment the traffic cleared, allowing them to cross safely to the other side of the road.

NANCY RICHLER

Your Mouth Is Lovely

Belarus, 1896.

Four years I stayed with Lipsa and four years I forgot I wasn't hers. I don't blame Lipsa. She was a busy woman. There were six children in her house – five of her own and me. Her husband was a peddler and was gone for days, sometimes weeks at a time. Lipsa plucked chickens, sold eggs, took in other women's babies and washing. One winter she packed matches for the factory in Mozyr. Another she made cigarettes to sell in the market. She had no time to remind me of my misfortune.

We worked, all of us, packing matches, rolling cigarettes, pushing carts of laundry to and from the river, but we had our pleasures too. I took mine from the eggs I cleaned for market. Delicate and fragile they were, each one heavy with the secret of life. I removed dirt and feathers with three-year-old fingers without ever breaking a shell.

In my fifth year, my father remarried. It was unusual for a widower to have waited so long, unusual for a man to have lived alone – a young man, at that, and for so many years. There had been talk, of course. None of it good. My mother was thought to be behind his unnatural behaviour. She had walked into the Pripet river immediately after my birth and her body had never been recovered. There was no saying where her restless spirit hovered.

A woman in my father's position would have been forbidden to marry. *Agunah*, we would have called her, an abandoned wife. Our village had two. Sima, whose husband was surely dead – his blood-spattered coat had been found in the forest shortly after his disappearance – and Fruma, whose husband had left for America ten years earlier and forgotten to send for her. Unfortunates those women were. They remained bound to an absence for the rest of their lives. Abandoned men, however, could more easily obtain dispensation from their marriages. And in the fifth year of my life, my father obtained his.

Tsila was the name of his bride. Avram the Hero's eldest daughter. He was called The Hero because fifteen years earlier when his house had caught fire in the middle of the night he had run outside alone and sat on the snow, head in his hands, rocking and weeping, while his wife ushered their five children to safety.

Tsila was twenty already when my father married her. A tall girl, she was slender as a reed and had long, velvet hair the colour of honey. Hard working and practical, with clever hands and a strong back, all things being equal, she could have married much younger and found a far better match than a shoemaker whose first wife's spirit had never been properly put to rest. But all things are never equal: Tsila's face was marked by Divine anger. Across her left cheek and extending down to her chin was the unmistakable red handprint of the angel that had slapped her before birth.

In a sweet-natured girl, such a birthmark might have been talked away as a mistake, a momentary lapse in Divine judgement. "Look at her hair," a clever matchmaker might have pointed out. "Her eyes like emeralds. Her voice like a flute. And her disposition . . ." But Tsila wasn't sweet. Sour as spoiled milk, there were those who said that when the angel marked her face, he also placed a slice of lemon under her tongue, prohibiting her from sampling any of the more pleasant seasonings life might offer.

Their wedding took place two days after Purim, and my father sent for me soon after. Spring was early that year; the roads were rivers of mud. Lipsa walked with me along the planks of wood that had been laid across the mud to prevent us from drowning in it. "You'll be a good girl," Lipsa said as we walked.

I stared at the dark sludge that oozed through the spaces between the planks. "You'll be helpful and you'll do as she says."

The day was mild, the air thick with the smells it had held frozen all winter. "She's your mother now," Lipsa said. I inhaled unfurling greens, thawing excrement, softening earth. "You had no mother, but now you do."

Past the butcher's we walked, the smells of fresh blood, chicken's feet. Past Reizel's stand of rotting fruit. It was Thursday. Lipsa's husband would be home tomorrow. Sometimes, if he'd been away a long time, he brought us small gifts. Once he had brought us candies. Hard yellow balls so sour they raised sweat from my forehead. "I was never your mother," Lipsa said.

We turned down the narrow passage where Malka the Apostate had lived. I wasn't usually allowed in that passage. Malka's mother had long since died of shame but her wails could still be heard on certain nights of the year. A fat drop of water fell on my face. I looked up at Lipsa. Her eyes were black stones. More drops fell. Lipsa clutched my hand tighter and hurried us along. We were close to the outskirts of town now – the planks of wood didn't extend this far. With each step we sank ankle deep into mud. A lark sang but I couldn't see it. The mud was alive, sucking hungrily at our feet.

I hadn't been to my father's house since my birth, hadn't seen him except in passing, had never heard his voice. We started up the hill. I knew that when we reached the top we would be there. The rain was falling more steadily now. Lipsa adjusted her kerchief, gave her chin a quick pat. She had a tuft of coarse black hair that grew out of her chin like the beard of a goat. Saturday evenings, when the men were at *shul* and we waited at home for the three stars that would end Shabbes and start the week, she would take me onto her lap. The hair on her chin tickled my cheek when she laughed.

We reached the top of the hill and stopped in front of a one-storey house. It looked like any other house. The walls were logs, the roof steep, the windows on either side of the door were squares of yellow light in the darkening afternoon. Chickens scratched in the mud of the yard. From somewhere in the shadows, a cow moaned. Smoke piled straight up out of the chimney as if it wasn't sure where to blow. Lipsa released my hand and thrust a small cloth bundle in my arms. "You're a lucky girl," she said. "I couldn't have kept you forever."

Tsila was tending her stove when I pushed open the door. Down on her knees, her back turned to me. I knew enough not to approach a creature that wasn't prepared to face me, not to enter a new life that greeted me with its back. I stood in her doorway waiting.

"Don't just stand there dripping rain," she said without turning around.

I had known she wouldn't want me. Lipsa's oldest had warned me. "Why would she want you?" Rohel had asked. "A new bride like her just starting out and you, a misfortune from her husband's first marriage?"

"In or out," Tsila said. "Don't you know it's bad luck to tarry on a threshold?"

Against my own judgement, I entered.

"Do you know how to tend a fire?" she asked, still bent over her stove.

I determined it was better to hold my tongue.

"Are you mute?" she asked and turned half around.

The side of her face that she presented to me was unmarked, and although I had not seen beauty in my life until then, I recognized it immediately in the profile I beheld.

"Well, sit down then," she said and gestured vaguely towards the window.

I followed her gesture and saw the small table by the window that she had indicated. Alongside the table were two chairs. I stood between them, uncertain which to choose.

"Sit," Tsila said, pointing to the one closer to the stove and settling herself on the other. "Here," she said, and pushed a plate of cookies my way.

It was Thursday and the cookies looked fresh. Who had fresh cookies at the end of a week, unless there was a special occasion, a special guest, something to celebrate? I reached over and took one. They were almond bars, dipped in sugar then baked until they formed a sweet crust. At Lipsa's we would have dipped them in tea.

Tsila watched me eat, then took one for herself. "I suppose your father will have to make another chair now," she allowed.

At Lipsa's there had never been a moment in the day or the night when the sounds of human life unfolding could not be heard. Her home was one of several grouped around a small courtyard, each one filled to bursting with its noisy generations. Reb Sender's nightly tantrums, his mother's snores, the whooping laughter of the Halpern old maid, the low moans of the fish monger's wife – all that and more had filled the two rooms of Lipsa's house and passed freely through the walls that barely separated us from our neighbours. "There's time enough for quiet in the world to come," Lipsa said once to a neighbour who complained. "We don't have to invite it before its time."

But in the house where Lipsa had just left me, the house where I had had the misfortune to be born, quiet had already descended. I strained my ears, but nowhere was there the hum of human conversation, the shrieks of children playing, voices raised in anger or lowered in fear or in love. Even Tsila's intake and output of breath was unaccompanied by sigh or cough. I knew I had not yet crossed into the world to come, but I couldn't feel certain. I listened for human sound but all I could hear was my own blood racing through my head.

We sat for a long while, Tsila mending, me clutching my bundle of belongings in case Lipsa should come back to return me to the noisy world of the living. I was still wearing my coat and was both too hot and shivering at the same time.

"It's good you don't look like her," Tsila finally uttered. It was late in the afternoon by then and already dark. I started at the sound of her voice but felt a relief so great that I immediately began to weep. "Don't be silly," she said harshly. A harshness sweet and reassuring in its earthly tones. I wept harder. She looked at me without expression then laid her cool hand on mine. "Don't be silly," she said again. "A man doesn't like to be reminded of past misfortune every time he looks at his daughter's face."

She didn't speak again. She continued her mending, I clutched my bundle of belongings, the rain fell on the roof and windows. I cleared my throat once to check if my voice had taken flight. For some time I had felt it flutter in my throat as if it longed to break free, return to Lipsa and abandon me to the silence, but it had not, as yet. Tsila looked at me. *Eyes of a cat*, one of Lipsa's daughters had said about her. "What are you staring at?" she asked, then turned back to her mending.

Eventually I heard footsteps approaching. My father, I knew, though I had never heard his footfall before. I looked up as the door opened and met his eyes for the first time. *A man of the earth*, people said about him, and I recognized immediately the clay of the riverbank in the hues of his face and beard. His eyes were the colour of mud.

He looked away and began to shake the rain off his clothes. He stamped his feet a few times, took off his cap to shake it, then shook his clothes yet again.

"*Nu,*" Tsila said after a while. "Are you going to stand there all night shaking like a dog?"

My father took off his coat and hung it on the peg by the door.

"Maybe you can take your daughter's coat too . . . unless she prefers to sit wrapped up like an old woman as if I'm denying her heat."

I stood up, walked over to my father and handed him my coat. His hands were large, his nails darkly stained from the blacking of the threads he used for his work. I didn't dare raise my eyes to his face.

"A glass of tea?" Tsila offered getting up from her chair as I returned to mine.

My father said "please" – I had never heard a man say please to a woman before – and sat down in the chair Tsila had just vacated. I jumped up and joined Tsila at the stove.

"Sit," she said to me, then to my father, "She hops around like a wounded bird, but she doesn't talk too much."

My father nodded again and risked a look at my face.

My father, Aaron Lev, was still a young man at that time – no more than twenty-two or twenty-three – but already he had the bearing of one well advanced in years. His life had long become a wound from which he knew he would never recover and he bore it uneasily, in the stoop of his back – a slight hunch that swelled between the blades of his shoulders and pushed him inexorably downwards.

He was a strong man, but not well built. Out of balance, he was, as if the Creator had assembled him hastily at the end of too long a day, throwing in handfuls of this quality or that without considering necessary counters and complements. Intelligence he had been given, but not the tongue to express it; a large appetite, but the stomach of an invalid. His heart was too delicate for a man of his circumstances, his feet too small for a man of his size. Walking up the hill to his home, his large hulk stooped over his tiny feet, he gave the appearance, more obviously than most, of one perpetually teetering on the edge of his own destiny.

The Stutterer, he was called in our village, though he had long learned to hold his tongue. He had been born at the start of the typhus and was just learning to speak as the worst of the fever swept the village. Was it grief that strangled his tongue? Perhaps, though my mother also lost her parents to the fever and her tongue, by all accounts, was smooth and unfettered.

He was raised by his mother's cousin, a kind enough man, but one prone to bouts of melancholia so severe that only ceaseless recitation of the psalms enabled him to endure each new day that rose up against him. The cousin's wife was more able – she supported the family by selling the bread she baked – but her meagre stores of kindness had long been expended on her own children. Hungry, but not starving, literate but not educated, Aaron was apprenticed at nine and betrothed at fifteen to Henye, also fifteen – her dowry provided by the Society for Widows and Orphans. Henye resisted the arrangement at first. Her reasons were vague – premonitions, uneasy dreams. But she did at last acquiesce so that by sixteen, Aaron Lev was a bridegroom, and by seventeen, a widower and a father. A widower whose wife's body was never found and a father whose child brought him no joy.

My father drank his tea in small even gulps. The tea was hot – I could see steam rise off it – but he didn't pour it into his saucer or slurp it up with cooling sucks of air. He drank precisely, quietly, as if heat didn't burn his mouth.

Tsila placed a plate of potatoes and onions on the table and a pitcher of sour milk between us. I waited for my father to recite the blessing for fruits that have been pulled from the earth, but he thanked Tsila first. Before God. "Thank you, Tsila," he said, and I looked up in confusion.

I watched his eyes meet Tsila's. What passed between them was strange, certainly. There was a look on my father's face – a softness – that could have been part of a spell. But there was boldness as well, a boldness that didn't speak of bewitching. And wasn't it Tsila who looked away first? Her cheeks that filled with blood? I watched them look at each other and understood that the dangers in that household were many.

I tried to eat the meal she had laid before me, but her potatoes and onions seared the inside of my mouth. I took a sip of cooling milk, then turned the whole mess back into my plate.

"My food's not good enough for your daughter," she said.

I pushed my plate to the edge of the table. I didn't know why – the dangers in that room were many, but unnamed. My father watched me push my plate. Tsila watched me too. I pushed it over the edge and heard it land with a dull thud. Potatoes and onions splattered the floor and I waited for the blow to the back of my head that might have exploded what was building within me.

"No one's taught her anything," Tsila said, her voice dull with resentment. "She's been living like an animal, and now I'm to raise her."

I opened my mouth to protest but no words came and I couldn't fill my lungs. My father averted his eyes as if I was obscene.

"Well come on then," Tsila said to me. "Clean up your mess."

My father closed his eyes to recite the grace after meals, taking a long time, although only the short grace was required since we'd not eaten bread. When he finished, he remained with his eyes closed, his head nodding, as if reluctant to break off his communication with God and return to the scene before him.

There were those who said it was my mother herself who inhabited the air of that house. *He'd do well to find new quarters before bringing home a new bride*, they whispered, and maybe they were right. Was it my mother I was feeling tightening my chest, smothering conversation and laughter? I didn't know, but as I filled my lungs with the air of that place I felt my blood begin to starve.

My father pushed himself back from the table. I heard his chair scrape against the boards of the floor, then felt him standing over me. He was a giant of a man, very close now. I smelled the leather of his workday, saw the patterns of dried mud splattered up the legs of his pants. His hands hung at his sides. One hand – it was open and very large – began to swing towards me. A careful swing, deliberate and slow, a swing that might have turned into a slap or a caress. It stopped an inch from the skin of my cheek – I felt the heat of him, my own burning skin radiating out to meet his – then it swung back to hang again, clumsy and useless as an oversized paw. His step was heavy as he retreated to the door.

"Will you be late?" Tsila asked him.

The wind was up and from the north. I heard it against the rear wall of the house.

"Don't wait up," my father said.

I stared at them, uncomprehending. The wind was high – surely they must hear it – and coming from the swamps.

"The wind," I said, but Tsila was already on her feet approaching my father in the doorway. She stood close to him, her face turned up towards his. Something glinted in the mud of his eyes. He stroked her cheek once, easily, then stepped out into the night.

Our village sat on the edge of the Polyseh swamp. To our south were pine forests where the air was sweet and trees grew straight and thick, but to our north stretched an endless tract of roadless swamp. The Pripet river meandered through the Polyseh, flooding freely over most of its flat course and turning here and there to avoid any obstacle that might disturb its lazy flow. Our village occupied one such obstacle – a slight rise in the land that the river curved around rather than cutting a path through. We sat in the crook of the river's curve – a few streets, a crowd of wooden houses, some cultivated fields that flooded every spring, a market, several churches, two synagogues.

Why our town existed, no one knew; how it had started, no one remembered. The trees, probably. In the forest were thick pines that men could cut, then float down the river to the steppes of Little Russia where they had the grain that we lacked, but no lumber. From such endeavours others grew: a few mills, the match factories – so that by the time of my birth in 1892 there were almost fifty Jewish families eking out their lives in that clearing on the edge of the swamp.

The swamp was an unhealthy place – a wilderness where snakes lurked in black waters, vapours and mists befouled the air, and the earth opened itself like water to swallow the foot that dared to walk upon it. There were lights in its vapours, lights anyone could see. They moved about in strange, weaving patterns and sometimes they moaned. Those lights were the souls that had departed our world but not yet entered the next, souls without peace that were detained between worlds for reasons only He could know. Lonely and comfortless, they waited for north winds so they could ride into town and look for solace among the living. It was on such a wind that my mother would come for me. Rohel had told me. You could smell them coming, damp and musty as they wafted in from the swamp. We closed our windows against them.

"The wind," I said to Tsila when she shut the door behind my father. I had never known anyone to venture out when the wind from the north was blowing so strong, but Tsila seemed unconcerned. She looked at me for a long time, impatience growing all the while.

"Your head is filled with *bubbe meises*," she said. "What *wind*? The wind is wind. That's all it is."

I didn't answer, but her impatience grew. "I'm not interested in the foolishness Lipsa taught you."

It wasn't just Lipsa, and Tsila knew that. The streets of our town were all but deserted on nights such as this, for who could say with perfect confidence that the souls of their loved ones had found their final place of rest?

"Do you think your mother is waiting to snatch your father?

Is that what you think? That she'll rush in to snatch him now when she never wanted him in life? Idiocy," she said, but she did rub her fingers on the amulet she wore around her neck, whether from habit or to ward off the evil her scornful words might have invited, I couldn't know for certain. "Your mother wasn't one to tarry," she said.

She led me then to a corner of the room – behind the stove, against the back wall of the house. There was a wooden bench there, small and narrow as I was, and upon it, a straw mattress, a quilt and a pillow. The quilt was the colour of young leaves and stitched with blue. The pillow was white and unstained. I had not seen such brightness in the objects of Lipsa's home.

"You'll sleep here," Tsila said, and I closed my eyes.

"Now what?" she asked, but how could I explain?

I had occupied until then the middle furrow of a tamped down mattress, wedged between Lipsa's two middle girls. Our blanket was rough but warm, leached of all colour and ripe with the smells of our accumulated nights. There I had drifted easily into sleep, the warmth of living flesh keeping me from drifting too far, the breath of other lungs leading my own breath into morning. What Tsila led me to was my bed, I knew, but how could it offer me rest when I was expected to enter it alone?

Tsila watched me undress then ran her hand across my naked back, my neck and through my loosened hair. Her touch, unburdened by affection, was lighter than Lipsa's. She probed at my temples and between the partings of my hair but found neither louse nor flea.

"I'll bathe you tomorrow," she said.

I turned away from her to recite my *Shema*, the same prayer that I had recited every night from the first moment my lips could form the words. "Sleep is a perilous journey," Lipsa had instructed. If death should overtake us before morning we should enter its embrace with praise of His Name on our lips.

"Are you finished?" Tsila asked. I hadn't even shut my eyes yet, had not begun to summon the necessary concentration. Out the corner of my eye I saw the brightness of the bed. I shut my eyes to clear my mind of distractions that were leading me away from Him.

"*Nu?*" Tsila said.

"*Hear O Israel*," I began, but as I did so my mind exploded with colours. The pale green of the quilt, the blue of its stitching, the honey of her hair, the crimson of her birthmark – new life, eternity, sweetness, anger – each colour had a meaning, and more beyond. I fell silent before it.

"Even this she didn't teach you? *Hear O Israel*," Tsila prodded.

"*The Lord is our God*," I continued, then stopped. White now, as brilliant as the new pillow on which I was to rest my head, refracting to the emerald of her eyes, the unyielded copper that had glinted in his. Longing – but for what? – swept through me like wind. Then fear – of what, I didn't know. It was a sin, I knew, to summon His presence only to defile it in this way.

I felt Tsila's hands on my shoulders. She turned me – a half-turn – to face her. My eyes were still closed, but upon them I soon felt a presence, a pressure, cool and calming. Tsila's hand. My eyelids fluttered against it.

"*Hear O Israel*," she began and I listened, word by word, my mind ablaze. "*Blessed is the Holy Name*," she continued, praise of His Name calming the colours, each in its turn until they rested, still vivid, but quiet beneath her hand.

She removed her hand and met my eyes with her own. She shook her head slightly as if dismayed by what stood before her. "We'll begin tomorrow," she said and extinguished the lamp by my bed.

When I awoke the next morning harm had befallen me. The storm had passed with the night, and sunlight flooded the room. My skin felt hot, as if the air of the room had scorched it, but my core had grown cold in the night and I shivered underneath the bright quilt. I felt a pain in my throat, but did not yet understand its meaning. Tsila was tending the oven. Her hair, unbound, fell golden across her back.

"*Nu?*" she asked when she saw my open eyes.

I pushed back the quilt and swung my legs over the side of the bed. The floor was smooth and solid on the soles of my feet, but the room spun around me.

"*Modeh Ani*," Tsila prodded. The prayer upon waking. This too Lipsa had taught me, but when I attempted to utter the words, I could not. The prayer was there, lodged in my heart, but the instrument for its delivery had been taken from me.

"*I stand before Thee*," I rasped. The theft had been incomplete. A ragged shard of my voice still remained, but it hurt to use it, so raw and sore was the place from which the rest had been torn.

I waited in terror. Afraid of Tsila's anger, yes, but more of the damage that had been done to me.

"*King of the Universe*," Tsila went on. "*Who has mercifully returned my soul to me . . .*"

"My mother," I whispered to Tsila without thinking, understanding at once who had swept through me the night before as I stood by my bed trying to recite the evening prayer.

Tsila looked up from her oven. I saw her as from a great distance away. She was kneeling as she had knelt the day before, but her face was turned to me now. She put down the poker she had been using, arose and walked over to me. Her hand was rough on my forehead.

"You have a fever," she said. "Get back into bed."

I obeyed her, as Lipsa had told me I must, drinking the tea that she gave me and allowing her to wrap a warm towel around my neck, but she was misguided to think that tea and a towel might bring back what had been taken.

"Sleep now," she told me, and I did. Through that day, and the following.

I awoke at one point to the sound of whispers. It was night then, the lamps extinguished and darkness pressing against the windows. I lay in the darkness confused, a stream of whispers drifting towards me from the alcove where my father and Tsila lay. I began to shake and pulled my quilt closer around me. Tsila's laughter rose from the whispers and I heard his laughter too now, a low rumble. And yet more whispers. My body shook under the quilt, but my cheeks burned.

I curled myself into a ball – only my hot forehead exposed. I lay like that, burning and shivering all at once until I felt a breath on my skin. Balm that breath was, soothing as a cool hand, and though I had not felt her touch until then, I knew at once whose it was.

I must have called out – but how? and with what? – because when I opened my eyes both Tsila and my father stood by my bed, Tsila's hand on my brow now.

"My mother," I whispered. Come for me, at last.

"It's the fever," Tsila said.

"Should we not call Lipsa?" I heard my father suggest as I fell back into sleep.

Lipsa's lips were pinched tight, her eyes unnaturally bright – two dark stars glittering out of a milky face.

"How long has this been?" she asked, then without awaiting an answer told Tsila to boil water with the lemons and honey she had brought.

"My mother," I whispered to her, but she placed her finger on my lips to silence me.

"*My mother, my mother*," Tsila complained. She was suddenly by my bed, waving her wooden spoon around. "What kind of curse have you brought into my house?"

Lipsa rested her hand on Tsila's waving arm. "Go stir the lemon. It shouldn't boil too hard." She removed her hand from Tsila and lay her fingers on the point of violation. My throat fluttered beneath her touch. I waited for her to appeal to my mother. I had heard her make such appeals before. Just the week before my father's wedding I had accompanied her to the cemetery where she had begged Channa-Gitl to loosen her hold on her daughter's heart. Two years after Channa-Gitl's death, the daughter was still so stricken with grief that she was barren and unfit as a wife. *Have mercy on your poor daughter*, Lipsa cried out to Channa-Gitl. *Release her from her mourning. Free her for the life that is still hers to bring forth.* I closed my eyes now and waited for a similar appeal to my mother.

"Your mother wouldn't do this," Lipsa said quietly. She removed her fingers from my throat and I felt a damp warmth. A towel. She was laying a towel at my throat, no different from the towels Tsila had been laying throughout the week. "Your mother doesn't need your voice," Lipsa said to me. "What would she need with your voice?" But Lipsa's own voice trembled and there was fear in her face.

"It's your father who needs your voice," she said to me. "Your father who needs to hear your sweet voice."

"What, sweet?" Tsila muttered. "She has the voice of a crow."

"And Tsila, Tsila needs it too," Lipsa said.

"What do I need with her voice?" Tsila asked. "She wants to be mute all her life? Excellent." She handed the concoction she had boiled to Lipsa. "Let her be mute. Deaf too if she wants."

In Tsila's voice too, though, there was the tremble of fear and it was from her that I understood just how close the angel of death hovered. *Leave her be now*, Tsila was imploring. *She is ugly, unloved, not worth your trouble. Go and find yourself a sweeter child.*

Lipsa brought a spoonful of syrup to my lips and I swallowed it. Hot, sour and sweet, it stung my throat as it passed through.

"Your father and Tsila need to hear your voice," Lipsa said as she continued spooning syrup down my throat. "What's a household without the voices of children?"

She pushed a lock of damp hair off my forehead.

"The next time I see Tsila, I want to hear you've been singing for her. Do you understand me?" I nodded miserably, hot tears sliding down my cheeks. "Tsila's your mother now," Lipsa said.

Mud filled my throat, a thick and sticky layer of it. It gurgled and thickened with each breath I tried to take. I strained for breath, gulping air in huge and useless swallows, but the mucus only spread across my throat, blocking the passage to my lungs.

Tsila forced steam through my nose and mouth with towels so hot they burned the skin of my face. But though the steam filled my nostrils and mouth, it couldn't penetrate the mud. I strained harder, clawing at the air, then at my throat that wouldn't admit it. With each failed breath my legs kicked up from the bed, then fell back. Tsila gripped my head against her lap, pressing harder with her hot, rough towels.

I heard Lipsa's voice again then felt her hands upon my head, and though her touch was gentle, the very hairs on my head ached beneath her fingers.

"Master of the universe," I heard her say.

"Save this child . . ." The prayer continued, but in Tsila's voice now.

I opened my eyes. It was daytime and nighttime at once. Candles burned in the room, yet light poured through the window. Moonlight or sunlight, I didn't know, but in that one beam of light I saw the suspended dust of the room begin to dance in a slow and swirling pattern. It circled my ankles once, twice, then again and again, gently tugging and lifting my now weightless legs from the bed. And though I did not see my mother among the particles of dust, I knew she was there, lifting and pulling me towards her. In the shadow behind me, though, Tsila clutched me against her hard and bony lap, holding me to the roughness of life.

Around the edges of my eyes a darkness began to gather. The dust still swirled, but it moved within a shrinking circle of light. Faster and wilder as the darkness pressed in around it – I watched, entranced, until the cool smoothness of Tsila's hand shut my burning eyelids. "Lord of my fathers, I beseech you," I heard from the shadow behind me. "Guide my hand in the act I am about to perform." My head was pulled back, my throat bared like that of a calf prepared for slaughter. "*Hear O Israel* . . ." Tsila whispered in my ear, preparing me to die. My mind followed the path of her words.

In peace will I both lay me down and sleep. For thou, Lord, makest me dwell alone in safety.

My father sat by my bed when he thought me asleep, softly reciting the psalms. Time had passed. I don't know how long. A cold wind still blew through the chinking of the walls, but Tsila had begun her Passover cleaning.

My fever had left me, and with it my strength. I awoke each morning and placed my feet on the floor, and each morning the air of that place pushed me backwards into my bed. The wound in my throat where Tsila had cut through the mud still hurt me, but air moved freely through my throat to my lungs. Every few hours Tsila boiled a new towel in water and laid it upon the wound.

The Lord is nigh unto them that are of a broken heart . . .
None of them that take refuge in him shall be desolate.

My father recited in darkness. His work days were long; he was never in the house in daylight except on the Sabbath. I would hear him early in the morning, before the sun rose and at night again, after the first calling of the nightingale: *I am come into deep waters and the flood overwhelms me. I am weary with crying; my throat has dried.*

I had not spoken since my illness. It was not from stubbornness, though Tsila accused me of that. Where my voice had once been, there was now only pain. I showed Tsila without words the ache that I felt there.

"Pain is no excuse for your stubbornness," she scolded me as she brought me cup after cup of honeyed tea. Her face was pale and strained, her eyes rimmed with red as vivid as her birthmark. "Life is painful, but you don't see people lying down dead in the streets because of it."

"Should we not call Lipsa?" my father suggested.

"Has that woman not caused enough damage already?" Tsila asked.

My father's eyebrows arched with surprise but he didn't answer right away. He took a swallow of tea, then another as he considered the question put before him. "What damage?" he asked finally. "What damage?"

Tsila's eyes, flat with exhaustion from all the weeks of my illness and convalescence, lit now with anger. "What would you call cutting us off from a living? Doing us a good turn, perhaps?"

Tsila was a seamstress, but all the weeks of my illness no one had come to our house to be fitted for a dress or to pick up an order. No one had crossed our threshold at all, except Lipsa. My father still left for work before dawn each morning, but Tsila sat idle save for keeping house and nursing me.

"People were afraid, Tsila," my father said.

"Afraid of what? And by whose tale-bearing?"

My father closed his eyes as he often did when faced with an argument with Tsila. He pinched the bridge of his nose between his thumb and forefinger as if that might somehow give him the strength for the harsh words that loomed.

"It was safe for Lipsa to cross our threshold all those weeks but not my customers? What, Lipsa can't infect other children but my customers can?"

"Lipsa is a healer. She can't heal the sick without going to them."

"It wasn't Lipsa who healed your daughter, Aaron Lev. And I didn't see her calling for a quarantine when Freyde's Itche burned with fever last summer."

"It wasn't diphtheria."

"*Diphtheria.*" Tsila spat the word. "Don't give me diphtheria. Lipsa thinks I've stolen the child from her so now she tries to starve us."

"Tsila, Tsila," my father chided. "She's not trying to starve us. Why would Lipsa try to starve us? She's a good woman and besides, she knows the child is ours."

"Yours. She has always known the child is yours, but when five years passed and still you didn't call for her . . ."

"I always meant to."

"Still, you didn't until you married me."

"I don't think . . ."

"You never think," Tsila spat back. "Just what business do you think Lipsa still has here? In my home."

My father didn't answer.

"You don't answer because you don't know anything. I am the one who knows. I am the one who watches her scuttling up the hill, hunched and oily as a cockroach rushing to do her evil sorceries. I am the one who knows what she wants. She wants the child back in her clutches, Aaron Lev – on my own good health I swear this to you . . ."

"Don't," my father said, but too late.

"Her potions are nothing. Do you understand me, Aaron Lev? You think she has a potion that will return your daughter's voice, but I am the one who can return your daughter's voice. I am the one who saved your daughter from death."

"Only the Eternal One . . ."

"You know nothing," Tsila spat and my father fell silent.

"The child will speak again. Trust me, Arele. Have I not loosened your own tongue and freed it from its fetters?"

My father did not answer.

"Your daughter will speak, Aaron Lev. I will lead her to words."

"Water," I called out that night in my sleep. The first words I had uttered since falling ill. When I opened my eyes, Tsila was standing beside my bed. "Water," I said again, and she handed me a glass of the cool water I had called for. I drank it empty and handed it back to her.

"What do you say?" she whispered.

"Thank you," I said.

"Again?"

"Thank you," I repeated, and she dropped to her knees beside my bed.

"Your mouth is lovely," she whispered to me, the same words I had heard Lipsa say to her two youngest boys when they uttered their first words.

Help us guard his little mouth from obscenities, Lipsa had said. *May he never lie, but speak only words of Torah and wisdom, pleasing to God and men. Amen.*

Tsila said none of that. She stayed half-kneeling against my bed, her face close to mine, her long soft hair falling around my head. "Your lips are a crimson thread," she whispered, softly tracing the outline of my mouth with her finger.

We started then, the very next day, with Bes, the second letter of the alphabet.

"Aleph was chosen to be first, it's true, but what came of it?" Tsila asked.

She looked at me, awaiting my response, but I had no response. I didn't know about the letters.

"Bes came second. A disadvantage, no?" I nodded and that seemed to satisfy her.

"But look," she said, pulling an egg from the basket beside her. "Baytzah," she pronounced as proudly as if she herself had created it. She placed the egg in my hand. It was warm, and heavy with promise. "Baytzah," I said as I handed it back to her.

"Bayis," Tsila said next, sweeping her hand to indicate the house that encased us. "Bimah," she said. "Are you listening?"

"Bimah," I repeated. The podium at the front of a shul. But now Tsila wasn't satisfied. "We've hardly even started and already you're daydreaming."

"I'm not daydreaming," I protested.

"You can't afford to daydream," she said. "Other girls, yes, they can daydream all they want, but you – you cannot afford to daydream when I am trying to teach you the Aleph-Bes. Do you understand me?"

I did not understand her, but nodded my head anyway.

"Do you want to end up like Simple Sorel?"

It was said that something had scared Sorel in her infancy and that was why she walked around with her hands covering her ears and eyes humming lullabies to herself all day.

"I'm not like Sorel," I said.

"Sorel wasn't like Sorel either until she started daydreaming and scaring herself half to death. Now you pay attention."

"I am paying attention."

"So then what else starts with the letter Bes?"

I thought about it, making the sound B over and over again. Tsila tapped her long fingers on the table.

"Bagel," I said.

"Bagel," Tsila repeated. "And what else?"

"Bracha," I said. "Binyamin, Booba . . ."

"Good," she said, with obvious surprise. "Bagel, Bracha, Binyamin, Baytzah – a lot of words, no?"

I nodded, but she wasn't looking at me.

"But most of all," she said, "most important of all the words Bes leads into the world . . . Can you think what it is?" She looked at me with hope. I wanted to satisfy her, but couldn't. She opened the Chumash on the table before us, opened it to the first page of the first book. Genesis. The beginning.

"Breshis," I said before she could.

She looked at me. Her eyes were flashing emerald light. Her colour was high, obscuring the mark of anger in her cheek. "Breshis," she repeated. "The beginning. Do you see?" she asked, excitement swelling her voice. "Second in line after the letter Aleph, yes, but chosen by God to begin the Torah, to begin all creation. Do you understand?"

I was only a child, and an ignorant one at that, but I sensed a blasphemy in the charged atmosphere of our lesson.

"And where's the Aleph?" she asked. "The great first letter?" Her eyes were lit as if by fever.

"*Nu?*" she prodded.

"I don't know," I said.

"Exactly." She took my finger, the second finger of my right hand and pointed to the third letter in the word "breshis."

"Aleph," she said. "First in line, but silent now after Bes."

She sat back in satisfaction and I waited for her to bring out the sweets she would now lay before me, the drop of honey she would now place on my tongue. Lipsa's boys had been carried to *cheder* their first day, Lipsa herself had baked the sweets and provided the honey. A light golden honey, she had chosen. "Knowledge is sweetness," she whispered to her boys as the letters of the Aleph-Bes paraded before them for the first time.

"I'm not your mother," Tsila said, her face still flushed, her eyes flashing sparks of light. "I mean no cruelty, but I am not your mother. You and I have an understanding on that, no?"

I nodded my head, though uncertain as to the nature of the understanding I was entering.

"I will raise you and teach you to be a human being among human beings." She paused as if to digest the significance of such a promise. "But as for your mother . . . This is your mother now." She indicated the letters before us, a long line of unnamed letters, their mysteries still unrevealed.

"Your first mother was unfaithful to you."

I wouldn't nod my head to that. I knew the commandments even if I could not read them.

"But you mustn't blame her," Tsila went on. "All mothers are unfaithful to their daughters."

Another blasphemy. I felt it in the knotting of my stomach and the flutter in my throat.

Tsila looked at my face and laughed. "You mustn't close your ears when I tell you the truth." Her laugh was light, almost kind.

"I'm going to tell you many truths. And what I'm going to give to you will be faithful. Far more faithful than your mother could be."

Knowledge, she meant – I understood that. But mine would not be sweet. I had expected honey, but my mouth tasted of bile. Fear and dread, but also excitement mingled on my tongue.

"Knowledge will be your mother," she said. She took my finger then and pointed to the third letter of the alphabet. "Gimel," she named it. "For *Gibbur*." Strength.

About the Authors

Andrew Gray lives in Vancouver. He is a graduate of the M.F.A. program at the University of British Columbia and is now the director of Booming Ground, an annual writers' conference held at UBC each summer. His stories have appeared in *Chatelaine*, *The Fiddlehead*, *Grain*, *Prairie Fire*, and *Event*. "The Heart of the Land" is part of a collection of stories entitled *Outside*, which will be published by Raincoast in the fall of 2001.

Lee Henderson was born in Saskatoon in 1974, has performed with John Cage, conceived and drawn the animation for a video by the band Sonic Youth, and played the villain in a made-for-TV movie; his stories have been published in *Rampike*, *Grain*, and *The Fiddlehead*, and he regularly contributes non-fiction to *Mix*, a *Vancouver Sun* supplement; "Sheep Dub" won honourable mention at the 2000 National Magazine Awards; he now lives in Vancouver, where he is at work on a collection of stories and a novel that looks like it will be very, very long.

Jessica Johnson is a graduate of the University of British Columbia's creative writing department. Her work has appeared in *Prairie Fire*, *Event*, and *Geist*, and has been shortlisted for the CBC/*Saturday Night* Canadian Literary Award, a Canadian Authors Association Award, and the Pushcart Prize (for the story that appears in this anthology). She lives in Toronto.

John Lavery has studied English at McGill and the University of New Brunswick, and linguistics at the Centre de la linguistique appliquée de Besançon. His stories have been published in a number of journals, principally *PRISM international*, *Grain*, and *Quarry*, as well as in *Canadian Forum* and the *Ottawa Citizen*. He appeared in *Coming Attractions 99* (Oberon Press), and his first collection of short stories, *Very Good Butter*, was published by ECW Press in the spring of 2000. He lives in Gatineau, Quebec, with his wife and three young children.

J.A. McCormack is a Toronto writer who daydreams a lot. "Hearsay" was her first published short story. One of her stories has since received an honourable mention in *The Fiddlehead*'s 1999 Fiction Contest, judged by Alistair MacLeod. Another story is forthcoming in *Descant*.

Nancy Richler was born in Montreal and now makes her home in Vancouver. Her stories have appeared in *Fireweed*, *ACM* (*Another Chicago Magazine*), *The New Quarterly*, *The Fiddlehead*, *Prairie Fire*, and *Room of One's Own*. Her first novel, *Throwaway Angels*, was a finalist for the 1996 Arthur Ellis Award for best first crime novel. "Your Mouth Is Lovely" is an excerpt from her current novel-in-progress.

Andrew Smith lives in Toronto. "Sightseeing" is his first published short story. As a non-fiction writer, he has won a Western Magazine Award for travel writing and has co-authored *Highlights: An Illustrated History of Cannabis*. He is working to complete a collection of short fiction.

Karen Solie was raised on a family farm in southwest Saskatchewan and is completing her Ph.D. and teaching English at the University of Victoria. Her poems have appeared in a number of literary journals, including *The Malahat Review*, *Indiana Review*, *The Capilano Review*, and *The Fiddlehead*, as well as in the anthologies *Breathing Fire* and *Hammer and Tongs*. Her first collection of poetry will be published by Brick Books in the fall of 2001. "Onion Calendar" won *Other Voices'* 1999 fiction contest.

Timothy Taylor lives in Vancouver. His first novel, *Stanley Park*, will be published by Knopf in spring 2001. His short fiction has appeared in *Grain*, *Canadian Fiction Magazine*, *The Fiddlehead*, *The Malahat Review*, *Event*, and *Descant*. One of his stories is included in *00: Best Canadian Stories*. Three other stories will appear in Oberon's *Coming Attractions* 2000. "Doves of Townsend" won Silver at the 2000 National Magazine Awards. He is working on a second novel.

R.M. Vaughan is a Toronto-based writer and filmmaker originally from New Brunswick. His books include the poetry collections *A Selection of Dazzling Scarves* and *Invisible to Predators* (both ECW Press), and the novel *A Quilted Heart* (Insomniac Press). Vaughan was the 1994-95 Playwright-in-Residence at Buddies in Bad Times Theatre, and his play *camera, woman* will be published by Coach House Books in 2000. Vaughan writes visual art criticism for *eye Magazine* and political commentary for CBC Radio. He is at work on a second novel.

About the Contributing Journals

Descant is a quarterly magazine that publishes poetry, prose, fiction, interviews, travel pieces, letters, photographs, and literary criticism. Editor: Karen Mulhallen. Managing Editor: Nathan Whitlock. Submissions and correspondence: P.O. Box 314, Station P, Toronto, Ontario, M5S 2S8. E-mail: descant@web.net Web site: www.descant.on.ca

Event is published three times a year by Douglas College in New Westminster, B.C. It focuses on fiction, poetry, creative non-fiction, and reviews by new and established writers, and every spring it runs a creative non-fiction contest. *Event* has won regional, national, and international awards for its writers. Editor: Calvin Wharton. Assistant Editor: Ian Cockfield. Fiction Editor: Christine Dewar. Submissions and correspondence: P.O. Box 2503, New Westminster, British Columbia, V3L 5B2.

The Fiddlehead, Canada's longest-running literary journal, publishes poetry and short fiction as well as book reviews. It appears four times a year, sponsors a contest for poetry and fiction with two $2,000 prizes, including the Ralph Gustafson Poetry Prize, and welcomes all good writing in English, from anywhere, looking always for that element of freshness and surprise. Editor: Ross Leckie. Managing Editor: Sabine Campbell. Submissions and correspondence: *The Fiddlehead*, Campus House, 11 Garland Court, P.O. Box 4400, Fredericton, New Brunswick, E3B 5A3. E-mail (queries only): fid@nbnet.nb.ca

Grain magazine provides readers with fine, fresh writing by new and established writers of poetry and prose four times a year. Published by the Saskatchewan Writers Guild, *Grain* has earned national and international recognition for its distinctive literary content. Editor: Elizabeth Philips.

Prose Editor: Dianne Warren. Poetry Editor: Sean Virgo. Submissions and correspondence: P.O. Box 1154, Regina, Saskatchewan, S4P 3B4. E-mail: grain.mag@sk.sympatico.ca Web site: www.skwriter.com

The Malahat Review publishes mostly fiction and poetry, and includes a substantial review article in each issue. It is open to dramatic works, so long as they lend themselves to the page; it welcomes literary works that defy easy generic categorization. Acting Editor: Marlene Cookshaw. Assistant Editor: Lucy Bashford. Submissions and correspondence: *The Malahat Review*, University of Victoria, P.O. Box 1700, Stn. CSC, Victoria, British Columbia, V8W 2Y2.

Other Voices is an independent, semi-annual literary and visual art journal that has published out of Edmonton, Alberta, for over twelve years. In addition to presenting exciting work by established writers and artists, *Other Voices* is proud to showcase many new and emerging artists in each issue. While our magazine is not limited to the publication of work by women artists, we are proud of our strong feminist roots and encourage submissions by women. We also welcome work that speaks from diverse cultural, sexual, and regional perspectives as well as pieces that challenge the reader/viewer through innovations in form and content. *Other Voices* is committed to helping underrepresented voices find the space to be heard. Submissions and correspondence: *Other Voices*, P.O. Box 52059, 8210–109 St., Edmonton, Alberta, T6G 2T5. E-mail: info@othervoices.ab.ca Web site: www.othervoices.ab.ca

Prairie Fire is a quarterly magazine of contemporary Canadian writing that regularly publishes stories, poems, and book reviews by both emerging and established writers. Its editorial mix also occasionally features critical or personal essays and interviews with authors. Some of the magazine's most successful issues have been double-sized editions on cultural communities, important authors, or literary genres. *Prairie Fire* publishes writing from, and has readers in, all parts of Canada. Editor: Andris Taskans. Fiction Editors: Heidi Harms and Susan Rempel Letkemann. Poetry Editors: Robert Budde and Melanie Cameron. Essays Editor: Joan Thomas. Submissions and correspondence: Room 423–100 Arthur St., Winnipeg, Manitoba, R3B 1H3. E-mail: prfire@escape.ca Web site: www.prairiefire.mb.ca

PRISM international, the oldest literary magazine in Western Canada, was established in 1959 by a group of Vancouver writers. Published four times a year, *PRISM* features short fiction, poetry, drama, creative non-fiction, and translations by both new and established writers from Canada and from around the world. The only criteria are originality and quality. *PRISM* holds four exemplary competitions: the Annual Short Fiction Contest, the Earle Birney Prize for Poetry, the Maclean-Hunter Endowment Award for Literary Non-fiction, and the Residency Prize in Stageplay. Executive Editor: Belinda Bruce. Fiction Editor: Chris Labonté. Poetry Editor: Andrea MacPherson. Submissions and correspondence: Creative Writing Program, The University of British Columbia, Buchanan E462, 1866 Main Mall, Vancouver, British Columbia, V6T 1Z1. E-mail (for queries only): prism@interchange.ubc.ca Web site: www.arts.ubc.ca/prism

This Magazine is Canada's best-known alternative magazine of politics and culture. *This* publishes a unique mix of literature, poetry, investigative journalism, and analysis, plus literary journalism and arts reporting. Devoted to publishing the best new work of emerging and established writers and poets, *This* continues to win both National Magazine Awards (nine in 1997 alone) and other kudos for its intelligence, wit, and innovation. Editor: Sarmishta Subramanian. Submissions and correspondence: *This Magazine*, 401 Richmond St. W. #396, Toronto, Ontario, M5V 3A8. E-mail: thismag@web.net

Submissions were also received from the following journals:

The Antigonish Review
(Antigonish, N.S.)

The Capilano Review
(North Vancouver, B.C.)

The Dalhousie Review
(Halifax, N.S.)

Exile
(Toronto, Ont.)

The Gaspereau Review
(Wolfville, N.S.)

Green's Magazine
(Regina, Sask.)

Kairos
(Hamilton, Ont.)

Matrix
(Montreal, Que.)

NeWest Review
(Saskatoon, Sask.)

The New Orphic Review
(Vancouver, B.C.)

The New Quarterly
(Waterloo, Ont.)

Pottersfield Portfolio
(Sydney, N.S.)

The Prairie Journal
(Calgary, Alta.)

Queen Street Quarterly
(Toronto, Ont.)

Queen's Quarterly
(Kingston, Ont.)

Rampike Magazine
(Toronto, Ont.)

Storyteller
(Kanata, Ont.)

Taddle Creek
(Toronto, Ont.)

TickleAce
(St. John's, Nfld.)

*The Toronto Review of
Contemporary Writing
Abroad*
(Toronto, Ont.)

Urban Graffiti
(Edmonton, Alta.)

Windsor Review
(Windsor, Ont.)

Zygote
(Winnipeg, Man.)

The Journey Prize Anthology
List of Previous Contributing Authors

* Winners of the $10,000 Journey Prize
** Co-winners of the $10,000 Journey Prize

1

1989

Ven Begamudré, "Word Games"
David Bergen, "Where You're From"
Lois Braun, "The Pumpkin-Eaters"
Constance Buchanan, "Man with Flying Genitals"
Ann Copeland, "Obedience"
Marion Douglas, "Flags"
Frances Itani, "An Evening in the Café"
Diane Keating, "The Crying Out"
Thomas King, "One Good Story, That One"
Holley Rubinsky, "Rapid Transits"*
Jean Rysstad, "Winter Baby"
Kevin Van Tighem, "Whoopers"
M.G. Vassanji, "In the Quiet of a Sunday Afternoon"
Bronwen Wallace, "Chicken 'N' Ribs"
Armin Wiebe, "Mouse Lake"
Budge Wilson, "Waiting"

2

1990

André Alexis, "Despair: Five Stories of Ottawa"
Glen Allen, "The Hua Guofeng Memorial Warehouse"
Marusia Bociurkiw, "Mama, Donya"
Virgil Burnett, "Billfrith the Dreamer"
Margaret Dyment, "Sacred Trust"
Cynthia Flood, "My Father Took a Cake to France"*
Douglas Glover, "Story Carved in Stone"
Terry Griggs, "Man with the Axe"
Rick Hillis, "Limbo River"

Thomas King, "The Dog I Wish I Had, I Would Call It Helen"
K.D. Miller, "Sunrise Till Dark"
Jennifer Mitton, "Let Them Say"
Lawrence O'Toole, "Goin' to Town with Katie Ann"
Kenneth Radu, "A Change of Heart"
Jenifer Sutherland, "Table Talk"
Wayne Tefs, "Red Rock and After"

3
1991

Donald Aker, "The Invitation"
Anton Baer, "Yukon"
Allan Barr, "A Visit from Lloyd"
David Bergen, "The Fall"
Rai Berzins, "Common Sense"
Diana Hartog, "Theories of Grief"
Diane Keating, "The Salem Letters"
Yann Martel, "The Facts Behind the Helsinki Roccamatios"*
Jennifer Mitton, "Polaroid"
Sheldon Oberman, "This Business with Elijah"
Lynn Podgurny, "Till Tomorrow, Maple Leaf Mills"
James Riseborough, "She Is Not His Mother"
Patricia Stone, "Living on the Lake"

4
1992

David Bergen, "The Bottom of the Glass"
Maria A. Billion, "No Miracles Sweet Jesus"
Judith Cowan, "By the Big River"
Steven Heighton, "A Man Away from Home Has No Neighbours"
Steven Heighton, "How Beautiful upon the Mountains"
L. Rex Kay, "Travelling"
Rozena Maart, "No Rosa, No District Six"*
Guy Malet De Carteret, "Rainy Day"
Carmelita McGrath, "Silence"
Michael Mirolla, "A Theory of Discontinuous Existence"
Diane Juttner Perreault, "Bella's Story"
Eden Robinson, "Traplines"

5
1993

Caroline Adderson, "Oil and Dread"
David Bergen, "La Rue Prevette"
Marina Endicott, "With the Band"
Dayv James-French, "Cervine"
Michael Kenyon, "Durable Tumblers"
K.D. Miller, "A Litany in Time of Plague"
Robert Mullen, "Flotsam"
Gayla Reid, "Sister Doyle's Men"*
Oakland Ross, "Bang-bang"
Robert Sherrin, "Technical Battle for Trial Machine"
Carol Windley, "The Etruscans"

6
1994

Anne Carson, "Water Margins: An Essay on Swimming by
    My Brother"
Richard Cumyn, "The Sound He Made"
Genni Gunn, "Versions"
Melissa Hardy, "Long Man the River"*
Robert Mullen, "Anomie"
Vivian Payne, "Free Falls"
Jim Reil, "Dry"
Robyn Sarah, "Accept My Story"
Joan Skogan, "Landfall"
Dorothy Speak, "Relatives in Florida"
Alison Wearing, "Notes from Under Water"

7
1995

Michelle Alfano, "Opera"
Mary Borsky, "Maps of the Known World"
Gabriella Goliger, "Song of Ascent"
Elizabeth Hay, "Hand Games"
Shaena Lambert, "The Falling Woman"
Elise Levine, "Boy"
Roger Burford Mason, "The Rat-Catcher's Kiss"

Antanas Sileika, "Going Native"
Kathryn Woodward, "Of Marranos and Gilded Angels"*

8
1996
Rick Bowers, "Dental Bytes"
David Elias, "How I Crossed Over"
Elyse Gasco, "Can You Wave Bye Bye, Baby?"*
Danuta Gleed, "Bones"
Elizabeth Hay, "The Friend"
Linda Holeman, "Turning the Worm"
Elaine Littman, "The Winner's Circle"
Murray Logan, "Steam"
Rick Maddocks, "Lessons from the Sputnik Diner"
K.D. Miller, "Egypt Land"
Gregor Robinson, "Monster Gaps"
Alma Subasic, "Dust"

9
1997
Brian Bartlett, "Thomas, Naked"
Dennis Bock, "Olympia"
Kristen den Hartog, "Wave"
Gabriella Goliger, "Maladies of the Inner Ear"**
Terry Griggs, "Momma Had a Baby"
Mark Anthony Jarman, "Righteous Speedboat"
Judith Kalman, "Not for Me a Crown of Thorns"
Andrew Mullins, "The World of Science"
Sasenarine Persaud, "Canada Geese and Apple Chatney"
Anne Simpson, "Dreaming Snow"**
Sarah Withrow, "Ollie"
Terence Young, "The Berlin Wall"

10
1998
John Brooke, "The Finer Points of Apples"*
Ian Colford, "The Reason for the Dream"
Libby Creelman, "Cruelty"

Michael Crummey, "Serendipity"
Stephen Guppy, "Downwind"
Jane Eaton Hamilton, "Graduation"
Elise Levine, "You Are You Because Your Little Dog Loves You"
Jean McNeil, "Bethlehem"
Liz Moore, "Eight-Day Clock"
Edward O'Connor, "The Beatrice of Victoria College"
Tim Rogers, "Scars and Other Presents"
Denise Ryan, "Marginals, Vivisections, and Dreams"
Madeleine Thien, "Simple Recipes"
Cheryl Tibbetts, "Flowers of Africville"

11

1999

Mike Barnes, "In Florida"
Libby Creelman, "Sunken Island"
Mike Finigan, "Passion Sunday"
Jane Eaton Hamilton, "Territory"
Mark Anthony Jarman, "Travels into Several Remote Nations of the World"
Barbara Lambert, "Where the Bodies Are Kept"
Linda Little, "The Still"
Larry Lynch, "The Sitter"
Sandra Sabatini, "The One With the News"
Sharon Steams, "Brothers"
Mary Walters, "Show Jumping"
Alissa York, "The Back of the Bear's Mouth"*